STORYHACK
ACTION & ADVENTURE
ISSUE FIVE

Bryce Beattie, editor

CONTENTS

The Last Word by H. A. Titus .... pg 3
The Singer's Tale by Jon Mollison .... pg 19
The Lair of the Old Ones by Stanley W. Wagenaar .... pg 35
Acme Denton: Out of Time by Michael Haynes .... pg 47
The Last Contract by Dominika Lein .... pg 65
Makani and the Vulture God by Paul R. McNamee .... pg 77
Night of a Thousand Eyes by Deborah L. Davitt .... pg 85
Black Dog Bend by JD Cowan .... pg 95
Swimming with the Devil by William Eckman .... pg 105

ART

Zefanya Maega .... Front Cover
Ari Syahrazad .... pg 2, 104
Gian Luca .... pg 18
Mike Bogdanovic .... pg 34
Art Anon Studios .... pg 64
Dvir Avromovitch .... pg 46, 84
Emilio Florencio .... pg 76
Anna Foubert .... pg 94

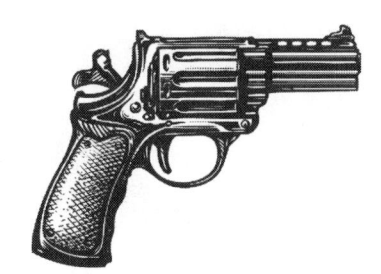

StoryHack Action & Adventure Issue Five is © copyright 2019 Baby Katie Media, LLC. All stories appear with permission. Copyright of individual stories remains with the story's author.

The Last Word
by H. A. Titus

It's all in an evening's work when the owner of a speakeasy asks Owan Craig, half-fae private eye, to deal with a little problem. Trouble is, that problem is attached to fae mobsters--just the sort of folks Owan likes to avoid.

THE LAST WORD
By H. A. Titus

By the way all the stories start, you'd think it was always rainin' in New York City just before the hero gets dragged into a mess of trouble by a pretty girl.

But I swear, it really was rainin' that evening when I stepped into the Howler, a club just far enough off Main Street to not be the spot, but close enough that the hoity-toities didn't mind drinking there. Most of the folk there couldn't understand how the Howler kept itself from gettin' raided, given the Prohibition and all. I knew.

Giselle, the owner, was fae.

She stood behind the bar at the right side of the room, resplendent in a tight red dress that clung in all the right spots without looking trashy. Her hair was cut in a daring bob, and her heels made her taller than the rest of the women in the room. The top of her honey-blonde head was almost level with mine, and I was no slouch.

She looked up and made eye contact with me, and I immediately felt the glamour swirling around her. Fae glamour kept normal folks from seeing the bar as it really was. At the same time, it pulled them in with a powerful urge, making the Howler one of the most popular speakeasies around. Being half-fae myself, I could see through the glamour and resist its pull, but I figured since Giselle obviously wanted to talk to me, I should probably oblige her. After all, she gave me free drinks in return for the occasional pro bono job. I walked over to the bar and shucked my coat and hat, tossing them on the seat next to me.

"Evenin', Giselle."

One side of her lips curved up into a flirty smile. "Owan. The usual?"

I nodded carefully. So far, she seemed to be in a good mood, but I'd been around long enough to know that could change on a dime.

She set a glass down in front of me and poured in a measure of Irish honey whiskey. The rich amber color reflected off the polished surface of the bar as I picked up the glass and took a sip.

Giselle leaned her elbows on the bar, watching the door over my shoulder. Though ever the gracious hostess, there was a nervous energy in the way her glamour swirled through the air, sparkling off the low-lit lamps and candles on the tables. She caught me watching and ran her fingers through her hair, sweeping golden strands behind her pointed ears.

"So what did you need me for?" I asked.

She raised one elegant eyebrow. "What makes you think I need you, shamus?"

The term for private detective made me grin—Giselle rarely used slang.

"I dunno. It's just that every time you're in need of a little off-the-record help, my feet turn here of their own accord. D'ya know that tonight, I'd actually planned to go home and read? Rex Stout's new book came out last week, and I've had a copy sittin' in my flat for two days. Haven't even cracked the cover."

"Hmm. Sorry, baby." Her smile widened.

I kept grinning, even though my stomach turned. I'd been trying for five years, ever since I first met Giselle, to figure out how she'd laid a charm on me that set my feet to doin' whatever she asked. It went beyond the normal requirement of owing a favor—I was pretty sure I'd paid that debt to her long ago.

It wasn't in the way she prepared the drink, 'cause I'd watched her close, and she put no glamour into that whiskey. It wasn't when she touched me, 'cause I'd've felt it right away—instead, it had taken me near to six months of these "spontaneous" visits and the coincidences pilin' up before I realized the problem.

Folks didn't call Giselle a sly vixen for nothin'.

I downed the rest of the whiskey. No use in delaying the inevitable. "Whatcha need this time, doll?"

Lugh's Spear, she hated when I called her that. I could see the thunder clouds gathering in her pretty whiskey-colored eyes, turning them a burnt-sugar brown. Then she blinked, and the smile and the twinkle in her eyes was back in full force.

"There's a new hire. Roe Gillam." Giselle reached out, traced a circle on the back of my hand. "She's having a bit of an issue with a patron."

Her touch was cold as ice. I forced myself still, though the tickle of her fingers sent chills up my back and made the hair on my arms rise. My eyes focused on her lips, her soft smile. She was gorgeous tonight. Things around me faded to a fuzzy gold, and I leaned forward slightly.

Outside, thunder crackled, and I jumped. The movement jarred Giselle's hand off my arm, and the glamour snapped. My heartbeat sped up. She'd almost had me there. I met her gaze, took a deep breath.

"So what d'ya want from me?" I asked, keeping my eyes locked on hers.

"Just a little lesson. Nothing much," she purred. "But enough that he'll leave the girl alone."

"You can't block him from entering?" I checked the red-and-gold-shaded lamp hanging beside the door. It was one of the stronger anchor points for her glamour wards. A thick flurry of glamour floated around it, meaning the wards were in good working order.

She pouted. "No."

I raised an eyebrow. Saints. "You can't just change Roe's work schedule?"

"He always seems to know."

I swore and wished I hadn't already finished the whiskey. "I dunno, Giselle ..."

Her red lips pushed outward in a pout, and she traced another circle on the back of my hand. This time, I could feel the slight nudge of power she put into it. I raised a second skin of my own glamour along my arm.

Again, the thunderstorm in her eyes flared, along with a crack of more thunder outside. "Come, now, Owan. This guy's done nothing too forward yet, but Roe's scared. She doesn't even like to walk home by herself anymore."

"Appealin' to my chivalry is a low blow, Giselle."

Another grin. "So you'll do it?"

I sighed. "Aye. Where's the girl?"

Giselle nodded at a point in space somewhere over my left shoulder. I spun to my right, swinging the barstool all the way around so I could lean my elbows on the bar. No use in askin' for bad luck by going around widdershins.

A jazz quartet was setting up at the other side of the room on the small central stage, while another guy in a newsie's cap was sweeping and polishing the dance floor. It was near seven o'clock, and most speakeasies would be bouncing by now, but the Howler served fae and those who dealt with them. Things really got movin' here closer to what normals would consider breakfast time the next morning.

Some of Giselle's girls were weaving among the tables, serving the few customers that had already showed up. Giselle only employed women as waitresses, but she treated them well, and usually had no issue with kicking out wise guys who tried to get too handsy. The fact that she wanted me to take care of this guy for her made me uneasy.

"Which one's Roe?" I asked.

"The redhead."

Redhead was a bit of an understatement—Roe's hair was gloriously bright and curly, with the kind of soft shimmer that made a man want to run his fingers through it. She wore it swept up and secured with pins and a sequined headband. Even halfway across the room I could see the freckles dotting her nose and cheeks, adding a touch of warmth to her pale skin.

"Pretty, isn't she?" Giselle asked.

I picked up my drink, trying to figure how best to answer.

"Baby," she whispered, lips tickling my ear. "You forget, I can feel it when your heartbeat speeds up."

I eased my arm away from her grip and kept watching Roe.

Despite the wide grin on her face, she seemed skittish. Her blue eyes darted about the room, bright and birdlike, even as she chatted with customers.

So the problem guy wasn't here yet, else she'd be looking at one spot a lot more. I turned back to Giselle, keeping my eyes fixed on the big mirror behind the bar. I could just see Roe in it.

If Giselle couldn't ban the guy, that meant one of two things: she was afraid of him, or he was more powerful than any glamoured wards she could muster.

I couldn't see Giselle being scared of anyone. Wary, maybe. She should've been able to keep this guy out, if she wanted. But she obviously didn't, and so she'd called on her pet watchdog.

I growled under my breath.

Giselle's lips curved up in an impish smile. "Excuse me, baby, but I've got to go greet a few people."

Giselle moved away and motioned to Roe to come take her place behind the bar. As Roe passed me, she smiled, a warm and open smile that spoke of genuine friendship as opposed to Giselle's flirtatiousness. "Evening," she said, in a slight drawl of a Midwestern accent. Not a native, then.

"Evenin'," I replied.

Behind us, the band started to play a jazzy ragtime number. Roe turned and pulled a couple of bottles down from the mirrored shelving behind the bar.

The bell over the door rang. I deliberately didn't move, but Roe straightened, and her lips parted as she sucked in a sharp hiss.

"Roe! Baby doll. Let's see a sidecar, would ya?" The voice was loud and brash. Its owner moved into my peripheral vision—a tall, slim guy with dark hair parted to the side. He wore a nice suit, gray with darker gray pinstripes. He dropped his hat on the bar and straddled a bar stool. As he leaned his elbows on the bar, I could see the outline of a knife press into his jacket. His ears were just this side of fae—not fully pointed, but not rounded like a full human's. Half-fae, like me.

Roe set a glass down in front of the man with a sharp clink. Liquor sloshed over the side, dripping to the bar. "Why are you here again?" she demanded.

He leered, brushing his thumb along her knuckles as he moved the glass closer to himself. Roe started to move away, but— quick as a wink—the guy's hand snaked out and pinned her wrist to the bar. His chuckle sounded like grinding gravel.

I clenched my hand under the bar.

Roe put her free hand on the guy's arm and dug her painted, sharp nails into him. He winced, and his expression shifted from a mocking smile to thinned lips, eyes fixed on Roe.

"That hurts, doll."

"Giselle and I've both warned you, Eric," she whispered.

He laughed derisively. "Your boss don't care, Roe, otherwise she would've banned me. 'Fraid you're on your own here."

Roe gritted her teeth.

Eric stood, brought his right hand up to her face, and brushed a curl away from her ear. She tried to jerk away, but his fingers went around the back of her neck. He pulled her forward, lips almost touching hers, and whispered, "Roe. C'mon, kitten. What're you afraid of?"

"Not you," Roe snapped, the quickness to her words belying the faint tremble in her voice.

He laughed again.

I didn't like that laugh. It had a nasty tone. And I didn't like the dark look in his eyes. Dammit, Giselle knew me too well. I couldn't let this continue.

"All right, I figure that's about enough," I said, swinging around to face Eric.

Eric glanced at me out of the corner of his eyes, then looked back at Roe. "Why don't you fade, pal. This don't concern you."

"You're speaking loudly enough that it could be the entire place's concern," I said.

"Go get a white ten-gallon hat, bruno."

I looked at Roe. "He botherin' you?"

"Very much so," she replied between gritted teeth.

"You heard the lady. I think it's time for you to fade."

Eric released Roe and turned to fully face me. "Tryin' to be smart? Listen, it's just a spat between me and my dame here, no reason to get worked up."

Giselle came up beside Roe and put her hand on the bar between us. "Gentlemen. If you're going to continue this discussion, might I suggest you take it outside? You're beginning to disturb my other customers."

I tried not to wince. With how fast she'd gotten between us, any fool would be able to see that she'd been waitin' for something to happen.

Eric looked between Giselle and me, and his face hardened. "I see how it is. Can't even stand up to me yourself, huh, Giselle? Gotta have one of your boys do it." He snorted and snatched his hat from the bar, then headed for the door.

Well, so much for makin' it look like Giselle ain't involved.

Giselle darted a half-panicked look at me. "Go after him!"

"Why?" I said. "He's gone, ain't that what you wanted?"

Giselle gave me a meaningful look, and before I realized what was happening, my feet were carrying me after Eric. I stopped and braced myself, expecting to feel a painful tugging at my heart, a rolling in my gut, something ... but I felt completely and totally normal.

Until I realized I was halfway out the door.

I sighed as I stepped out into the light rain. Thunder rumbled again, and lightning flickered over the tall buildings around me. Heavier rain was coming. Unless I wanted to get drenched, I'd better finish this quickly.

Something hard struck the back of my head. Spots of light burst in my vision. I staggered to my knees, skidding my palms on the wet sidewalk.

Eric stood next to the door, holding his dagger tight in one hand, pommel toward me. He glared. "Didn't think you'd actually be stupid enough to follow that chippy's orders."

I rose, holding my hands out. "Look, I don't want—"

He sneered at me. "Then walk back inside, and next time I come around, don't see fit to stick your nose in my business."

My chest tightened. I'd really hoped to resolve this without physical conflict. "Sorry. Can't do that."

His eyes flickered, and he lunged forward at me. I sidestepped, knocked his arm to the side. He punched me in the ribs with his free hand. I huffed out a short breath and pulled away. That'd be a bruise tomorrow.

The knife blade glittered in the lamplight as he slashed at me. I twisted and it ripped along my right bicep, stinging as it dug into flesh. Should've had my gun, but it was back in my coat pocket. Inside. Stupid.

Eric jived back and forth and came at me again on my wounded side. I grabbed his arm with my left hand and spun so my back was to him, the arm braced over my shoulder. He punched me in the lower back, but this close he didn't have the power for a good, solid shot.

I cracked his arm over my shoulder.

He howled. The knife clattered to the ground. I spun, pushed him away, and punched. One, two, three to his face, grabbed his hair and smashed my knee into his nose.

His head bounced like a rubber ball, and he collapsed to the ground.

I stood panting, my hands raised defensively, waiting for him to get up.

He didn't move. I walked over and knelt down beside him. The rain was washing away the blood on his face. I'd broken his nose, and probably his arm.

I grabbed his arms and dragged him into the alley off to the side of the Howler, then crouched down again and began going through his pockets. I found his wallet, but all it held was a few dollar bills. No driver's license, just my luck.

I took the bills—heck, Giselle wouldn't pay me for this job—and replaced the wallet, then finished rifling through his pockets. In Eric's breast pocket, something sharp jabbed my finger. I hissed and pulled whatever it was out of the pocket.

The dim light of the lamp revealed a small tie pin in the shape of a fairy-star flower. My heart sank. I stood and carried the pin to the mouth of the alley for a better look. The lavender enamel glimmered with a golden sheen in the rain and the lamplight.

"Damn," I muttered.

I returned the flower pin to Eric's pocket, propped him up against the wall so he wouldn't choke to death on his own blood, and went back inside. I hadn't seen anyone walk past during our brief fight, but apparently searching through Eric's pockets had taken longer than I'd thought, because the place had gained several new customers since I'd left.

Roe stood behind the counter where I'd left her, scrubbing the copper bar harder than looked necessary. She looked up at the jingle of the bell, and her eyes widened in surprise.

Before she could speak, Giselle hurried over to me with my hat and coat in hand. "Here, take these," she said, shoving them into my arms. She spun me around and pushed me back toward the door.

"Hey, hey," I said loudly. "C'mon, Giselle, I just beat up a guy for you, don't you think that earns me another drink?"

She raised her eyebrows and set her jaw. "You're scaring my patrons," she said in a low voice.

I didn't look away, just stared her in the eye. She stared back, blocking the door with one arm, eyes that dark burnt-sugar brown again. I clenched my teeth. Something in my chest tightened, and I realized that even though I knew Giselle had been charmin' me all these years, at some point I'd begun to think of her as a friend.

My mistake.

"Do you know who you've gotten me in trouble with?" I said in a low, terse voice. "Do you know who Eric was working for?"

She shrugged dismissively. "Thank you for taking care of it, Owan."

"Wait, Giselle—"

She shut the door in my face.

I stared at the wooden door for a moment, anger and betrayal warring in my head as my face and neck grew warm. I closed my eyes briefly, then placed my hat on my head and walked down the street, shrugging into my coat.

I was about a block away when I heard wet, splashing footsteps behind me. I turned, my hand going to the gun in my coat pocket.

Running down the sidewalk after me was Roe, her trench coat flapping around her and an umbrella threatening to tug free from her hand. She stopped in front of me, smiled hesitantly, and said, "Thank you. For what you did. I don't know if beating him up will teach him not to come around anymore, but thank you."

I glared at her. "Thank your boss. She's the one who asked me to do it." I turned and started walking. Maybe she didn't deserve my anger. Or maybe Giselle had sent her to cozy up to me, cool me down a bit. That would just be like her.

She caught up, half-running to keep up with my long strides. From the corner of my eye, I could see her frown. "Giselle did? But that doesn't make any sense. She told me she couldn't do anything about him."

"Yeah, of course she couldn't," I muttered.

"Which never made sense to me, because Giselle's far more powerful than Eric."

I stopped on the street corner and turned to her. "Look, don't play a dumb Dora to me, okay? I found the lavender fairy star in his pocket."

A little wrinkle appeared between Roe's fine eyebrows. "What?"

As if she didn't know. "The pin. You know, the sign that he's part of Niall Byrne's gang?"

Roe's face went deathly pale. For a second, she looked like she was about to faint, but she put her hand on my arm and steadied herself. "Niall Byrne? But..." She lifted her hand from my arm. "You're bleeding!"

I looked at my arm. Blood had soaked through the sleeve, leaving a large red stain that was spreading with the help of the rain. "Just a small cut." I started to turn.

"Wait! Mister ..."

"Craig."

"Mr. Craig." She caught up to me again. "Let's at least bandage that up. It's not far to my place."

I eyed her. She still looked white as a ghost, the freckles on her nose and cheeks standing out against her pale skin. Her curls had started to sag from their pins with all the rain. I sighed. Maybe she really, truly didn't know that her ex-beau had been one of Niall Byrne's men. Maybe.

I held out my elbow, and she placed her hand on my good arm. We set off down the street.

Roe lived in a fifth-story apartment in midtown. Instead of going through the front door, she directed me around to the back and up the fire escape. There, she pried open the window she'd left barely cracked, hiked up her skirt, and ducked into the apartment. She had nice legs.

"Curious way to get into a place," I said, climbing after her.

She blushed. "Sorry. I didn't even think. I've been switching around my paths home lately, because—" She bit off her sentence and looked away.

She's hiding from Eric.

"Besides, my next door neighbor is nosy. If she saw me bringing home a man at this hour!" Roe forced a laugh.

I looked around the modest apartment. Off to the left of the kitchen area, there was a battered white door, and a little hallway that I guessed led to the bedroom. No pictures hung on the white plaster walls, and just a threadbare sofa sat in the living room.

Roe went to one of the kitchen cabinets and pulled open a drawer. "May as well sit down. Should I get a kettle going? Do you like coffee, or tea?"

"Coffee, please." I tossed my coat and hat over the back of a chair. I rubbed my hand on the faded floral tablecloth. "So. How long ago did you move here?"

Roe started a kettle of water on the stove, collected a small leather satchel from a cabinet, and sighed as she came over to the table. "Not very long—maybe a month? Eric knew where I lived and ..." she hesitated.

Time to change the subject. "What're you doing in the Big Apple anyway? Your accent don't fit."

She snorted as she pulled a chair out beside me and sat down. "Springfield, Missouri. Is it still that obvious? I've been living here for a year."

"Still obvious, sorry."

She motioned at the long sleeve of my previously-white button-down. "I'm not going to be able to do much with that still on."

I felt the tips of my ears color. "Umm..."

"Oh please. I grew up on a farm with five brothers. Wouldn't have pegged you for such a bluenose."

"Hey, that finally sounded like proper NYC talk," I joked.

Roe laughed she began unwinding a ball of gauze. This laugh sounded easier, genuine.

I unbuttoned my vest and shirt and pulled them off, then rolled up the sleeve of my undershirt so she could easily get at the cut. Peeling away the wet, rain-and-blood-soaked fabric pulled the wound open again. Roe pressed a wad of gauze to it as she pulled a tin of salve from the bag with her free hand.

"Okay, so, farm girl," I started, trying to distract my mind from the fact that I was sitting here in my undershirt with a very pretty fae chick. I breathed deep, relaxed my shoulders. "Why'd you move to the grand ol' NYC?"

"I'm studying antiquities."

Okay, this dame was full of surprises. "Studying antiquities" was slang for "working with relics," and I only knew one group fool enough to do that nowadays.

"You're a curator?" I asked.

She nodded.

I mimed raising a glass in a toast. "That's a crazy bit of work."

"Crazy, but necessary." She didn't sound disapproving, just firm. "There's been an influx since the Great War, and it's more necessary than ever to have a firm handle on them."

"I'd believe it."

"Have you ever encountered a relic?"

"No. But I'm not dumb. I've heard the stories." Stories of plagues unleashed by one person wearing the wrong necklace. Stories of folks' minds being taken over with just a touch. Relics were objects that had been imbued with one single-minded purpose, and they made glamour nearly irresistible to full-bloods. To humans and half-fae like me... I shuddered. Yeah, I was perfectly happy to let the curators handle those sorts of jobs.

Roe peeled the wad of gauze away from my arm and frowned at the cut. "That'll need iodine for certain." She opened the cap on a dark bottle and dabbed some iodine out on a clean piece of gauze. "How about you, Mr. Craig?"

"Me?" I grinned. "Mostly I spend my days tracking down lost puppies and errant husbands. I'm good at findin' lost stuff, you might say."

"Giselle mentioned that you were a private detective. Any police work?"

I jumped as she pressed the iodine-soaked gauze to my arm. "Ouch! Lugh's Spear, woman, you could've warned me!"

She grinned. "Aww, is the big tough shamus scared of a little sting?"

I rolled my eyes. "How long did you date Eric?"

Her movement slowed a little, and she glanced away. "A couple of months. One of the girls I used to room with set us up on a blind date. He was sweet at first, but he got really possessive after a while. Hit me once, when I went out with other friends without asking him for permission first."

I raised my eyebrows. "What'd you do?"

"Gave him a black eye."

"Sounds like growing up with five brothers was good for you."

"Thanks."

We talked a bit more as she finished cleaning up and bandaging the cut—mostly about life in New York, how she'd met Giselle, our various favorite parts about living in a big city. I couldn't help but compare her lively, cheerful personality to Giselle's ice-queen attitude. She got me coffee, and our talk drifted to our tastes in books and theater. With theater, at least, we agreed, and it took all my self-control not to ask if we could go to a play sometime. I figured that was the last thing she needed, since she was still dealin' with Eric.

After a time, I glanced at my watch and realized it was nearly ten o'clock. "I'd better go. Can't have your neighbors thinking we'll keep them up all night with our chatter."

She laughed. "The walls aren't that thin."

"Nah. I got a Rex Stout book I'd like to dig into and besides, you need sleep too." I stood, pulled my shirt back on and buttoned it up.

Roe began clearing the table, and I caught her nervously glancing at the door. Of course, her snoopy next door neighbor. I sympathized.

"Don't worry, I'll leave the same way I came in," I said. "Say, Roe, would you like me to meet you at the Howler tomorrow night? What time do you get off work? I'll walk you home."

"Oh, I don't want to inconvenience you."

"No inconvenience. I want to make sure your lousy ex got the picture."

She started to run her fingers through her hair, then winced as she got caught on a bobby pin. "I can't believe Giselle convinced you to go to all this trouble just for me. And to get yourself possibly involved with a gang ..."

I shrugged. No need to bother her by saying that I hadn't been able to resist Giselle's "request."

"Well, if you're certain, I wouldn't mind it. I'm pretty sure Eric doesn't know where I live—I've been able to slip away each time he's tried to follow me—but it wouldn't hurt." She held out her hand. "Thanks for everything, Owan."

I shook her hand, smiled. "See you tomorrow night." I pulled on my coat and hat and slipped out the window.

Roe shut and locked it behind me, then waved as I climbed down the fire escape.

The rain had stopped while we'd been in her apartment, but everything still dripped. I walked down the alley, kicking a few pebbles along in front of me as I thought.

I couldn't figure Giselle's angle. Obviously she hadn't wanted a fight in her speakeasy, since she'd kicked us out once Eric had gotten angry. And the fact that she'd quickly shoved me out after the fight suggested that she didn't want to be associated with Eric's lesson in manners. Had she known who Eric was? It sure seemed like it. She'd been afraid to ban him from the Howler.

But why would she think that getting beat up would get through Eric's thick skull?

I sighed. I'd been in over my head the moment I'd set foot in Giselle's speakeasy, and if I could travel back five years ago and tell myself to just walk on by, that the Howler wasn't all it was cracked up to be, I'd do it in a heartbeat.

Although then I'd have never met Roe.

I snorted at myself. C'mon, Owan. You barely met the girl, she's still dealing with a nasty ex-beau, and you're already thinkin' that 5 years of trouble was worth meetin' her? Gimme a break.

I rounded the corner of the building, and the hairs on the back of my neck rose. I stopped. Scanned the street ahead of me. It looked empty.

It was the night for me to fulfill clichés, because I didn't even bother glancing up.

Something heavy and scratchy dropped over my head. I yelled and flailed at it, trying to drag the material—a blanket?—off of me. I could hear the muffled sound of footsteps, and the spring and creak of the metal fire escape above me. Arms wrapped around me, pinning the blanket in place. I struck backward, my elbow finding someone's ribs, drew my arm forward, and went to strike again.

A kick to the back of my knees dropped me to the ground, and another in my gut made me curl up, feeling like I was about to vomit.

I forced myself upward, wrapping an arm around my gut. Something cracked into the back of my head. My vision swirled into black.

I awoke sitting in a wooden chair, my wrists tied to the arms and my ankles bound to the chair legs. I tipped my head back and blinked hard. I sat in a corner of what looked to be a warehouse, surrounded by stacks of wooden crates and boxes. There was a small open space around me, with a desk and wooden filing cabinet to one side, like someone used this as an office in a pinch.

"Hey, boss-man, he's awake!"

I glanced right, where the voice had come from. Two men sat on overturned crates, using a third as a table to hold their cards and a lantern. Another lantern hung near the desk.

"Hey, boss!" One of the guys got up and disappeared behind the stacks of crates.

The other ignored me and proceeded to pick up his buddy's cards and look through them.

I looked down at my wrists. Rough hemp rope pinned them securely to the chair arms—they had pushed up my sleeves, not even leaving me the wiggle room that fabric could create. I twisted my hands anyway and cringed as the rope bit into my skin.

The echo of footsteps brought my head up again, and I watched as two goons with actual swords slung at their sides stepped into the little space. Following them was a tall, slim fae wearing his curly dark hair in a ponytail.

Behind him was Eric, bruises on his face and his arm in a sling.

My heart sank to my feet.

"That him?" the taller fae asked.

Eric spat and stalked forward. "Think you're smart now, wise guy?" His fist cracked against the side of my head.

The blow knocked me to the side, rocking the chair. I tasted blood at the back of my mouth, but I shook it off and straightened. "Shame ya couldn't do that earlier tonight."

Eric drew his fist back again. And yeah, I'm not ashamed to admit that I cringed a bit. Stars burst in my vision. My head snapped to the side, and this time I stayed there. My temple throbbed in a growing headache. If he kept this up, I was gonna pass out again.

"That's enough, Eric," the tall fae said.

"But—"

"I don't need to repeat myself, do I?"

The fae's calm, cool voice sent a chill down my spine.

Eric stepped away from me, head bowed. He nodded to his boss, then turned and left the room. At a nod from the tall fae, one of the swordsmen followed Eric. I heard the sching of metal on leather, then the sound of ripping flesh, a strangled gasp, and a limp body hitting the floor. The swordsman came back into the room, cleaning blood off his blade.

He'd just ordered Eric killed. Just like that.

I closed my eyes as shivers spidered down my back. Then I firmly pushed my fear to the back of my mind. I'd deal with it later. Now, I needed a cool mind.

The tall fae walked past me and settled on the desk, his ankles crossed as he studied me. His gloved fingers slowly tapped out a rhythm on the desk's edge.

I straightened up. "Hi. I'm Owan Craig. I'd say I'm pleased to meet you, but ..." I shrugged, tried to lift my hands.

He snorted. "Yes. Owan Craig, private investigator. And I'm Niall Byrne, as I'm sure you've already guessed."

"I had a sneakin' suspicion, yeah."

Niall crossed his arms. "Care to explain why you beat up one of my men at the Howler tonight, Mr. Craig?"

I shrugged again. "Didn't like his tone toward one of the waitresses."

"Ah yes. Roe Gillam." Niall glanced at the two goons who stood by their abandoned card game. "Eric's ex-girlfriend, isn't it?"

The taller of the two men shrugged. "To hear it, boss, they're still together, she's just bein' cagey."

Niall rolled his eyes. "All this trouble over a skirt." He eyed me. "What's your score in this fight?"

"Nothin'. Giselle just asked me to help out."

Niall laughed. "And out of the goodness of your heart, you agreed? She didn't even tell you who he was, did she?"

I shook my head.

Niall nodded, smiling. "Good. I appreciate you being forthright. It'll make this a lot easier." Niall went around to the back of the desk and opened a drawer, began slowly moving aside the contents. "Do you know what my biggest import is, Mr. Craig?"

I shifted in my chair. "Not particularly. I mean, a guy in my line of work can't help but hear things, but I'd just as soon keep my nose clean and outta any gangster's business. 'Less, of course, I get hired to be nosy."

His nostrils flared, and for a second, I thought that my usual banter—be sarcastic, let the bad guys know that I knew their dirty laundry, be flippant—wasn't gonna work on this guy. Maybe I'd read him wrong. Maybe it annoyed him too much.

Niall laughed, and I sagged in relief, feeling like my limbs had gone to gelatin.

Niall plucked a long, thin bundle, wrapped in white muslin cloth, from his drawer, closed it, and walked around to stand in front of me again. He picked at a knotted string around the bundle.

"I import elfwine, Mr. Craig. You're familiar with that, surely?"

"Sure." I was bluffing. I'd heard the term, but I'd always thought it meant liquor so fine that the fae could've made it.

Niall clicked his tongue against his teeth. "And here we were being so honest with each other. That's really such a silly thing to lie about." He paused in unwrapping whatever it was in his hand and looked up at me.

"How are you doing that?" I asked. "I'm a pretty good liar. Gotta be, in my business."

"No, Owan, you're really not."

"Yeah, just go ahead and insult a guy about his job, that's fine," I muttered.

He ignored my last comment. "Elfwine is distilled in Europe, by a certain monastery in the Alps where half of the members are fae. The secret was carried with them from Tir Ni-all when the paths were closed. The recipe has, from what I gather, largely unchanged since then, although I imagine its power has waned a bit along with the rest of our ... abilities."

He finished unwrapping the object and held it up, twirling it in his long fingers. My stomach curled at the sight of the black blade coated in a thick, flaking orange rust.

Cold iron was a right nuisance to full fae, making them sick, burning them, and eventually killing them by collateral damage. Rusted iron? Rusted iron was poison to my kind. All this guy needed to do was cut me with that blade—didn't have to be a big cut either—and he could sit and watch my veins blacken. My heart would fail, and I would die gasping and in horrible pain.

Niall made no move toward me. He leaned against his desk, twirling the knife through his gloved fingers, eyes fixed on me.

I didn't like to admit it, but his intimidation was working. I balled my fists, feeling the sweat on my palms.

"So ... there's a big market for elfwine, is there?" I asked, more to occupy my mind with something other than that stupid, twirling, orange-bladed knife.

Niall smiled thinly. "You'd be surprised at how much politicians are willing to pay to influence their opponents."

"Nah, I'm not. Sounds like the bloodsuckers."

Niall chuckled. "You know who else pays handsomely for a bottle of elfwine now and again?"

The answer hit me like a freight train. I gritted my teeth, lowered my head.

"That's right, the lovely owner of the Howler, that remarkable speakeasy you seem to enjoy frequenting even though it always gets you into trouble." He twirled the knife again. "Giselle's a smart broad, I'll give her that. She knew the type of opportunity she had when she opened the Howler. Elfwine, the drink that mimics anyone's favorite liquor and slowly enthralls them."

"Just my luck," I muttered.

"So some poor, unlucky sap gets himself enthralled and is basically doing free bouncer work for Giselle," Niall continued. He stopped twirling the rusted knife and studied the blade. "And then he's asked to take care of a nuisance for one of the waitresses, because Giselle knows who the guy works for and doesn't want to ban him for fear her supply of elfwine will be cut off, but can't let him continue for fear it'll give other guys ideas. What was she hoping? That it would look like some random white knight? Or that you'd kill him?"

"She should know better by now," I muttered. Stupid. All those years being enthralled, being too lazy to actually figure out how Giselle had a hold on me. Heck, now that I thought of it, part of the enthrallment was probably to keep me from askin' too many questions.

All I could be thankful for was that I'd left my gun in my coat pocket and hadn't killed Eric. Maybe that would earn me some leniency.

Niall stabbed the knife into his desk. The thud made me flinch. "The problem I face now, Mr. Craig, is what to do with you. Personally, I'd be all for letting you go. But you beat up one of my men."

"Who you just killed," I said quietly.

Niall waved the comment away. "Eric was a liability. Still, if it got out that you jumped him—"

"It won't from me," I assured him. "Look, Niall, we can deal, right? Surely there are terms we could come to."

Niall studied me for a moment, his eyes

half-closed as if considering. Then he straightened from the desk and left the room, his bodyguards trailing after him.

I was left alone, feeling sick and hollow.

Even though I knew Giselle had been charming me along, I'd still thought she was my friend. Some part of me had still trusted her.

I started twisting my left wrist. The rough cord chafed and tore my skin. Niall seemed reasonable for a gangster, but I wasn't about to takes chances. I didn't want to die—not here, with a gunshot to the back of the head, or in the harbor my feet bound to a sinking chunk of cement. And definitely not with rust poison seizing up my heart.

Blood streaked my wrist and I stopped, breathing hard. Panic welled in my gut. I tried to push it to the back of my mind, tried to stay calm. I'd been shot at while in the police force, and I hadn't panicked this much.

Then again, I'd never been tied up and threatened with rusted iron either.

I'd dealt with one case a few years ago where half-fae had been killed with rusted iron. I'd seen the dark, bulging veins on their bodies. The pain and terror, frozen forever in rigor mortis, on their faces. I didn't want to die like that.

Maybe if I drank elfwine that Niall Byrne gave me, my loyalty would switch to him. Should I offer that?

I immediately felt sick that I'd even thought such a thing. Giselle might be manipulative, but better be enthralled to her than to a killer like Niall.

"Owan!" The voice was a soft hiss from above me.

I whipped my head around, searching the shadows as I tugged harder on the rope around my wrists.

Roe scrambled into view on the top of a stack of crates. "Owan, stop! You're hurting yourself!"

"Roe!" I gasped. I sagged against the back of the chair and let out a strangled laugh. "How did you get here?"

"Rode on the back of the car, on the luggage rack." She clambered down, crouched beside me and starting pulling at the knots pinning my wrist.

"But how did you even hear—"

"You may not realize this, Mr. Owan Craig, but you kick up more fuss than a pair of tomcats when you're mad."

The phrasing made me laugh. "Okay, okay. Thank you." Even as I thanked her, though, my insides twisted in worry. Now I had to make sure she got out safe too. If Niall found the ex-girlfriend of his dead gang member here... I shoved the thought away.

"Thank me when we actually make it out."

After a few more seconds, the rope around my right wrist came loose. Roe moved onto my ankles as I undid the rope on my other wrist. As soon as I was free, I scrambled to my feet, then dropped back down. My legs were numb. I leaned over and started rubbing the feeling back into them.

"Roe, can you find my coat?"

"Can't you just lea—"

"That coat has my blood on it," I said sharply. "You ever been on the bad side of a fae? A blood curse is no picnic in Central Park, let me tell you."

"Oh." Roe bit her lip. "I'll look." She went around behind the desk.

I felt a little bad for barking at her, but with every second that passed, my shoulders got more tense. What would happen if we were caught?

"Here. It was half under the desk." Roe shoved it into my arms.

I stood, slipped it on and checked my pocket. The gun was still there. I caught Roe's hand and squeezed it gently. "Sorry."

She nodded, a faint smile coming to her lips.

We slipped into the shadows of the maze of crates. Roe immediately pulled my arm to the right. Beyond the lantern sitting at the mouth of the makeshift office, the warehouse was dark, with only glimmers of light showing here and there through the stacks of crates. I was completely lost in the maze, but she guided me with confidence, our feet barely making a sound.

Roe's free hand came to my chest, pushing me to a halt. "The entrance is just here," she whispered, pointing to the end of the corridor we stood in.

I nodded and stepped in front of her, glancing around the corner.

Several guys, all dressed in the rough clothing and caps of dock workers, stood in front of the entrance, talking in low tones. One flicked a silver coin back and forth in his fingers, but the others had their hands free or in their pockets. Any one of them could be armed.

I reached into my coat pocket and gripped my pistol. Hopefully we could get past them without a shootout, but it still made me feel better.

A shout echoed from inside the warehouse. Roe gripped my hand tighter.

"It'll be okay," I whispered, and risked another glance around the corner.

The four goons had straightened, their attention caught by the shout. And it was just my luck that most of 'em were looking right where I poked my head out.

"Hey, you!" One of them yanked a gun from his belt. The others dove for various weapons in the area.

I shoved Roe back.

The shot sparked off the cement inches from my foot.

"This way!" Roe dragged on my arm, pulling me up. We ran down the aisle, and she screeched to a halt beside a smaller stack. She grabbed the straps holding the crates in place and clambered upward, wedging her feet into the cracks in the wood until she was on the top of the stack.

I scrambled after her, and we dropped down the other side to a new, narrower corridor. Footsteps rushed past on the other side of the crates.

At the opening of this corridor, a square of lamplight shone on the cement floor. Freedom was within reach.

I pulled my gun from my pocket and swung around the corner, making sure no one stood there watching for us. As I swept the open area, nothing moved.

"Okay, I think we're clear." I reached back, gripped Roe's hand. "Ready to make a run for it?"

She nodded.

"One, two, three—" I squeezed her hand. "Go!"

We dashed for the door.

Halfway across the open floor, I spotted movement. Someone—something—running straight for Roe.

"Look sharp!" I dodged to the side and pushed her out of the way. She went tumbling.

Something struck me hard in the back, and hot spikes of pain jammed into my shoulder. I screamed. My hand went limp, and I lost the grip on my gun. My knees sagged.

I struggled, trying to see who had stabbed me.

A creature loomed over me in the lamplight, fangs bared in a mostly human face. Dark skin covered its left arm. A púca. I glanced down at the claws protruding from my shoulder. I was very lucky that it hadn't pierced an artery.

The púca began to lift me to my feet. I gasped, put my hand up to my shoulder, black tunneling my vision.

A shot rang out, and the púca lurched backward. It dropped me. I rolled to my back and pushed myself away. The púca paid no heed—its eyes were fixed on Roe, who stood across the loading bay, my pistol clutched in both hands.

"You think that bothers me, sister?" He snickered. "Try again."

"You asked," Roe said, and shot it in the chest.

The bullet knocked the púca back a few steps and to one knee. He pressed a hand to his chest, gasping.

"Owan, don't just lie there! Run!" Roe shouted.

I forced myself to my feet and staggered after her. The sounds of running steps and shouts echoed close by in the warehouse.

The street outside was muddy, slick from the rain earlier. The fish-and-refuse smell of the harbor hit me, now that I was outside and away from the sawdust in the warehouse. I glanced around. Roe yanked open the side door of a low-slung black car, scrambling inside. I ran around to the driver's side as she cranked the keys. The car rumbled to life as I slammed the door shut.

A bullet tore through the fabric roof. I yelped and grabbed Roe's shoulder, pushed her down to the seat as I worked the pedals and gearstick. The car's tires spun, then gripped, and we shot forward.

I drove fast through the maze of warehouses and buildings that made up the dockside district and didn't slow until we were on a main road, heading for my apartment. I glanced over my shoulder. There were no other vehicles on the road. I sighed and leaned back against the seat, then instantly regretted it as pain shot through my shoulder.

Roe pulled off her coat and pressed it to

my shoulder. Then she gave a strange, hiccuping gasp and covered her mouth with her hand. I glanced over. Tears rolled down her cheeks.

"Hey, hey." I reached over, out my arm around her shoulders, and gave her a gentle squeeze.

She let out a deep breath. "I ...I'm sorry. I just... I shot someone."

I gripped her hand on my shoulder. "Without you, I'd probably be slowly dying from rust poison right now. Or sinking into the harbor. Thank you."

I drove in silence for a moment, watching Roe out of the corner of my eye. Her jaw was set, but as we passed the street lamps, I saw tears still glimmering in the corners of her eyes. I squeezed her hand a little more. Nothin' I could say would make it better, but just to let her know that I was there. I'd been right where she was, first time I'd shot someone.

I pulled up to the curb several blocks from my apartment and shifted in the seat. Roe's hand fell from my shoulder, and I reached up to keep her coat pressed against the wound. "I'd better get inside and take care of this."

She nodded, eyes on the floor.

"Roe." I reached for her, gently put my hand on her shoulder. "I need to ask you something."

She looked up, brushed away the tears on her lashes, and took a steadying breath. Her makeup was smeared and her hair frizzy, but to me she looked just as pretty as she had at Giselle's speakeasy.

"First off, are you gonna be okay?"

She nodded. "It's not the first time I've shot someone. It was just ... it startled me. I didn't think I'd ever be able to hold a gun again."

Full of surprises, our little Missouri spitfire. I chuckled. "You did swell. Now, listen—Niall Byrne told me he imports elfwine. Does Giselle have elfwine in her speakeasy?"

Understanding bloomed on Roe's face. "That's why she wouldn't ban Eric."

"And she gave that elfwine to me so I'd be more compliant. So she could get work outta me for free."

Roe sighed and pinched the bridge of her nose. "Owan, I am so sorry, I didn't know ..."

"Don't be apologizin' for things your boss did." I pulled the keys from the ignition and pushed open the door, wincing. "C'mon. Let's get my shoulder cleaned up, then I'll take you home."

Without even being asked, she came around to my side of the car and put her hand on my arm. I accepted the support willingly as we walked down the street. This, I could get used to.

I spent the next two days at home, nursing my wounded shoulder and reading my new Rex Stout novel.

Or, tryin' to read, anyway.

My brain kept spinning around with the problem of what to do with Giselle's hold on me. Already I could feel an empty gnawing in my gut, something that told me that pretty soon, I'd be craving that perfect, amber-colored honey whiskey like nothing else. I even went out and bought myself a new bottle of the real stuff at another, human speakeasy. I paid through the nose for it and it didn't have nothin' on the elfwine version.

Roe came by and told me she was moving again, since Niall's men knew where she lived.

"Seems like a good idea," I told her.

Roe curled a piece of hair around her finger. She was wearing it down today, and I could barely stop myself from reaching out to run my fingers through it. She rubbed her eyes. "I can't stop thinking about how Giselle used you," she said softly. "She knew that Niall wouldn't like you roughing up one of his men."

"Funny you should say that." I straightened from my slump on the couch and winced as the stitches in my shoulder pulled. "I've gotta plan for that. Interested?"

She leaned forward, blue eyes showing a spark. "Tell me."

I told her. She laughed and said Giselle deserved it.

That night, I placed two phone calls to the police—one anonymous, and one in my official capacity as a private investigator. Then I got dressed and limped my way over to Giselle's speakeasy. Giselle greeted me as usual, eyes sparkling, a wide grin on her painted lips. She offered me a glass of my favorite honey whiskey. I accepted, put it on the bar.

"Well, baby?" She tipped her head to the side. "Not gonna drink it?"

My hands trembled, and I shoved them into my pockets. "That trash? Not bloody likely."

"Well, you're in a foul mood." She tossed a towel over her shoulder and turned, walking off. "Let me know when you've decided to be better company, baby."

I waited until she was at the other end of the bar, engaged with other customers. And then, casually, I picked up my drink, got up from my barstool, and walked over to the window.

Sure enough, there were a few more cars parked along the curb than usual, and some guys in suits were sitting along the benches and loitering on the corners.

I reached into my jacket pocket, popped the top on the lead-lined flask that I carried, and emptied the iron shavings into the lamp hanging beside the door. Sure 'nough, just as I'd thought, the golden, shimmering sparks in the air flickered. Some of them winked out. It was enough—now anyone, even full humans, could see the Howler as the speakeasy it truly was, rather than the drab storefront it masqueraded as.

Giselle's head snapped up, and she looked straight at me.

I smirked and stepped out the door. Try as she might, she wouldn't be able to weave enough glamour to cover it that quickly. Once I was outside, I raised my hand—the agreed-upon signal.

Plain-clothes detectives ran for the door, slammed it open, and poured inside, guns drawn. Shouts and screams echoed from inside. I watched the scuffle for a few minutes until two cops dragged Giselle out of the building, cuffs on her wrists. She looked over to me and bared her teeth. How had I always missed the monster under the glitz and glamour?

"Owan!" she shrieked. "How dare—help me, you worthless fool!"

I staggered forward two steps before I stopped myself. Focusing hard on keeping my feet planted, I raised the glass of elfwine and saluted her. "I am no longer your thrall, Giselle." Then I dropped the glass, allowing it to shatter across the sidewalk.

A faint golden thread appeared, stretched in the air between us. It snapped, and I felt a gentle pop in my chest. She screamed again.

I turned around and walked away.

I didn't slow my pace until I got to the street corner, away from the noise and confusion. Then I stopped. There was a low, snuffling sound behind me, and it made the hairs on the back of my neck rise.

The púca stepped up beside me. Even in humanoid shape, no one would ever mistake him for a human. Too-sharp, too-long eyeteeth glittered against pale skin. He wore no hat, and his white hair was slicked back straight from his forehead, revealing the ragged points of his ears.

"Figured one of Niall's goons would be lurkin' around." I adjusted the brim of my hat against the rain nonchalantly. "What's he have to say?"

"He wished you to know that the police raid found very little, as we'd anticipated your move. But even so, he's interested in a mutual truce."

" 'Fraid I could make his life too hot for him?"

The púca snorted. "Make no mistake, Mr. Craig, Niall Byrne could order your death without blinking an eyelid. But he rather admires your ...gumption, I believe he called it. This is his offer."

"You tell your boss sure, I'll bite. Truce. But he better not come knockin' at my door, or Miss Gillam's, anytime soon."

The púca flashed his bright white teeth again. Without a word, he turned and slunk away into the shadows of the alley.

I straightened my shoulders, pushing back a shiver. No need to show that I was scared to anyone who might be watchin'.

I went across the street to the little diner where Roe waited for me. I ordered coffee at the counter, then joined her at her booth by the back window.

"Looks like you're out of a job," I told her. "Sorry about that."

"She had it coming." Roe tapped the side of her coffee cup, the tired tension evident in her hunched shoulders.

"Ya know," I said casually, "why don't you come work for me?"

She looked up, eyes widening. "What?"

"Sure. Why not? It's about time I find a partner anyway."

"You mean secretary," she said.

But I could see a small, hopeful gleam in those pretty blue eyes. "No." I blew on my coffee. "I mean partner. You've got guts, and you showed yourself pretty handy with a gun the other night. Sometimes a doll can get places a guy can't. Besides, havin' a curator—"

"In training," she corrected again.

"—would come in handy, since it looks like we're gonna get a whole lot more business with the fae now that Niall knows who we are."

"Craig and Gillam, private detectives," she mused. "I like the sound of that. Will my name be on the front door?"

"Right beside mine."

She grinned at me, her eyes twinkling, and lifted her coffee cup up to mine. "To Craig and Gillam," she said.

"To partnership."

My cup clinked against hers, and the sound echoed in my mind, pushing away the fog of the elfwine. Come what may, Roe and I could watch each other's backs, I was sure of it.

I looked up the street at the activity at the Howler and chuckled. And it sure seemed like I'd had the last word over Giselle after all.

H. A. Titus, when not spinning storyworlds in her head, can be found moutain biking, skiing, or having adventures with her husband and young sons. She's been obsessed with fantasy and mythology since she was young. She is the author of a celtic urban fantasy novel, Forged Steel.

"Hold up, Ted. It looks like another action story is about to roll through."

BROADSWORDS and BLASTERS
Pulp Magazine with Modern Sensibilities

"The Mad Scientists of Modern Pulp"

Issue 11 Fall 2019

Stories by
J.C. Pillard
C.J. Casey
E.K. Wagner
Gary Robbe
James Kane
Aaron Emmel
Erica Ruppert
Kevin M. Folliard
Benjamin Chandler

Art by Luke Spooner

NEW ISSUE OCTOBER 2019!

Come check us out at
BroadswordsandBlasters.com
and search for us on Amazon.

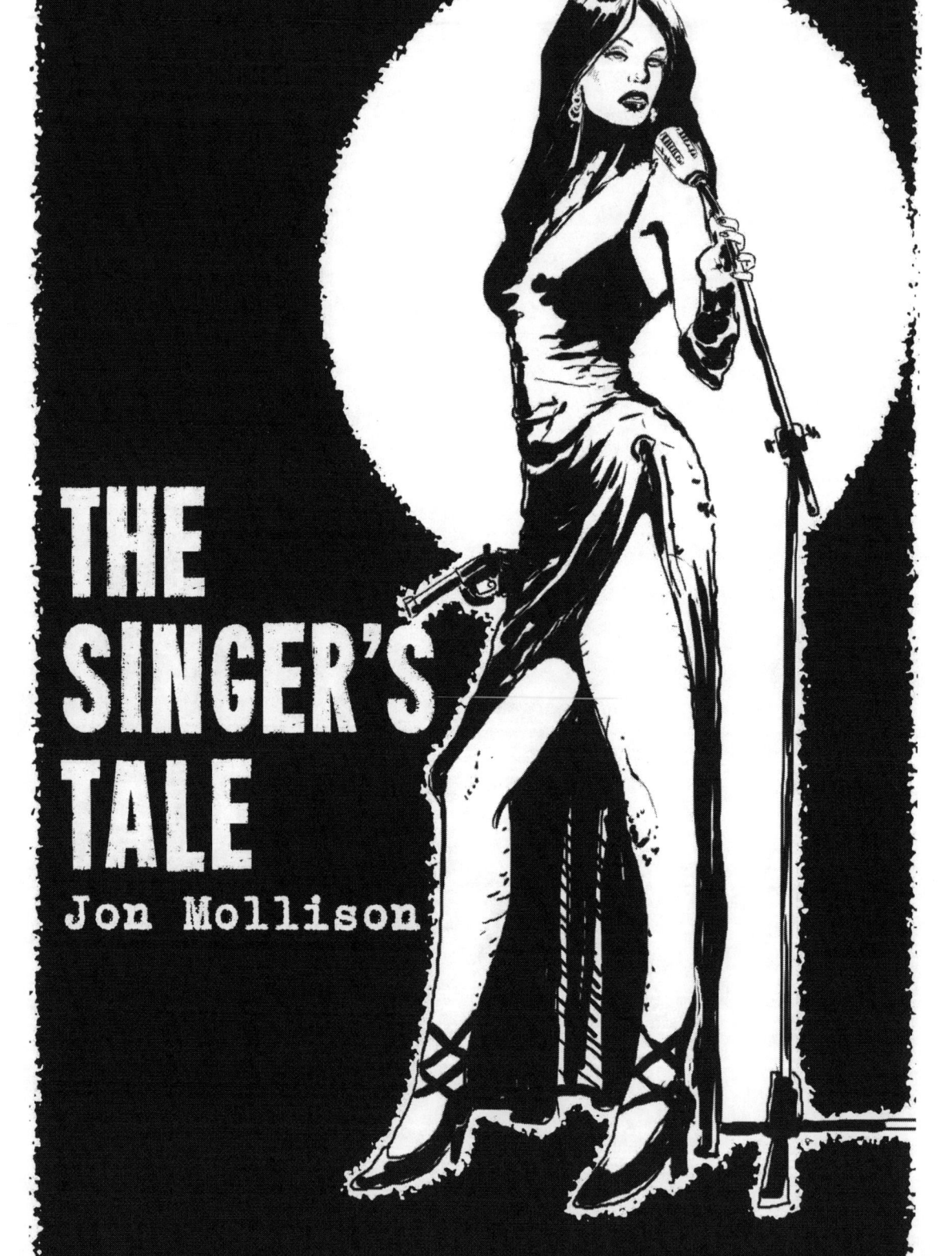

THE SINGER'S TALE

Jon Mollison

An alluring chanteuse uses everything she has to amass fame and glory in a mafia nightclub. How many lives is she willing to destroy to reach the top?

Part 4 of "Last Night at O'Reilly's"

The Singer's Tale

1

Putty in her hands.

The crowd roared in approval as she entered the Main Room of the most exclusive night club in town. All of the action at O'Reilly's ground to a halt when the headliner took the stage, even on a night like tonight. The usual crowd of local movers and shakers swelled with the addition of dozens of out of town businessmen and politicians. Partially blinded by a bright spotlight that illuminated her glossy red dress, the one with the lowest neckline in her wardrobe, and added bright waves of sheen to the curls of her pitch-black tresses. Ever the professional, her face betrayed no trace of discomfort at the hot lights. She paused at the first booth she passed to favor "Arctic" Aidan MacArralt with a blown kiss – the silver haired fox with the cool blue eyes sat pressed in the center of the booth between two red-headed tramps and a pair of his suited goons so she couldn't press any closer – and then waved genially to the rest of the crowd.

Somewhere in the shifting silhouettes of the backlit crowd stood O'Reilly himself, but Scarlett spared him not a glance. She saved her best performances for Arctic. And why wouldn't she? He was the power behind the O'Reilly throne, and as long as she kept Arctic wrapped around her little finger, O'Reilly couldn't touch her. But if things went well, after tonight she wouldn't have to play games with either of them.

She climbed the short steps of the stage, accompanied by a fanfare from the jazz quartet that sat down stage left. Kim hit an awkward note on his sax, fumbling the arpeggios again, and she smiled and blew the four tuxedoed idiots a kiss. The crowd wouldn't notice the ice in her eyes any more than they would the sour note, but Kim would get the message. He should have gotten the hint after she stormed out of their last rehearsal, but he was a sax player. You couldn't count on them to tie their shoes when there was a pretty woman in sight.

The room grew silent once the last tones of the fanfare died away. In accordance with her demands, the operations of the entire club came to a halt when she took the stage for the first time. The waiters stood attentively near the door to the kitchen. The dealers in the upper gallery halted their games. Behind them, the twin bars flanking the entrance fell silent as even the show-offs schlepping drinks paused their antics.

She drew a deep breath and held it for a twinkling. One last moment of suspense, and then she filled the silence with a half-sung and half-moaned opening lyric. As the sound of her voice died away, the snare drum picked up the song, and the quartet joined in, one at a time, adding a soulful accompaniment to the aching lament of a woman scorned who cannot bear to stop loving the man who done her wrong.

It was the perfect song to begin her set, allowing her to croon and sigh and slink around the stage like a pool of crimson seduction brought to life by an angel of desire. She used the twin spotlights to brilliant effect, turning and arching her body against the polished silver of the microphone stand. She showcased her best assets and used her dress to add curves and arches that appeared and disappeared as she lithely twisted about.

She played to the crowd for the moment. In part because she had yet to identify the national music producers who were her prey tonight, and in part because she wanted to prove to the two men that the crowd loved her with all the ardor she deserved.

She certainly deserved more than this crowd. She deserved her name in lights, and it wouldn't happen here. Exclusive the nightclub might be, but it wasn't the sort of place that could afford a flashing marquee or to run advertisements in the local Penny Saver.

That might be the Police Chief sitting next to the Fire Commissioner at table three, and the DA might be sitting in a back booth with his latest intern-slash-mistress.

This town was filled with holier-than-thou hypocrites that would have howled to the heavens in protest if they ever found out about O'Reilly's, and would have shut it down out of jealousy that they were never invited. They just didn't understand that the rich and famous needed a place outside of the harsh glare of public life to kick back, relax, and enjoy life without all of those pesky rules that the common mob was expected to follow.

And so there was no blazing sign out front with the name "Scarlett Greene" to the heavens, beckoning men and women alike inside. Her name had never graced an overhead marquee. No newspaper had ever enticed a crowd with the sultry image – so like that of a pin-up painted on the nose cone of a bomber – of the best thing that ever happened to O'Reilly's.

If she could just figure out which table held those two producers, all of that would change. She could charm the mitre off a bishop, and once those two big shots got a taste of her, they'd be as malleable to her whims as the rest of this crowd.

The last chord of her first song died away and the room filled with the applause and shouts of approval that filled her heart with pride. The crowd was bigger than usual tonight – a good sign for her prospects.

And if the two big shots couldn't recognize what she had to offer them? Well, she had other plans. There was always another way to get what you wanted out of men, all you had to do was push their buttons. If the men who ran this joint wouldn't give her a shot at the big time, she would just have to find a way to make it in their best interests to do so. Given the nature of O'Reilly's, it was a sure fire bet Arctic and Rye-Rye were running all of their finances under the table.

If she could just dig up a little dirt on this place and get it out without being caught, she could hide it someplace safe and start calling a few shots around here. Arctic was connected – he could throw his weight around and get her a recording contract, she just knew it.

It was a bold plan. Risky, and she knew it. She never would have even thought of it a few months ago, but ever since she had brought one of the two massive bouncers at the club under her spell, she felt safe and protected. She threw him a wink. Eric stood near the door to the kitchen, hands clasped before him. He looked good in his tight tuxedo – his broad chest stretched the fabric tight, and his long blonde pony-tail fell over one shoulder, making him look like a modern day Viking. A ghost of a smile crossed his normally stone-set face when she threw him that look. Yeah, she could trust him.

Not like Larry, that creeper in the kitchen. If she ever did find something she could hold over Arctic's head, it would be a lot safer in Eric's pockets than in Larry's greasy hands. She could barely remember why she had started stringing Larry along when there were so many better looking and more successful men around. Something about the desperate way he followed her about was like an ugly runt of a puppy. He was fun to play with for a while. But once a pure-bred like Eric showed up, she forgot all about Larry.

The next two songs went as well as the first two, and then it was time for her second act. She descended the stage steps to mingle with the crowd as the jazz band dropped out of their "Main Stage Sound" and into "Background". Kim managed to get through the songs without another mishap – a minor miracle. She wondered if maybe he knew about the producers and was deliberately trying to sabotage her big chance. He would, the little snake.

Once again, she started making her rounds with Arctic, but he was no help. He refused to make with the goods, despite all of her hints. Maybe he was too clever. She couldn't stay long at the boss's table. She had a whole room to work tonight and couldn't linger for long at any one table, especially when she was supposed to be encouraging the paying customers to drink.

She sighed inside, careful not to let her seductress mask slip, and decided that if Arctic was too clever to let her know which table held her producers, that O'Reilly probably wasn't.

She laughed along with a table full of Japanese businessmen – they preferred blondes, but were hardly immune to the charms of a six-foot statue – then circulated through a series of tables of mixed couples. She got a variety of reactions out of the women as she toyed with their men, tugging their ties and ruffling their thinning hair. She had grown used to the men's clumsy flirtations and eager puppy-dog stares, but she would never stop enjoying the jealous and angry looks from the dumpy women. Ha! They should thank her for getting their men's blood riled up like that – those women were in for the first night of real passion out of their cloddish husbands in weeks.

Her heavy lidded eyes scanned the crowd as she worked it. There were just too many sausage parties in attendance tonight for her to easily find her intended targets, and she didn't want to waste time with men who could do nothing for her. She tried to maneuver closer to one of her aces in the hole, Eric, so he could point them out. The big blonde bouncer with the pony tail was the one who had told her they were here tonight during a brief tete-a-tete in her dressing room before her first set.

Before she could reach the big handsome lummox, O'Reilly intercepted her.

"Great sound tonight, Scarlett," O'Reilly told her. He lightly placed a hand on the small of her back and steered her away from Eric. Toward the stage. A solidly built man in his late fifties, he stood half a head shorter than her, forcing her to look down her nose at his slicked back hair and the gray streaks converging in a pronounced widow's peak. He probably thought that white sport coat looked dashing with the red tie and kerchief, but she always thought it made him look like a small time Italian mobster in a low budget seventies flick. Hell, that wasn't too far from the truth of things. "...the crowd is getting restless," he was saying, "Why don't you get back on stage?"

She lightly slapped his arm and laughed, "Of course these men are restless, Rye-Rye. They get that way when I make them wait. But it's worth it, isn't it?" She stopped and leaned over a table with a pair of young suits. She leaned over to whisper loudly in one's ear and gave the other a clear view down her plunging neckline. "Are you boys in from out of town?"

The two men barely reacted, just a raised eyebrow and an awkward cough. Probably gay.

"Don't tell me you don't recognize the Anderson brothers," O'Reilly cut in. "They run the biggest plumbing supply chain in the city. They come in every week."

Damn. Now she remembered. Andy and Sandy Anderson. She actually went out on a date with Andy last year, a real snoozefest. Or was it Sandy? She laughed to cover her tracks and stood. "Don't be silly, Rye-Rye, of course I remember. I just like to keep these boys on their toes."

She spun away with a last lascivious wink and retook the stage. The night was still young. She could get through a forty-minute set and then take a break. Eric would find her back in her so-called dressing room and then she could pump him for more information. Meanwhile, she decided to give the crowd the show of her life. She found a way to work the Senator into a song, which elicited appreciative laughs from the crowd, and then disaster struck.

During her spectacular rendition of Femme au Chocolat, a fun little number Scarlett improved upon by adding a sultry flair to its sweet melody. Since she sang it in its original French language, most of the rubes in the audience probably thought it's random and nonsensical lyrics were actually a great protestation of desire and comparisons of a woman's love of chocolate for her love for a man. What could have been a flirty little number was transformed into an epic seduction in Scarlett's presentation.

Then, just as she was working her way up to the song's climax, the crowd turned away from the stage. She was used to them only half-listening, but this was something different. Something in the gallery had completely captured their attention.

Kim's saxophone faltered and the quartet stopped playing altogether. Scarlett had no choice but to stop singing. The song required the resonant chords to work.

She shielded her eyes with the back of one white gloved hand and followed the crowd's eyes. Sure enough, a commotion in the upper gallery had ruined her song. Three short steps up a wide stair led to a row of six gambling tables. Their green felt covers shone under spotlights just beyond a dark wooden railing.

The patrons in the last row of booths craned their necks to peer through the ornate wooden posts – completely forgetting the real star of the evening.

Furious, Scarlett bit back the retort that formed on her lips. It was then that she noticed Eric and O'Reilly and the second bouncer, the big black former boxer everyone called Bomber, converging on one of the blackjack tables. It was hard to make out through the lights, but – yes, yes of course.

It was Dawn's table. Dawn was a bitch. This was probably part of some plan of hers. The boys had broken up a fight or something. It looked like had separated a couple of greasy gamblers, and now they dragged one of them out through the door to stage left.

Nice. That meant the poor bastard was either being thrown out into the back alley or tied up and left to sweat out the night in The Box. Across from her dressing room was a little closet they used to store cleaning supplies. Sometimes when Arctic was really mad at a guy they'd leave him in there for a few hours to think about what was going to happen next. Whatever it was, it was never pleasant. Eric told her about how they'd rough up some of the guys and how they'd dragged a few guys – spies for a rival mob or guys caught cheating at the gaming tables, and once even an undercover cop - up to the third floor to wait for The Surgeon.

He said it just like that, too. "The Surgeon," complete with capital letters. It sounded so dangerous and sexy when he talked like that.

As Eric and his partner dragged the greasy little man in the cheap suit out of the Main Room, O'Reilly made an announcement she couldn't hear, but the band took the hint. They wisely started a new song, something light to take advantage of the excitement that ruined one of her best songs.

At the end of her set she decided her break could wait until she got a little payback. She breezed through a couple of tables and then ascended the short flight of stairs to the gaming tables.

Normally, she left the gamblers to their games and focused on the winers and diners in the lower seating area, but tonight wasn't normal. Dawn needed a little reminder of who headlined this joint, and who was just a hired card flipper.

Fortunately, Dawn was stationed at the first table to the left of the red carpeted stairs. In an instant, Scarlett took in the five remaining players and the dishwater blonde dealing the game. Dawn wore the black skirt, white tuxedo shirt, and thin black tie of all of the menial staff of O'Reilly's. Her face stayed carefully neutral as Scarlett interrupted the game.

Throwing their money away for a night in her presence, the players consisted of a middle-aged couple, a battle-axe of a woman and her nebbish husband, an aging cowboy accompanied by a much younger woman desperately clinging to her no-longer-youthful looks, and a fifth player. The last caught her attention for a couple of reasons. Not just his good looks. He was clearly a single guy, and wore a blazer and blue jeans – the only pair of blue jeans in the joint – which lent him an air of casual rebellion against the rat-race score-keepers that dominated the crowd at O'Reilly's. Mostly, though, she couldn't help but notice how he and Dawn both stiffened at her approach.

That was it. He was Dawn's Achilles heel. Scarlett had most of the staff of O'Reilly's wrapped around her little finger, but Dawn had proven a tough nut to crack. But now, Scarlett had seen enough awkward moments and subtle signs at tables occupied by revelers who didn't want the world to know who was actually sleeping with who to recognize that little look. He and Dawn were some kind of item, and he was all the leverage Scarlett needed.

She leaned over the end of the table, causing all three men's eyes to drift to her low-cut top and the delights it skilfully left just barely concealed. The henpecked man yelped as his thick wife elbowed him.

Dawn flicked a pair of cards his way and announced, a little too loudly, "Twelve."

Bingo. This was going to be more fun than Scarlett thought.

"Is Dawn taking good care of you boys tonight?" The singer sighed as she leaned over the green felt of the table. She waved a long finger at each pile of chips, as though to count the ones in front of each player. "One of you is certainly getting lucky tonight," she purred.

The good looking gambler tapped his cards for another hit, and glanced at the dealer who responded by flipping him a King, which pushed his tally to a heart-breaking twenty-two.

Scarlett stuck out her lower lip in an exaggerated pout and purred, "Ohhh, that's too bad. You see?" She sidled around the table, and ran a finger through the man's hair, then she leaned her face close to his and breathed into his ear, "Some girls just don't know how to treat a man." She moved to his other ear. "Don't you worry, gambler, Scarlett knows." She walked two fingers across first of the gambler's shoulders, not stopping until her hand walked clear across his shoulders, hopped the gap to the old cowboy's shoulders and then wrapped around the older man's neck. "But then, from the way you boys watch me on stage," she leaned in close to the Texan's cheek, "You already realized that."

The cowboy's aging wife boldly reached over and took Scarlett's hand from her husband's shoulder. She held it with two fingers and flicked it away in a melodramatic gesture of disgust. It did nothing to hide the woman's jealousy at Scarlett's obvious hold over her man's attention.

Scarlett merely laughed in response and stood to her full height "You boys look...thirsty. You should really do something about that."

She sauntered away, knowing the three couples at the table couldn't help watching her leave, and clearly hearing the harrumphs of the women as their men proved powerless to resist Scarlett's allure.

That would show Dawn who was boss once and for all.

Speaking of showing people who was the boss...

At O'Reilly's approach she placed the back of her hand against her forehead and waved dismissively. "Oh please, darling. I've been going for over an hour. I'm taking fifteen." Without waiting for a response, she breezed out of the Main Room, strode past the door to her dressing room with its clichéd glitter star on it, and instead entered the last door on the right.

O'Reilly's office.

A window the left was too grimy to see through, not that there was anything worth looking at in the alley beyond it anyway. There wasn't much worth looking at on this side of the window, either. An institutional gray steel desk with a green blotter dominated the room. Behind the desk, a wall filled with small black and white framed photos of O'Reilly shaking hands with random faces – big shots, none of which Scarlett recognized.

The desk faced the door and a deep leather couch sat against the wall. The wall opposite the window held a tacky landscape painting of green rolling hills above a windswept sea. The gold frame tried and failed to lend the hotel-room quality painting a touch of class.

Scarlett sneered, glad of the elbow length white gloves she wore, and sat at O'Reilly's desk. This would have to be quick.

The side drawers held nothing of interest. A worthless unlabeled bottle of amber booze. Pointless paperwork. Scissors. The usual detritus of any desk.

The top center drawer revealed a surprising treasury.

A heavy pistol rattled against the front of the drawer. A revolver for the tough gangster. She snorted – O'Reilly was a big softy. With the way he let Arctic push him around all the time, she doubted he had ever even fired the thing.

More interesting still were the three red ledgers. A quick thumbing through the pages of the top leather bound book revealed something strange – the book was already full. The final date was six weeks away, but every row and column had been filled with numbers and records of deliveries and payments and income.

These books were fake.

Why would an underground nightclub that didn't technically exist need fake accounting? Was O'Reilly skimming money off the top? She could definitely use that against him!

Then she noticed dust on her fingertips. A square of the bottom of the drawer also testified that the books hadn't been moved or touched in a long time. If O'Reilly was skimming money, he would have to update these on a daily basis. No luck there.

She slumped back in her chair and glanced around the room. A black file cabinet to one side held more boring manila folders stuffed with tiresome paperwork. Seriously, how much record keeping did a club like this need? It's not like it had to file reports with tax agencies or the EEOC.

Maybe she had underestimated O'Reilly. His office was as boring as the man himself, without a trace of anything untoward or illegal. Other than the fake ledgers, which couldn't be used to prove anything, it was no different from the offices at the small time clubs where she had started her singing career.

She cracked open the office door and made sure the coast was clear. The hallway was empty, so she returned to her dressing room momentarily, then went back out into the main room for her second set of the evening.

The band started low and mellow, the better to ease into the attention of the revelers. Performing for a crowd was a lot like seducing a man. Sometimes you needed to grab them by the ears and force them to pay attention, and sometimes you needed to sneak up on them and slide into their awareness before they realized you were there. If done right, they would slowly forget about their petty problems and trivial conversations and give you their undivided attention.

They were four songs into the second set, and Scarlett was feeling good about things – she had reacted to the interruption with aplomb after all – and lost herself in her performance. Now, with the crowd eating out of her hand once more, she turned her attention to scanning for the music producers. She had it narrowed down to three tables, and during her next break in singing she would spend a lot of time at those tables fishing for more information.

Not that she ever doubted it, but it looked like she might salvage tonight after all. The crowd sat rapt as she held them spell bound, inspiring feelings of love and loss and triumph and longing in them. Their eyes were glued to her statuesque form, a vision in glittering red made all the more dramatic by the bright lights and the black curtain backdrop.

Then disaster struck a second time. Another altercation in the upper gallery. Shouts this time, and once more O'Reilly and his two security men converged on Dawn's table. Worse, the commotion disrupted the spell she had cast on the crowd. Again they turned away from where she stood to the back of the room.

Scarlett stepped away from the microphone, forcing her band to scramble to vamp for a few measures as she composed herself to try and finish out the song despite the confrontation. Then O'Reilly actually waved to the stage and the band stopped playing.

Stunned, she couldn't even trail off – just cut off in the middle of a phrase like some sort of amateur. She moved out of the spotlight to get a better look at Dawn's table and planted a fist on one cocked hip.

It was that same gambler from earlier – the good looking one who hadn't been thrown out. She couldn't hear what was happening, but the much smaller man tried to attack O'Reilly and was immediately overwhelmed by the two bouncers. She loved seeing Eric rough up patrons and toss them around like rag dolls. This time Eric and Bomber didn't stuff the man in The Box like they had the other one, they trussed him up and dragged him out the front door. Even from here, she could hear the clatter of glass and trash as the man was bodily heaved out into the dirty alley.

Dawn looked stricken. She had one hand raised to her neck and winced at the crash. That figured. She and he were involved in same way, Scarlett knew it. Now she just needed to figure out how to use that information against the bitch.

O'Reilly pointed to the band and they started in on the next song. An instrumental jazz version of "Kung-Fu Fighting" seemed a little on the nose to her, but the crowd chuckled its approval, and it gave her a minute or two to reset and prepare for the next song in the set. She played it up by sketching out a few karate dance moves, not easy in her tight fitting dress. Hiding her irritation at the second interruption helped her win back the crowd and the next two songs passed without incident. She didn't manage the same sort of total attention Dawn had ruined, but she checked her emotions enough to keep the show going.

As she sang, she watched O'Reilly take Dawn out of the Main Room and back to his office. Gail, one of the boring waitresses filled in at Dawn's blackjack table. That was strange.

Dawn was a stone-cold ice queen who never missed a day of work. She refused to play Scarlett's games. She would never leave her position willingly.

Maybe she and that gambler really were working together, and O'Reilly had figured it out. Maybe he was going to stuff her in The Box with that other gambler.

It was all so exciting she forgot all about her irritation at Dawn's antics tonight. She really wanted to know what was going on back there, so she cut the second set short. She descended into the crowd, and the moment O'Reilly left his office she slipped past Arctic.

To her disappointment, Dawn wasn't tied up and strapped down in The Box. It just held just one gambler – the greasy one.

After he peek, she decided to check O'Reilly's office, and it held an even bigger surprise.

Not that Dawn was present. Scarlett expected that. What she didn't expect was finding the petite blonde dealer standing with one hand on the large landscaped painting, which stood open – the thing was set on recessed hinges and hid a wall safe. A wall safe that Dawn had one hand inside. She had turned at the sound of the door and now stood, wide eyed and scared.

Busted.

Scarlett cocked an eyebrow and leaned against the doorjamb. She folded her arms under her ample chest and grinned.

2

Scarlett deliberately shut the office door and sidled over to Dawn, who stood frozen with her hand still inside the safe. It was wrapped around three red leather ledgers that looked exactly like the ones in the top drawer of O'Reilly's desk.

"Well, well, well," Scarlett breathed. "It turns out little miss goody two shoes isn't as pure as the fresh driven snow after all."

Dawn snatched her hand off of the books and tried to shut the safe, but Scarlett prevented her by bracing a hand against the small iron door and looming over the shorter woman.

"It's not what you think." Dawn tried to sound tough, but her voice sounded timid, even to herself.

"Don't even try, dear," Scarlett chided. "You've been caught with your hand in the cookie jar." Next to the ledgers sat several envelops stuffed full of green bills wrapped in neat little bundles. She pulled out one of the envelopes full of cash and rifled through it. "I'm impressed. I guess your 'cool and detached' ice queen thing is all just an act. Pretend to be the emotionless, loyal servant until you stab O'Reilly in the back, and for what? A little money? Why you're nothing but a petty thief!"

Dawn opened her mouth, but hesitated.

"Well," the singer purred. "Tell me why I shouldn't scream for O'Reilly right now." She lowered her eyes menacingly. "You know what they do to thieves, don't you?"

Scarlett noticed the dealer's eyes flick to one side. Scarlett had forgotten the stringy gambler tied up in The Box. She laughed, "Oh no, dear. They'll just rough that sad little gambler up a little, put a scare into him, and threaten to kill him if they ever find him in this city again. For those caught stealing from the till, they have...special rewards." She took Dawn by one hand and caressed it gently with her thumb. "Such long and lovely fingers. Better enjoy them while you can."

This was more fun than she had had in a long time.

Dawn snatched her hand away and tried to move, but Scarlett blocked her path, still holding the envelop full of cash, which she placed on the edge of the safe. They stared each other down, Dawn wavering on the edge of fear and anger, Scarlett mocking and contemptuous.

A commotion in the hallway startled them both, and Scarlett fumbled her hold on the envelope full of cash. She bent to recover it as Dawn swung the painting closed and leaned back against it. Scarlett heard the door rattle, loud voices in the hall. With no place to hide the thick envelop on her person, kicked it under the sofa and she stood and leaned against the desk.

The noises moved down the hall and something thumped into the closet next to O'Reilly's office.

"I could have you killed for this," Scarlett hissed. "You owe me!"

Dawn inhaled, but said nothing. Then her face softened and she slowly sat down, crossed her legs, and spread her arms across the back of the small couch. "Have me killed for what? I've just been sitting here all this time."

Astonished by the sudden change in Dawn's demeanor, Scarlett's eyes narrowed. They flicked toward the door, but Dawn's voice stopped her cold.

"I wouldn't," the woman said. "It's your word against mine. And O'Reilly has been looking to replace you for months."

"Arctic loves me," Scarlett countered.

"I've got him wrapped around my little finger." She batted her eyes in mock innocence and pouted a little as she mockingly quoted, "Oh, Arctic, it was just awful! Please, you have to believe me. I'd do anything to earn back your trust."

"So you are a whore."

A hot wave of anger swept through Scarlett's chest. Nobody had talked to her like that since she stopped working the – her mind clamped down before it could finish that thought. Those days were behind her and would never return. Her mind refused to go down that path. Instead, she couldn't help herself, fists bared, she started to lunge for Dawn.

Before she could launch an attack, the door banged open.

"Scarlett?" It was Eric, all six-foot six blonde Viking in a tuxedo of him. "Here you are! What are you doing in here? Never mind – boss wants you both back out on the floor. Now." The man looked distracted. Agitated, he tugged at his tie and his cuffs and ran two hands to smooth his wrinkled, white shirt.

Scarlett smiled wide and said, "Of course, darling. After you, Dawn."

She rose from the couch, slowly and cautiously. She didn't like it, but anything Dawn said now would only have aroused suspicion in Eric. As the woman left, Scarlett sidled up to Eric and murmured just loud enough for her to hear, "Just one second, Eric. There's something I want to show you."

Scarlett smirked in triumph at the nervous look Dawn cast over her shoulder as she left the room. The door closed behind her, and Scarlett wrapped her arms around Eric's broad chest. She loved the way that he towered over her even when she was wearing her high-heels. She didn't want to smudge her lipstick, so she held herself to hugging the big, dumb ox.

"I need you to stall for me for just half a moment more," she sighed into his chest. "Go tell O'Reilly that I'll be out in two minutes."

He shifted on his feet uncomfortably. "I don't know if that's a good idea. He was pretty adamant, Scarlett."

She stiffened in his arms. In a flash of irritation, she stepped back and stabbed him in the chest with two firm fingers. "There's a lot of things you don't understand," she snarled. She didn't dare risk telling him about the ledgers or the cash. He was useful now, but soon enough he would be nothing but an anchor that needed to be cut loose. She had a new life filled with fancy West Coast parties ahead of her, and there wouldn't be any room for a lunkhead like Eric in that new life.

The bouncer stepped back under the assault of her ire, and she relented. Tough guys like this needed to be directed with a gentler touch. She placed her palms on his chest and slid them up and inside his black formal jacket. She stepped close and pressed the swell of her chest against his. She tucked her chin down and looked up at his handsome face through her long lashes. "Please, Eric. I just need to do one little thing." She rose up on her toes and pressed her cheek against his. Her lips tickled his earlobe as she whispered, "If you do this for me, I promise you a night you'll never forget."

As expected, he just couldn't resist when she really turned on the charm. She felt Eric shudder and then sag, all the tension gone from his body. "Okay, Scarlett. I just hope you know what you're doing." She stepped back and waved to the door with her fingers in a shooing motion.

"Trust me," she teased. "Have I ever steered you wrong before?"

The man rubbed the back of his neck with one thick hand as he actually considered answering the rhetorical question, but another flash of anger in her eyes warned him against saying anything more. His eyes widened in recognition of another oncoming storm of anger, and he turned to leave with as much dignity as he could muster.

"Darling," her voice stopped him at the threshold of the office. "You and I were never here – I've been in my dressing room this whole time."

He paused, thought about asking for an explanation, but noticed her words were an order and not a request. So he nodded and gently closed the door behind him.

Scarlett threw her head back and laughed. God, she loved men. So predictable. So easily misled. She was eternally amused that any of them ever thought they were in charge of anything in this woman's world.

Moving quickly, she snatched the fallen envelop of money from under O'Reilly's couch and returned it to the safe. She grabbed the three ledgers and stepped back to close the safe. On second thought, she snatched two of the envelopes stuffed with cash from the safe and then shut its door and swung the painting back into place as thought nothing had happened.

She peeked into the hallway – no one.

Clutching the ledgers and cash to her chest she slipped down the hall and into her dressing room. Just as the door closed, she heard voices in the hallway – Dawn and O'Reilly.

Her heart stopped for a moment. That idiot Eric hadn't bought her any time at all. She only needed a minute, and the man couldn't even give her that much. She sighed. Just another reminder of why it wasn't worth letting him ride her coat-tails out of O'Reilly's.

She hurried to drop the ledgers and cash into the bottom side drawer of her dressing table. Frantic, she covered them up using a pile of scarves and gloves and a random assortment of beauty products.

Her hands moved on auto-pilot – she was used to hiding things and keeping secrets – as her thoughts raced to craft a way to pin the missing books and money on Dawn. Hadn't Dawn been the only one in O'Reilly's office tonight? Scarlett had seen her taken back into the office after that fight at her table between those two greasy gamblers. And one of those men was a regular at O'Reilly's. She didn't know his name, but he spent an awful lot of time at Dawn's table – she must have stolen them and given them to that man the first chance she got.

The two voices passed the door to her dressing room, and she relaxed.

A shiver of anticipation ran down Scarlett's spine. She was doing it. She had everything she needed, and there was no going back. All she needed to do now was slip the books out of the club, and that would be an easy thing to do. Her last song ended twenty minutes before last call. She could change into street clothes, stash the books in the suitcase she used to bring her dresses in and out of the club, and then she would have Arctic under her thumb instead of just wrapped around her little finger.

She grabbed her lipstick, checked herself in the mirror, and realized she didn't need a touch up – she looked amazing already.

She blew her reflection in the mirror a congratulatory kiss, and swept back out into the Main Room with a predatory smile upon her face. She graced Arctic with a wink and a smile, relishing the thought that she would soon be in control.

She no longer cared which of the tables held the music producers. With the plan she had in place, she was getting out of this dump one way or the other. In a strange way, she almost hoped the music producers would fail to appreciate her talent tonight. It would make her appearance on the national music scene – helped along by an unwilling Arctic MacArralt – all the sweeter.

Before the scattered applause at her reappearance faded, and before Kim could ruin the moment with his screeching sax, she launched into her rendition of "Titanium", a high-flying song about rising up and succeeding in the face of all those little people who stand in your way and try to bring you down. She and the band had only rehearsed it a few times, and it wasn't part of their planned second set, but she didn't care. It fit the mood of the night.

To their credit, the band joined in after her first acapella stanza, almost as though they had planned it. They might be perennial second-raters, but they were still professionals, and a small part of her would miss them after she had moved on to bigger and better things.

Maybe not Kim, though. She had heard drummers that could play a better saxophone.

3

Her third set of the night went as well as the first two, but she no longer minded the interruption.

At least this time it came from a new direction. Instead of table three in the upper gallery, the disruption came from the kitchen. A clatter of dishes started off muffled, then rose in volume as the swinging door banged open.

A slender man in a stained white shirt and black pin-striped pants lunged out of the kitchen brandishing a wicked looking cleaver. Gangly and goggle-eyed, the long shanks of the man's hair along the sides and back of his head were held fast by a hairnet that covered the bald top of his head with a lattice of black. The crowd gave way as he brandished a knife at Scarlett and cried out her name.

The poor sap was one of the line cooks that worked and sweated alongside Larry, not even a sous chef, and she couldn't remember his name. He had carried her things out to her car a few times and she even teased him with promises of a date night sometime in the future – a silly game perhaps, but the man's goofy grin and hopeful eyes amused her.

They didn't look hopeful now. They looked downright murderous. But she wasn't worried. Eric had assumed his usual station near the kitchen doors to Scarlett's right – Bomber watched the upper gallery, and nobody was stupid enough to start anything off stage left while Arctic and his private goons were in the club.

"Is it true?" The crazed cook's plaintive voice cut through the faltering chords of the jazz musician's song. Then he grunted as Eric hit him from behind and dragged him to the floor.

The crazed cook only had time to take three steps into the Main Room before Eric hit him with a flying tackle powerful enough to bring down an NFL quarterback. She had no idea how the bouncer managed that trick in the close confines of the dining tables and the milling patrons, but he did it. The knife went rolling across the carpet and an instant later Bomber jumped on the cook as well.

Scarlett sighed and stopped singing when the jazz quartet faltered. Then she planted her wrists on her hips and cocked both her hips and her head at the commotion.

Robert and Eric hauled the cook to his feet as the man wailed, "After everything I've done for you!"

She gave the man an exaggerated look of sympathy, and even shrugged as the bouncers dragged him out of the room and back into the kitchen. The chef, a silver haired gentleman named Val watched them drag his man through the swinging door and then followed. Just like that, it was over. The entire event probably took less than a minute, but it left a mark on the crowd. They stood, uncertain and clearly worried that the night had seen three altercations. Nervous eyes looked about, wondering who else was likely to go berserk tonight. Just like that, a pall had been cast over the night's festivities.

O'Reilly must have felt it, too. The man was headed over to Arctic's table, and even through the blinding spotlight, she could see he had the hangdog look of a man walking to the gallows. Arctic may not have looked any different than usual, but Scarlett could imagine that the constant interruptions in the steady flow of food and drink and money had him on edge, too.

If they were pissed now, just wait until they found out what she had planned for them.

She laughed at the thought, and then as the sound of her laughter echoed through the subdued noise of the crowd, she realized that getting this party back on track was up to her.

She purred, "Now I know what you boys out there are thinking," and wagged one finger like a scolding schoolmarm. "You might be able to get my attention like that, but you'll never get anywhere with me by getting yourself beat up and dragged out of this club. No sir, if you want to get in good with a girl, what you need to do is get in good with her friends." She glanced at the band, willing them to take the hint. "And we all know who a girl's best friends are, right?"

A ripple of laughter spread through the crowd as the familiar strains of "Diamonds are a Girl's Best Friend" broke out. The geniuses behind the instruments had been ready for her, if only every man could so easily anticipate her needs she wouldn't have to resort to blackmail.

During the course of the song she really played the vixen act to the hilt. She bent a little lower at the waist to allow for a better view of her cleavage. She kicked one leg out, parting the long slit in the side of her dress, which let the skin of her calf and thigh shine white against the glittering red sequins of her dress.

To bring the women on board, she sighed and waved a pudgy businessman up to the stage. Naturally, he dutifully obliged, with a cigarette dangling from his mouth and hope shining in his eyes.

Scarlett explained to the crowd, "Some people look down a girl trying to use her assets," Scarlett put a special emphasis on the first syllable of that word, "to get ahead in this cold world."

She pointed to the cigarette in the man's mouth and held out a hand. He patted his jacket and brought out a half a pack. He shook it and extended the pack to her, one white cigarette poking out of the little box.

She rolled her eyes, held up two fingers, and waited.

"I say a girl should use the talents God

gave her." The man took the hint and lit the cigarette, then placed it between her fingers. They were amazing things, cigarettes. She could make the mere act of placing one against her lips and taking a drag then letting the smoke billow and writhe above her head seem like an invitation to far more dangerous bedroom activities. She studied the burning ember as she continued, "But then I don't say that often, because..." she paused. She placed the cigarette between her ruby lips and took another drag. She slowly exhaled, blowing a series of perfect rings of smoke out into the air over the heads of the nearest table.

"I don't give a damn about my bad reputation."

The drummer kicked into a quick tempo and the piano, sax, and bass joined right in on cue. Nothing won women over to her side like a Joan Jett song. She abandoned all pretense of sexiness and played to the women, flexing and striking poses that the dull-witted women in the crowd associated with strength and power. They thought this act was for them, but Scarlett understood men well enough to know that they loved the idea of claiming and subjugating a strong and independent woman as much as any other. She had let more than one ex-boyfriend think his tender ministrations had chased every last feminist thought from her mind.

"A girl can do what she wants to do, And that's what I'm gonna do," she sang the line staring directly at Arctic, who raised one curious eyebrow. He was smart enough to suspect she was sending a message, and she thrilled at the thought that he might think back on this moment after she laid down the law with him.

It worked. The crowd relaxed and remembered what they were there for – to unwind and enjoy her performance. With the night back under her control, she allowed the quartet a break from reading her mind and settled back into the usual third set song list. From here on out it should be the old stand-by's and a few more contemporary songs recrafted for a formal dinner nightclub. After one more song to really smooth things over, she decided that a little personal touch might be in order and gave the band the signal that they should take a break, too.

While flirting with the table of Japanese businessmen, she caught a quick flurry of activity out of the corner of her eye. O'Reilly, Eric, and Bomber all ducked into the hallway to her dressing room at the same time.

The blood drained from her face.

O'Reilly must have found his ledgers and money missing. Now he summoned his goons to ransack her dressing room, and Eric was too dumb to cover for her. Or had Eric sold her out? Was he jealous that she was stringing that cook along?

She excused herself from the table and set out for her dressing room before they found the incriminating evidence.

To her surprise, they weren't interested in her dressing room. The three men crashed out of the metal door at the end of the hallway and out into the darkness of the night.

Confused, she followed them as far as the threshold and held the door open a crack. She caught sight of O'Reilly, the last of the men to leave, as he turned the corner at the end of the alley, running after his security personnel.

But who were they running after?

The only thing that came to mind was that greasy gambler Eric had stuffed in The Box early in the evening. She checked the supply closet and found him still there and still tied to a rusting drain pipe. She shut the closet door and leaned against it, considering her next move.

If that greasy gambler was still in there, that left only Dawn, the snotty dealer Scarlett had interrupted in the act of stealing from O'Reilly's safe. Scarlett realized she hadn't seen the dealer on the floor in a while, but didn't know what that meant. She wasn't in The Box. Had O'Reilly dragged her back into his office at some point when Scarlett was distracted with entertaining the drunks?

She moved to O'Reilly's door, trying to make her footsteps silent – not easy in her stilettos – and whipped it open.

No one.

The landscape painting was flush against the wall. The wall safe was closed. The unlabeled bottle of scotch still sat in the of the green pad on the gray desk.

Scarlett stood and tapped a long, gloved fingernail on her teeth as she thought.

Something very strange was going on at O'Reilly's tonight. The constant interruptions of her act were just the most obvious signs. O'Rcilly had been acting funny all night, too. Constantly worried about Dawn, his golden girl, on the one night she was clearly off her game. He didn't have that other gambler, the one Dawn had the hots for thrown into The Box with the greasy one, either. O'Reilly might have been a softy, but he didn't usually let a slight like that go unpunished.

In fact, come to think of it, he had left Scarlett alone for most of the night, too. He typically rode her ass all night for spending too much time on the floor mingling with the patrons or for spending too much time in her dressing room, or for spending too much time having fun with the staff. Tonight, he had only nagged her once or twice. She had taken that as a sign that he was distracted, but now she wondered what exactly it was that had him distracted all night.

A terrible thought crossed her mind.

She moved around the desk and checked the long central drawer.

Sure enough, the ledgers were missing.

So was the gun.

But the missing ledgers were dummies – copies made and pre-filled out weeks in advance. Who would want those?

She wondered if Dawn had been stupid enough to steal the wrong ledgers, then realized that she had caught Dawn with her hand in the wall safe.

Dawn knew. The bitch knew.

So why were the ledgers gone now?

The night had gotten a lot more complicated. A few minutes ago, she had been the one in charge, laying plans and getting ready to strike at her unsuspecting victims. Now, she didn't know what was going on.

A second realization struck Scarlett like a brick.

The missing ledgers.

Slowly, she stood and moved back around the desk.

She pulled at the painting and it swung noiselessly open. The wall safe sat shut, and Scarlett's chest tightened. She couldn't remember if she had locked it earlier.

Swallowing hard, she put one hand on the handle. She took a deep breath and pulled.

The safe swung open, and she let out a short, barking laugh of relief.

Inside, a stack of cash stuffed envelopes slumped to one side, but the expected red ledgers were gone.

Scarlett slowly closed the safe, making sure it didn't lock this time. She swung the painting back against the wall, and left the office with a practiced casualness.

Inside, her nerves were thrumming like high-tension lines in a hurricane. Outside, she forced herself to move with the same lithe grace as always. Whatever happened, it was important to at least look like she was the one in charge.

Besides, it might not be too late to cover her tracks. She hadn't told anyone anything. Eric might suspect, but he didn't know anything.

She almost peeked out of the door at the end of the hallway to make sure Arctic was distracted, but with the quartet on their break in the kitchen, it was too quiet. She didn't dare risk tipping him off now that she resolved to put everything back the way it was and pretend like none of this had ever happened.

She returned to her dressing room and pulled the money and ledgers out of their hiding place.

Gazing at them, she thought that even though tonight hadn't worked out, she could always steal the ledgers again next week. She made it into O'Reilly's office, opened the painting again, and was reaching for the safe when a sudden thought struck her.

How would she steal these next week?

The safe would surely be locked.

So why wasn't it locked tonight?

She placed the bundles of money back in the safe, but hesitated when it came time to give up the ledgers. She stood, both hands wrapped around the three red books, and tapped her fingers on them as she ran down the list of possibilities.

Surely O'Reilly and Arctic wouldn't leave the safe unlocked intentionally. Just as surely, Dawn was no expert safe-cracker.

And yet, the woman had somehow managed to open a safe that, until tonight, Scarlett hadn't even known existed.

No – there was no way that uptight blonde glorified waitress could have opened the safe. She must have had help. That gambler? That didn't make sense either. He had been thrown out, too. She remembered that because Dawn had been so upset at seeing her man beat up by Scarlett's man that she needed to take a break...

Right here, in O'Reilly's office.

She must have let that guy back in so he could break open the safe.

But he couldn't have had the time to do it. O'Reilly had spent a long time back here with Dawn. Far too long to allow that gambler to get it, crack the safe, and get out with the real set of ledgers.

It didn't make sense. The only way it would work is if O'Reilly left the safe unlocked, but then he would be giving all of the evidence of his own crimes over to Dawn and that gambler.

But it was the only way. It was the only way to explain how Dawn had gotten her hands on the ledgers.

And Scarlett had figured it out.

Arctic was going to love this.

She couldn't wait to tell him that the man running his precious club was selling him out.

She turned to the door and then remembered that she still held the false ledgers in her hands. Mentally kicking herself, she turned to place them back inside the safe.

The door opened behind her.

She froze.

Strong hands grabbed her by the shoulders and flung her down onto the brown leather sofa.

Arctic stood over her, and hissed, "What have you done?" Fire blazed in his ice blue eyes, his face was contorted in a rictus of fury.

She tried to stammer an explanation, but he didn't wait. His hand slashed out in a sudden backhanded blow that sent her reeling down to the sofa, then he whirled to the safe. He ripped the door, heedless of an eruption of noise coming from the Main Room. Footsteps thundered in the alley outside.

Scarlett gave no thought to the commotion, either. Hot tears stung her eyes and she lifted one hand to the numbness of her cheek where Arctic's hand had struck.

He ignored the money and pulled out the ledgers, but immediately noticed something was wrong with them. He let two fall to the floor and ripped at the cover to the third. In a rush, he rifled through the pages, searching for something.

She lay on the couch with the gangster looming over her, dazed and uncertain of how to play the situation. Scarlett watched as his eyes danced across the pages. Anger faded to disbelief and shock, and the third ledger fell to the floor.

Arctic sagged and stumbled back against O'Reilly's gray desk.

Confused by the sudden change in his demeanor, Scarlett sobbed, "Arctic. What's going on?"

Jolted out of his reverie, his eyes snapped into focus and he sneered at Scarlett.

"You!" He snarled and raised a fist. He stepped toward the cringing singer.

He didn't make it.

A voice shouted, "Freeze!"

Four big men armored in black law enforcement fatigues, ominous black rifles at the ready, spilled into the small office. They piled onto Arctic and dragged him away like a common street hood.

They handled Scarlett with a little more delicacy, but nothing like what she deserved. Deep down, she knew that she should have protested. She should have cried and cringed and played on the SWAT team's sense of honor and chivalry. She should have played up her sex appeal and insisted she was just a working girl caught up in Arctic's schemes and just a victim in this whole situation.

She should have done something while they handcuffed her, read her her rights, and shoved her into a long line of handcuffed and intimidated men and women in evening wear. She should have done something, but she couldn't think of anything to do.

She was numb to it all.

It was all too much. It wasn't supposed to go like this, and having all of the control ripped from her grasp left her in a shock that she didn't truly wake up from until days later.

After the investigation. After being stuffed into a crowded van and hauled down to the station for hours of waiting in a jam packed holding cell. After hours of questioning in a small room that smelled of old coffee and sweat born of fear. After being released onto the Monday morning streets in her evening gown and black stilettos.

The newspapers told her that O'Reilly died in a shoot-out that night. They said two inside men – the dealer bitch and her gambler boyfriend – were cops who busted the Arctic mob. They told her Arctic was only avoiding a death sentence by pleading out to a series of lesser crimes that would see him up for parole in the year 3,791 A.D. The papers told her that dozens of state and city officials had also been swept up in the police raid that last night at O'Reilly's.

The papers didn't tell her what happened to Bomber or Eric.

In a dazed confusion she sought refuge in

her small downtown apartment. Somehow, she would find a way to get back at Dawn and her gambler and Arctic and every last one of them. She wasn't sure how, but her reeling thoughts circled around who to seduce, who she could manipulate into exacting her revenge for her, while she waited from a safe distance. She would figure something out eventually – she knew it.

And yet she knew not to leave her apartment until she had found a new champion. Someone like Larry or Eric, but stronger and richer and dumber. She closed the drapes and didn't venture out. Her choice of meals soon dwindled down to microwave popcorn or chicken broth.

She was still dreaming and plotting of a vague and bloody vengeance when a pair of Arctic's goons, two men who hadn't been caught, but who owed the man one last favor, found her seething in her apartment three days later.

And by then it was too late.

Science might keep food on his table, but fiction keeps Jon Mollison's soul nourished. A dilettante of an author, he mainlines science fiction and fantasy, but can never fully escape the lure of modern day adventure fiction. If you enjoyed this work, then look for his stories of Karl Barber, a man with a K-Bar and a thirst for justice in Issue Zero of StoryHack or from Milhaven's "Tales of Suspense".

"Well, we got some regular fiction over here."

"I'm not looking for regular, Clyde. I'm looking for superior, StoryHack-grade stuff."

LEARN TO WRITE
like the PULP masters

Pulp Era Writing Tips contains 17 articles from some the best writers of yesteryear. In this book, you'll learn:

- Several methods of plotting a story.
- How to make characters more interesting.
- Ways to target your fiction to a specific audience.

Bust out that laptop, tablet, pencil, or pen and start writing today. You know that story is in you, desperately trying to claw its way out!

The publishing world has undergone sweeping changes in the past few years, but excellent writing techniques will always be in style.

AVAILABLE NOW

At all major online booksellers

THE LAIR OF THE OLD ONES

by Stanley W. Wagenaar

A wandering adventurer encounters the daughter of a local ruling baron, helps her out in a scrap which embroils him in a wild adventure that takes him face to face with a gargantuan cosmic monstrosity.

The Lair of the Old Ones

By Stanley W. Wagenaar

Chapter 1.

The heavy war bow creaked ever so faintly as the brawny warrior drew the nock to his cheek. The wary young doe, the target of the concealed archer, heard the slight sound, but merely tensed and looked about without finding the source. The bow was constructed of laminated wood, buffalo horn and cat sinew, and the arrow launched from its rest towards the deer in a blur of speed with a sharp twang of horsehair bowstring. The doe was already in mid leap as the arrow reached it, and the shaft passed completely through the cage of ribs that protected the vital organs within. The doe bounded on for ten or more strides before falling to the grassy path, dead in mid-flight.

The hunter stepped out from the screen of bush and looked about the heavily forested path. He was a big man, not especially tall, but powerful and compact in build. His red hair was close cropped to his scalp, and he wore a short, dark red beard. But, his most outstanding feature was his eyes-a strange aquamarine green, set in a pale, white face made ruddy by the elements.

Gunnolf, wandering warrior of the Northrealm, walked over to the deer, drawing a long iron fighting knife in preparation to dress-out his kill. He cut the throat to drain what blood he could from the carcass, and opened the belly neatly to remove the entrails. As he worked expertly on the deer, he thought about making camp, building a roaring fire, and roasting fresh meat for his dinner. But his thoughts of dinner were shattered by a sudden scream.

Gunnolf's hand blurred to the sword at his side, and bright steel flashed in the late afternoon sunlight before the last echoes of the scream died away. The voice was a woman's, but it was not a scream of fear, but rather of rage and defiance. And it came from the dark woods not far from where Gunnolf stood, possibly no more than 100 strides away. The woman screamed again, and Gunnolf launched himself toward the sound, his powerful bare legs pumping beneath his leather kilt. He wore only a scale mail shirt for armour, and had no helmet on his head, but he had a blade in each fist as he ran towards the sounds of strife just beyond the slight forested rise in front of him.

He broke through the thick brush onto a ledge of granite, overlooking a small grassy clearing, and saw the source of the strident alarm. A woman stood on the far side of the little glade with her back pressed against the trunk of a gigantic oak. A long, slim rapier quivered in her grip, dripping dark blood from the razor edge. Her skin was dark, and her hair blue-black, twisted into a long braid. She wore a blouse of rough cotton, men's leggings of soft doeskin, and brown riding boots of polished leather. Standing in front of her in a rough semi-circle was the object of her rage, two score or so warrior trolls of the deep woods. All of this Gunnolf saw in an instant, and with a wild battle roar, he leapt from the ledge, sword glinting in the dim light. He landed among the inhuman troll warriors like the blast of a thunderbolt.

Left and right he struck with iron knife and steel sword, and the dark troll-blood spurted high into the air. Here, a hideous, dark green head jumped from its owner's shoulders, there, an arm was sent spinning into the woods, still gripping a sword. As Gunnolf waded into the snarling, smiting pack of trolls, the dark haired girl began swinging her rapier with renewed hope and vigor. The trolls were about five feet tall, thickly muscled with dark green skin. They wore rough clothes of crude homespun cloth, or stitched leather. Over these basics, they covered themselves with a smattering of armor; chain mail, horned helmets, iron studded leather and small steel bucklers on their free arms. The weapons they bore were of high quality steel.

Gunnolf swung a mighty blow with his curved steel sword at a howling troll, and it chopped deep into the creature's shoulder, split the upper chest and lodged itself into the thick spine. As the dying foe collapsed, Gunnolf's trapped sword was dragged from his blood-slippery hand. He caught a leaping troll by the throat with his free right hand, and drove the iron knife in his left hand deep into its lower belly. A twist and a heave upwards on the knife ripped it up to the breastbone, and the belly muscles opened like giant, grotesque mouth, releasing its contents in a bloody, slimy rush.

Gunnolf threw aside the corpse, and, unable to see his sword in the pile of green, bloody bodies, simply picked up one of the several dropped swords of his opponents. It was straight, double edged and the blade was about as long as Gunnolf's arm. It appeared to be forged of fine steel. He roared with wild laughter, and, whirling the glittering blade about his head, dove back into the bloody fray. The troll-blade whistled in the still air, and with Gunnolf's might behind it, nothing could stop it. Bucklers split, mail parted and helmets burst before the glittering steel in Gunnolf's fist, and the dark troll-blood sprayed high into the air like ocean waves bursting on a rocky shore.

Suddenly, the fight was over. Four remaining troll warriors broke and fled into the woods, leaving behind nearly two-score dead on the trampled, bloody grass.

Gunnolf turned his wild, battle maddened gaze upon the woman, and she took a step back. The green color in his wide eyes seemed to spark with ferocity. He was splattered with troll-blood. His exposed arms were big and muscular, with bluish veins thick and writhing like serpents beneath the pale skin. He blinked, and the green eyes became clear and sane.

"Are you hurt girl?" rumbled the warrior between deep inhalations as his breathing, rapid from exertion, began to slow.

"Nay, no troll-blade touched me at all, more than can be said of your hairy hide." said the dark haired woman, with just a ghost of a smile on her lips.

Gunnolf looked down on his thick torso, and only then noticed his condition. His shirt of scale-mail hung in tatters, a testament to the quality and sharpness of the troll weapons. However, most of Gunnolf's wounds were shallow, and would heal cleanly: the mail had done its job.

"I present a somewhat larger target for these creatures than your slim form does, and more of them came at me at once than faced your rapier." grunted the warrior.

"Yes, you are right, I may have killed one or two less than yourself." laughed the young woman. "But my form is much cleaner and effective, with far less energy expended in the doing. You stand before me blowing and snorting like a bull after a river crossing, while I am hardly winded, and ready for more!"

Gunnolf's eyes glinted ferociously, "Bring me a hundred more of these Trolls, and I will paint this glade with gore, and send them all to their ancestors. And still match steel with the likes of you, lass. "

He turned back towards the pile of troll corpses, and as he searched for his sword, he shot back over his shoulder to the girl, "And you are welcome."

Once again the girl laughed. "Relax, warrior. I but jest at your expense, for you seemed of thick hide and good humor. I am glad you showed up when you did, really."

Gunnolf retrieved his curved sword from the dead troll's spine, and wiped it clean with some rough cloth ripped from a corpse. He looked around the bloody battlefield, and found a leather and steel scabbard of the correct size for the troll sword still in his hand; he was impressed with the fine steel, and would be keeping this one. "I have a half-butchered deer just down the trail that I do not want spoiled by scavengers..."

"My father, the Baron, would be happy to have you stay at the Keep, for tonight at least." said the girl. "I am sure he will reward you well for your help, if you seek gold."

"Well, as long as he will share my deer meat, I could be convinced to drink some of his ale, and perhaps add a few coins to my purse." said Gunnolf. "Who is your father, and for that matter, what is your name?"

"My father is Baron Victor Falkenrath, lord and keeper of the lands hereabouts. And I am his daughter and only child, Victoria." she stated. "The keep is but an hour's march to the south from here. We can be there before sundown, and that would be a good thing in these troubled times."

"Very well." Gunnolf said, "Allow me to gather my gear and my kill, and we can be on the march shortly. I have been on the trail for some weeks, headed south, and have not slept with a roof over my head for long enough. Nor has ale passed these lips in far too long- let's get a move on lass!" he roared. His mood had swung again, and he was happy to meet new people and see new things. He clapped the girl on the back in a fit of joy, and nearly sent her headlong into the brush.

"Easy, you clumsy oaf!" shouted Victoria. Gunnolf only laughed gustily.

Chapter 2

As the sun slowly set, Gunnolf and Victoria strode up to the heavy oaken gate of a great stone keep. Gunnolf looked up at the great granite pile, towering high in the evening light, and he estimated the walls as being a good thirty feet high. The walls were built of great granite blocks, rough hewn, and levered into place without mortar. Thick moss and creepers burst from the seams, and the walls were stained with minerals leaching from the rock, the effects of a thousand years of rain, wind, frost and sun.

The walls had walkways on the interior which allowed defenders to fire arrows and such upon attackers. Even now, guards looked down upon the two as they entered the gate. Torches set in iron supports along the walls were just being lit, and orange flickering light sought to hold back the approaching darkness. Once inside the walls, Gunnolf could see the living quarters for the solders and their families; stone and mortar walls with thatched roofs. In the middle stood a great manor constructed of stone and huge peeled logs. The manor was three levels high, and looked large enough to house a dozen families. The living areas looked fairly new, at least compared to the main walls.

As they approached the main manor, Gunnolf noticed faint, heavily worn carvings on many blocks of the old stonework that made up the defenses. They were hard to make out, but may have been depictions of spiders, or possibly some other multi-legged invertebrates. Another looked like some winged creature or bat, but again, so worn as to be blurred to the eye. They all seemed vaguely horrific in their antiquity, and the warrior suppressed a slight shiver that ran down his spine. "Foolish superstitions, for children and fools!" thought Gunnolf. He turned his attention to the man approaching them from the open door of the manor.

"Victoria, Victoria. How many times have I warned you about wandering off into the forest alone, especially near nightfall?" the man said softly, almost whispering. He was tall, clad in black from head to toe. His face was nearly snow white, clean shaven and framed by slicked back hair the color of a raven's wing, and lank and snaky in form. His eyes were a pale, intense gray, underscored with dark pouches beneath, the eyes of a man who sleeps little and broods much.

"And what have we here, some barbarian wanderer you have befriended on some whim to make my life miserable?"

"Father, this man assisted me while I was attacked by troll warriors, and had he not shown up, I would doubtless be a prisoner, if not a corpse!" the girl said evenly, but with a trace of anger.

The man in black looked again at Gunnolf. "My apologies, warrior. It would appear I should be grateful for your interference." the baron's voice was slippery and whispery. "What is your name, and where do you hail from?"

"My name is Gunnolf, and I was born in the Northrealm, a member of the Broken Mountain clan." the warrior rumbled with just a hint of pride, for he was still a young man and proud of his heritage.

"I have heard of your kind, but have never met one before." stated the baron. "Your tribe is not prone to wander far into the Southlands, what brings you so far from home?"

"Unlike my gloomy brothers, I have developed a taste for wine, sunshine and adventure, of which little can be found in the frozen gray lands of my fathers." stated Gunnolf with a crooked grin.

"Excellent." whispered the baron, "Come inside to the fire. I have much wine, and we should talk a piece." The figure in black turned in a sudden swirl of black robes, then stalked off in the direction of the open manor door.

Gunnolf looked at Victoria, who seemed a little sheepish at her fathers brusque manner. "Wine. I very much like wine. And right now, I could drink a barrel-full!" He slipped the heavy traveling pack from his shoulders with a sigh, handed it to a waiting groom and strode towards the manor with great purpose and anticipation. Victoria only shook her head in mild despair, for her father had much wine indeed.

Chapter 3

Gunnolf sighed with contentment, and leaning back in his great wooden chair, stretched his legs out before him, towards the crackling hearth. In his hairy fist was an earthenware drinking jack, filled to the brim with the blood-red wine of the Southlands. The serving staff had just removed his food platter, once piled high with enough food for three men, now empty but for a few larger bones and a puddle of grease.

"Now, Baron, you said you would like to talk some, and I am much sated with food, but more than willing to hear what you have to say." Gunnolf said, "But keep the wine jug handy, for talk gives me a great thirst."

The baron raised an eyebrow ever so slightly, for the barbarian wanderer had already drank enough wine to stagger a small platoon, but nevertheless ordered the servant to broach a new cask of wine. "Warrior, you have done me a great favor, and I always repay my debts. My daughter means much to me, so you can name your price. What will it be; gold, women, lands...?" He let his voice trail off, curious to see if the light of greed should be seen in those cold green eyes.

"I have no need of lands, as I am on my way south." rumbled Gunnolf. "Women I will find aplenty in the Southlands, if half the tales I have heard are true. Gold...yes, I could use some, but only enough to to keep me going on my journey. And perhaps some supplies to load on my horse for the trip."

The baron was surprised, but did not allow his pale features to reflect that fact. "Most adventurers would have attempted to take all that they could, as few of these type of men can overcome their inherent greed." His voice was soft and oily, and Gunnolf could detect a slight disgust in it. He poured a long swallow of the expensive wine down his gullet, and allowed a little to dribble from his chin, just for the Baron's sake.

"There is just one other thing I would like, some... information." said Gunnolf.

"What sort of information? asked the baron, with a slightly wrinkled brow.

Gunnolf stood suddenly, and at the same time, drew from the scabbard at his side the sword he had taken from the battle ground where he had slaughtered the trolls and saved the baron's daughter. He drove the keen point deep into the thick wooden floor of neatly sawn logs at his feet, and released the grip to allow the sword to wave back and forth before the fire, gleaming with the light of the fire in the hearth. "Tell me about this fine steel sword, and the creatures that wield them." He did not sound like a drunk barbarian, nor did he move like one. He moved more like forest tiger than a man. The Baron blinked rapidly.

The sword was a fine weapon, the blade about as long as a big man's arm, doubled edged, with a wide, deep fuller that ran almost to the tip. It was a wide blade, with very little taper down it's length until a little before the end, where it came to a sudden, needle-like point. The hilt had room for a hand and a half grip, and was tightly wound with some sort of thin cord. The guard was an engraved piece of steel shaped in a slight semi-circle. The pommel was carved from silver, shaped like a dragon's claw grasping a sphere, heavy enough to offset the weight of the blade and give it balance and quickness. It was a special blade indeed, to those who knew the value of steel.

"Well," the Baron began, "the tale goes something like this; long, long ago, further back than anyone can imagine, these lands were ruled by a powerful sorcerer. As his ambition grew, he realized he needed an army to fulfill his desires, and he found it right here. This very keep was in fact the remains of an ancient city, populated by a non-human race of trolls, and ruled by, er, 'things'. The rulers died out and the trolls degenerated into beast-like cave dwellers. They shunned the light and avoided mankind. Until the sorcerer drew them out with his power, and forged them into an army. Although they were degenerate beings, they still retained the skill of forging fine steel, and the sorcerer commanded them to create the arms and armur to equip themselves for war and conquest. "

"Well, before the sorcerer could march his unholy horde against an unprepared human population, some event, some sort of cataclysm rocked the keep, destroyed the sorcerer and scattered the troll army back into the hills from whence they came. Mankind was spared the conquest, and the sorcerer, the trolls, and even the fine steel weapons were forgotten by most in the mists of time. "

"My Grandfather found the remains of the keep while exploring with his men, and began to re-build it, and eventually moved his family and men into the protecting walls you see here today." The baron sipped a little wine and continued. "And so my father become baron, and after him, I became the next baron. And our lands expanded, and our wealth grew, and now I have control of the people and lands for several leagues in all directions."

Gunnolf frowned into his cup. "What of these warrior trolls? Do they present a risk to the keep, and your holdings?"

"Nay," whispered the baron. "they are but a fraction of what they once were, and have no real leadership or direction. I will have them smoked out and annihilated within the year, like rats, or serpents."

"I see." stated Gunnolf. "And who was it that built these walls of stone?"

"The sorcerer, of course!" the baron snapped, ever so slightly.

"Nay, before the sorcerer began building his army of trolls, you stated he found this keep, in the remains of an ancient city." Gunnolf rumbled softly. "Who built the original walls?"

The baron looked slightly dismayed, as if he had found a hair in his soup. "I do not know, for sure. In fact, no one knows. Perhaps the trolls..."

"Unlikely," interrupted the Northman. "the trolls work some fine steel, but do not seem like masons and builders to me. And the carvings I seen worked into some of the stones... they are worn for sure, but they seem strange and disturbing. Alien. Not the work of trolls, or humans."

"No matter!" laughed the baron. "All that is lost to the mists of time, and means nothing to us here and now. I think it is time to retire, as I have much to do in the morn. My servant will show you to a room for the night, and we can settle on a reward for you when you arise."

Gunnolf rose once more from the wooden chair and stretched his muscular frame, easing the knots of travel from his powerful body. He pulled the troll-blade from the thick wooden floor, and deftly returned it home to its scabbard. Despite drinking all evening, he showed no sign of impairment, and his movements were feral and smooth. "Aye, I could use the sleep. I have to continue my journey in the morning, and I hope to be somewhat heavier with supplies, and gold when I leave." His eyes gleamed a strange aquamarine fire, and his teeth seemed very white and almost sharp in the dull orange glow of the dying fire.

"Sleep well, warrior." Said the baron in his soft, slippery voice. He watched Gunnolf follow the servant to the sleeping quarters and his mind turned like a worm in a gall. He smiled ever so slightly.

Chapter 4

Gunnolf's eyes opened in complete darkness. His breathing remained that of a sleeping man, while his hand sought out and found the leather wrapped grip of the dagger he kept under the rough blanket. He was instantly aware of where he was, and what had woken him up; the soft, heavy movement of a granite slab on well-oiled rails. And now he could smell intruders. There was a soft glow from a torch down a long, narrow tunnel where there had been no tunnel before.

He could now dimly see a bulky form

reaching out to feel for him, and as the hand touched his chest, he exploded into violent action. He surged at the form above him, and ripped murderously upward with his heavy iron dagger. It plunged deep under the lower jaw of his opponent, and crunched home into the brain case. Gunnolf hurled the corpse aside and met the next attacker.

The Northman blocked the lunge of a short-sword with his long dagger, deflecting it to the side and countering with a back-slash across the neck cords of his assailant. The troll, as Gunnolf could now see well enough to identify his enemy, staggered back with a wet gurgle, and Gunnolf hacked him in the throat again, nearly severing the head from the thick, spurting neck. The dying creature collapsed, and the third and final troll leaped on Gunnolf, stabbing madly and roaring like some hell-sent demon.

Gunnolf lost his dagger in the tackle, and went down under the troll. The attackers' blade sank into his side and deflected off his heavy rib bones. Blood gushed down Gunnolf's flank, and he fought madly to grasp the troll's weapon hand. Locking his powerful hand on the thick, dark green wrist, Gunnolf heaved and twisted. The troll's arm gave at the elbow, and broke with a sickening, flesh-muffled crunch. The troll howled in agony. Gunnolf gained his footing without releasing his grip on the broken limb, and swung the troll into the stone wall with a meaty thump. The Northman's heavy, mallet-like fist slammed into the troll's head, pounding it against the granite. Once, twice, thrice; Gunnolf smashed with his knotted fist. The troll's upper jaw, nose and eye-sockets collapsed under the battering in a splatter of dark blood and a crunch of breaking bone. Gunnolf spun and faced the tunnel mouth, wild eyed and snarling, but there were no more assailants.

There was a pounding at his door, and voices raised in alarm, ordering him to open the bolted door. Gunnolf slammed the bolt back and wrenched the door open, blood running in slick trails down his side and flank. The baron's men-at-arms reeled back from the doorway at the sight of Gunnolf, blood-slicked and wild-eyed, and he roared at them in a voice like a sea-storm. "What is the meaning of this! I have nearly been murdered by a pack of trolls in my bed–is the keep under attack?"

"Nay Lord," stammered one of the guards, "There have been no sounds at all tonight, until we heard the attack on yourself just now."

"Well, the green bastards have a way into the keep!" growled Gunnolf. "And this may not be the only room with a secret passage; best we organize a search of all rooms, and tell the guards on the walls to keep a sharp eye for trolls. I smell a trap, no doubt about it!"

More guards clattered down the main passage, and as they passed Gunnolf's room, they shouted, "The Lady is gone! Someone or something has taken her into the bowels of the earth through a passage we found in her quarters. Where no passage existed before!" The panic and fear was evident in the quailing voices of the guardsmen; something was very wrong. They ran on toward the baron's quarters.

Gunnolf buckled on the straight sword and picked up the short sword of the dead troll. The shorter blade would be useful in the narrow tunnel that ran downwards into the earth If it opened up down there, he would put the longer sword to good use. "Victoria, they have her." he said through gritted teeth. "Tell the baron I am following them while the trail is still hot, and to send men-at-arms after me. I will mark the path as best as I can. "He turned to the men and his face was split by a grim, wolf-like smile. "Follow me into hell, if you dare dogs! If I run into the devil himself, he had better stand aside, or I will cleave him in twain!" There was madness in those wild green eyes, and with the two blades, wearing only his boots and leather kilt, Gunnolf turned about and plunged down into hell.

Chapter 5

Gunnolf picked up the signs of the kidnappers soon enough, and beyond that point, the tunnel continued downward without break or deviation for some time. Twice he stopped to inspect signs of strife and bloodshed; Victoria was not going easily, that was obvious. Gunnolf chuckled grimly and continued quickly onward, head bent slightly for the low ceiling. "The lass has grit, may the Gods bless her!" thought the Northman as he stepped over a dead Warrior troll, dagger still buried deep in its eye-socket.

Eventually the tunnel stopped its downward plunge and became level and much wider. The space was dimly lit by some sort of glowing gems set in steel on the walls at about Gunnolf's eye level, and spaced out about 20 strides apart. The gems glowed strangely, without fire, but once a man's eyes were used to the dim, green light, one could see quite well. He touched one with the short-sword in his hand first, then with a finger, and found them cool to the touch; some lost science of old times, no doubt, or sorcery. Gunnolf had no love of sorcery, but was glad for the light just the same.

After what seemed like several hours and a few leagues travel, he could now hear something far ahead, some sort of chanting. It was deep and strange, rising in volume, then dropping to a whisper. Then there was a deep, hair-raising tone blasted from some sort of horn that rolled on and on, and seemed to vibrate the very earth beneath Gunnolf's feet. It sounded like the toll of doom itself, the call of the old ones that slept in the black slime at the bottom of the seas. Gunnolf liked it not, and his back crawled in uncontrolled reaction to that demon call, but he gripped his weapons tightly and continued on toward the source of the sounds.

Soon, he rounded a rocky corner and looked upon a gigantic dome of pure granite. All was lit dimly by the same cold gems scattered by the thousands on the vast curving walls. Also, some torches burned with a smokey orange glow in the middle of the huge room, set around what appeared to be a low block of blackened stone. An altar of sorts. All around the ebon block stood the warrior trolls, swaying and chanting together, hundreds strong in number.

As Gunnolf watched from his place of hiding, he noticed what appeared to be a great throne of stone set about twenty feet high into the wall of granite. And upon that throne sat the baron himself! His voice droned on in some strange, long forgotten tongue, and the trolls chanted along with their leader. The baron then shouted a command. From within the crowd Victoria was dragged forward towards the black altar. Gunnolf stiffened convulsively, and his knuckles whitened as he gripped his weapons in mute fury. How could he possibly fight through the crowd of trolls and secure her release without being cut down by the massed warriors? And at that moment the baron turned towards Gunnolf with his index finger pointed at him and roared to the trolls "Seize the warrior! Take him alive, and bring him to me!'

Gunnolf wasted no time trying to understand how the baron knew he was spying on them, but instead leaped into instant and ferocious action. He was among the warrior trolls in an instant smiting right and left, determined to sell his life at the highest price possible. The trolls fell back from Gunnolf's glittering steel, now clotted with troll blood. They roared in fury and frustration as they were restrained by the orders of their leader to take the Northman alive, even as they were cut down in windrows like ripe barley before the scythe. A lead ball ripped through the air, powered by a hard whipped sling, and rebounded off the temple of the blood-maddened Northman, sending him crashing to the cave floor with his wits dashed from his head. Darkness closed in...

Chapter 6

Slowly, painfully, Gunnolf returned to the land of the living. He found himself laying on a sandy floor, on one side of some sort of large, oval-shaped arena. He sat up, and waves of nausea washed over him as he carefully probed his swollen, blood crusted temple with his fingers where the lead ball had struck him.

Gunnolf looked about and saw he was surrounded by hundreds of trolls seated on rough-hewn benches carved into the sloping floors of the huge amphitheater. At the far end was a gigantic, iron-barred door in the mouth of a darkened passage. The door was fully three times the height of a tall man, and he wondered what horror lay beyond it.

"Northman!" shouted the baron.

Gunnolf spun about, and, tracking the echoing shout, craned his head upward. Some fifty feet above the sandy floor of the cavern was a small finger of flat stone that jutted out from the steepening stone wall about ten paces out, and five wide. Upon this ledge, seated on a chair of laminated human bones, was the baron. "Northman, are you prepared to die?"

"Every day. Are you?" rumbled Gunnolf. "But why wait till now, when you could have had me killed when you set your horde of troll-scum upon me earlier?" This comment triggered a deep grumble of resentment from the gathered masses seated all around him.

The black-clad baron chuckled,"Your death must be done in the correct manner, in order to maximize the sacrifice to the Old Ones. My plan was to sacrifice my daughter to complete the ritual, and your death will only sweeten the deal. The Old Ones delight in the suffering of a great warrior."

"In my homeland, when a parent is found guilty of murdering their own child, they are captured, tied up and taken out to the forest to have their heads bashed in with heavy stones. Like a mad dog." Gunnolf shook his head."Only civilized men would would kill their young for gain."

The Baron laughed and said, "But the blood of of your kin is the sweetest of all, to those whom I serve. With this final step, I will finish the spell that the sorcerer of old began, and I will then command the most powerful army in the western realms. But enough talk, the time approaches." He turned toward two trolls at the foot of the rock bridge who stood next to a huge iron wheel mounted to the wall. "Release the pet!"

With dry scream of rusted iron and corroded brass gears, the great gate began to open. The trolls strained at the iron wheel. Gunnolf looked about for a means to escape, but the walls, about ten feet high all around, were lined with spear-armed trolls who would simply prod him back into the arena if he leaped up and grasped the top edge of the wall. Gunnolf then sighted a weapon to defend himself with. A great axe, head down, leaned against the wall near the iron gate. He ran forward, grasped it in both hands and quickly backed away from the nearly open gate.

He took a moment to inspect the axe, and noted that the rusty, double bitted head was quite huge, and the thick ash handle longer than most. It was too heavy and cumbersome for the average man to wield, but Gunnolf hefted it up and took measure of its weight. His muscles swelled in anticipation of huge, murderous blows delivered with this ancient weapon. It would do.

At that moment, the occupant stepped out from the caged tunnel into the dim light of the arena, and Gunnolf's eyes widened as a giant shambled out towards him.

It was a huge mountain ape, fully twice the height of Gunnolf, and at least four times his mass. It was covered in thick, matted brown hair and the black leathery face split into a huge gaping maw filled with thick yellow tusks. It had only one eye, the other socket crushed and scarred by some battle wound. In fact, it was covered with rough, twisted scars that criss-crossed the thick torso and huge limbs. It trailed a length of rusted iron chain from a steel cuff around one ankle. The links of the chain were as thick as Gunnolf's wrist.

With an ear-splitting roar, it charged the puny man in the arena with every intention of crushing him to bloody pulp and plucking his head from his corpse. Gunnolf stood his ground till the last moment, then leapt to one side, rolling under the sweeping arm and regaining his feet behind the giant ape. Before the beast could spin about, the warrior swung a mighty blow at the one of the beast's thick legs. The axe clipped the limb, and blood spurted, but the hair was thick and the flesh tough. This was not going to be easy.

The ape spun around, snarling, and the chain that ran from ankle to the interior of the tunnel nearly knocked Gunnolf to the sand. The ape roared and charged again, and again Gunnolf escaped instant death by a slim margin. He could not keep this up for long, and the second blow he landed with the great axe did little damage. The ape turned, and crouched down to gather itself for another charge. As it roared it's frustration and pain, Gunnolf could see intelligence in the beastly countenance, and the stamp of a long life of pain and suffering at the hands of its oppressors. It had lived in horrible torment for ages, and Gunnolf was the target of that rage. It charged again.

Gunnolf dove between the thick, bowed legs, rolled, and rose up with the great axe held on high to deliver yet another mighty blow. As the giant ape turned, he swung the axe downward with all his strength, striking the iron chain trailing from the beast's ankle. Two more times in quick succession the heavy axe head was brought down, and then the rusted links parted. The gathered crowd of Trolls were silent. The great mountain ape looked at Gunnolf, then reached down with one hairy hand and lifted the shattered chain to his nostrils and sniffed cautiously. It looked straight into the green eyes of the warrior.

At that moment understanding flashed between the two. The scarred face of the ape split into a savage grimace that might have been a smile.

The gigantic ape roared in outrage and hate, spun about, and, with a running leap cleared the arena wall. The watchers exploded into action, trying to flee in all directions at once.

The great tortured creature raged among them, tearing and rending and slaying. The entire arena was in pandemonium, and Gunnolf used the opportunity to clamber up the wall himself and try to seek out Victoria. Above them all, the baron stood transfixed, rendered stupid by the events that transpired in the arena.

"No, no, this is all wrong!" he wailed. "The Old Ones will awaken, and they must have their sacrifice. I have already started the spell, and it cannot be undone!" He spun about, and pointing a bone white forefinger downwards towards the alter, he screamed, "Kill her! Kill her now! The precious blood must be spilled to appease the Gods! Do it now before it's too late!"

At the bloody alter, Victoria had already taken advantage of the uproar. She pulled her right am free of her bonds, snatched a dagger from one of the guards, and hacked his throat open. As the blood spurted from its neck, Victoria rolled to her left and buried the blade deep into the eye of a second troll as it attempted to restrain her while drawing his own sword. She slashed the rest of her bonds and rolled from the alter onto her feet, stooped, and drew a sword from the scabbard of the dying troll. A grim smile touched her lips.

"Gunnolf!" she shouted. "To me! We can cut our way free of these devils if we work together. Lets be quick about it!"

The Northman looked up toward the altar, and caught sight of the girl in the midst of the pressing crowd of warrior trolls. She still wore only her thin cotton sleeping shift. Her hair was tousled, she was spattered with blood, and she swung a blood-darkened troll-blade.

She looked every inch a warrior to Gunnolf. "Hold strong girl, I'm on my way!" he roared, and with the now blunted battle axe clearing a bloody path, he struggled towards the area of the altar.

At the same time, the great mountain ape, bristling with a dozen spears, continued the wreak havoc among the trolls. It hurled them left and right like dolls, smashing them to ground meat and splintered bones. Here, it swung a troll by its feet against a thick column of granite, bursting the body like a rotten wineskin. There, the ape grasped a troll with its foot, and plucked the head from the torso like ripe fruit. But even this giant had limits, and the spears began to take their toll. It collapsed, and with a great, final roar, crushed several trolls in its powerful arms as the spears were driven home deep into its vitals.

As the Trolls attempted to rally together and overpower Gunnolf and Victoria, something new caused a ripple of fear to run through the ranks. The very earth shook and rumbled, causing loose stones and granite dust to rain down from the lofty ceiling. From the deep cavern where the mountain ape had been caged issued a great, gusting bellow. It was the voice of something gargantuan. It was like the voice of a dying mountain or a shifting continent. The voice of something alive. It bellowed again, closer.

Gunnolf finally reached the alter where Victoria was dispatching one last troll with her captured sword. As she turned to him, he could see she had been wounded by a sword thrust, just below her left breast. She smiled a ghastly grimace at him, and her lips were bright red with bloody bubbles; she was lung rent. Gunnolf had seen wounds like this before on the battlefield. She would be dead within the hour, likely less. And Gunnolf was shocked by the feeling of pending loss that stabbed him; he did not know why he cared so, but he felt it.

"Come with me lass, we'll cut our way free of this lot and make for the surface. At least you can die in the open air, instead of in this nest of vipers." Gunnolf reached for her arm.

"Nay," Victoria mumbled through scarlet lips. "I will never make it. Besides, I wish to send my loving father to the bowels of hell before I leave this world. Flee, warrior. Live to tell the tale of a father who would sacrifice his child to a Black God for personal gain and power." She turned and staggered toward the steps that climbed up the high throne of the baron.

Gunnolf would have stopped her, but was

forced to turn at bay and engage a knot of furious trolls who sought to drag him down and spill his blood for the glory of the Old Ones.

Victoria gained the top of the stairs and slowly walked towards the baron, her father and her murderer. He babbled incoherently, about a spell, a Black God and the blood of loved ones. He did not even see the lightning thrust that killed him, but felt the cold burning pain of a pierced heart. Victoria withdrew her sword without a word. He fell to his knees. Grabbing a handfull of the black, snakey locks, Victoria pulled back the dying man's head and chopped deep into his throat with the razor edge. It took two more blows from the weakening girl, but the head came free in her hand, and the spurting body fell to the side.

Victoria looked out over the milling warriortrolls, raised the dripping head high, and screamed out,"See this, creatures of the night. See the one who would lead you. See now he is dead, and your doom comes upon you from below!" She hurled the head far out over the crowd. And as her eyes sought out and found Gunnolf wrenching the giant ax from a troll skull, she smiled and died on her feet.

The spell was broken, and the trolls scattered in all directions to flee the thing from the depths. The ground shook, solid granite cracked and burst, and great gouts of flame and smoke filled the air. Over all was heard the call of the Black God, the shuddering roar of The Old Ones.

Thick black tentacles, a hundred feet long and thick as a man whipped out from the black depths of the earth. They crushed trolls to meaty slime, or tore them asunder like a child with a grasshopper. All was pandemonium, and Gunnolf was forgotten for the moment. He cast his eyes about, seeking an avenue of escape, a way back to the surface. And he found it. A crumbling stairway cut into the wall of the rock, running upwards above the great black crevice from whence the tentacles issued. He did not hesitate, but leaped instantly toward the stairs, and hopefully, freedom.

But before he reached the base of the stairs, it began to flow from the great crack in the earth. He could not tell what it was, but it was gargantuan; bigger than the baron's manor. It seemed to be made of heavy, black, rubbery flesh, but also soft and slimy, like a jellyfish. It looked like a bizarre mix of squid and fish. And maybe bat. It had a single eye of huge size set high in the "head" portion, and below that was a gaping maw filled with thousands of triangular teeth like a shark. It smelled of rotting corpses and ocean floor sea-slime, and the earth shook with the mind-numbing bellows that issued from its mouth.

Gunnolf could not hope to kill it, for was it not a God? But he would not stand still like a sheep before the butcher, and hoped only to strike one blow before he died. He ran towards it with the war cry of his people ringing in his ears. As he ran, he reached way back with the great ax in his right fist, and flung it upwards at the leviathan with every ounce of power he could muster from his straining sinews. The ax tumbled end over end and the heavy iron head sank it's full mass deep into the huge single eye. The wet, bulging orb burst like a ripe grape underfoot. The Old One screamed.

Rock exploded in all directions, great chunks and whistling splinters killed trolls by the score. Gunnolf was knocked down by the blast, but was back up in an instant, blood pouring from his torn scalp where a shard of flying granite had grazed him. Past the writhing, flopping thing he ran, and up the stairs towards the surface, and life. If he could make it. The earth shuddered, mountains moved, and molten magma burst upwards in flaming red fountains. And upwards ran the warrior.

Chapter 7

Gunnolf leaned on his troll sword and looked back towards the keep. It was no longer there. In its place was now a great crater, a hundred feet deep, and a thousand strides across. A towering cloud of dust and smoke rose high into the morning sky, and small shudders still shook the area. The entire cavern deep below the keep had collapsed, and no trolls emerged from the ground. Most of the people on the surface had fled when the walls shook and the earth opened to swallow whole houses. Gunnolf stood alone.

He was torn and cut, bleeding and bruised. A great flap of scalp hung over his left eye, and he flipped it back in place and held it there with a scrap of silk. He was breathing heavily, and his thick limbs trembled with exhaustion from the force of his exertions. He wore only a leather kilt and boots. His only possession was the great troll sword gripped in his bleeding fist. Victoria was gone, covered by a hundred thousand tons of granite deep below the surface. But she died a warrior, dealing death to her evil father even as she died on her feet. No warrior could ask for a better death, and Gunnolf knew that she feasted with the fallen warriors in the Hall of the Gods. And one day he would too, but not today.

Gunnolf turned his back on the smoking crater, and once again continued his journey to the Southlands, with less than he had just one day earlier. But he still had the sword, and something else; great confidence and conviction. Had he not just tangled with a God and blinded it with mere mortal weapons and lived to tell the tale? Oh, what stories he would tell in the taverns and wine shops of the south. He laughed gustily and quickened his step.

Stanley W. Wagenaar is a long time reader/fan of Howard, Burroughs, Wagner and the like. He's 54, and only recently started writing and submitting fiction because he could no longer contain the spirit of tale-teller within himself.

Acme Denton: Out of Time
by Michael Haynes

A mid-20th century PI finds himself transported to an old west where magic is real, and really deadly.

Acme Denton: Out of Time

By Michael Haynes

I kept the phone jammed between my shoulder and head. My other hand rubbed my temples as if it could wipe away the pounding within.

"Well, I just don't want you to forget, Acme," my wife said.

I counted to five before answering her. "I know, Carol. I'll stop by the store on my way home. I promise."

She made that little clicking sound with her tongue that gets on my nerves so bad. I know there was a time I thought it was cute, but those days are long past.

"Fine." A small sigh. "Do you want to say good night to Timmy? He's had his bath already."

"Sure, put the little fella on."

"Daddy!"

"Hey, Timmy, you being good for mom?"

He giggled. "Uh-huh."

"Is that what she's going to tell me?"

"I dunno." There was a silence on the line for a few seconds and I thought maybe he'd given the phone back to Carol but then he asked, "Give me a good night hug when you get home?"

"Sure thing, kid."

We said good night and this time he did put the phone down. While I was waiting for Carol to come back to it, I reached into my pocket. I found a few pennies in there, but the only silver looking up at me from the palm of my hand was a quarter and a couple of those new Roosevelt dimes. Damn. I could've sworn I had a second quarter.

"Okay, I'm going to get our stinker in bed," Carol told me when she got back on the line.

I didn't answer. I was staring at those coins.

"Acme?"

I bit my lip. Hell.

Charlie downstairs might've let me borrow a buck until I had it to spare. But he'd be back home in Park Forest by this time of night.

"Yeah, about those groceries, Carol... If, uh... If I had to get just the bread or the milk, which one would you rather?"

Silence stretched out over the line, so quiet that I wondered if we'd lost our connection. "Carol?"

"Acme Denton..." The words came out like a curse. I waited, afraid to hear what she'd say next, afraid to make it worse by interrupting. "When are you going to do right by me and Timmy?"

"Carol, I'm not sure --"

"No. Don't not sure me. I am sure. I'm sure that I'm tired of living on whatever you scrape together from week to week. There's plenty of jobs out there where you'll get a steady wage. Isn't it time you made yourself a real provider and gave up on this ridiculous private eye fantasy?"

Her words stung and the wound they made was all the deeper because they echoed the same things I said to myself every day as I sat here in this office waiting for a client to walk through the door. But then I'd get to thinking that all it would take was one real break, something where my name got around -- in a good way -- and I'd be my own man, not responsible to any boss. I wasn't ready to give up on my dream. Not yet.

"We'll talk about this later, Carol. Maybe... Maybe after the New Year, if I'm not seeing any progress --"

"After the New Year?" Her voice was shrill in my ear. "Acme, that's two months away. Do you really think we can keep living like this? And what about Christmas?"

Christmas. Another opportunity for the department stores and the advertisers to make you feel guilty if you weren't buying all the right things.

Into my silence, Carol kept right on going. "Timmy's four now and Christmas is going to be really special for him this year."

"You know, Carol, I really don't give a damn about Christmas right now."

She gasped and the line went dead for real. After a few seconds, I hung up the receiver. I banged my fist hard against my desk but all I got for my trouble was a sore hand. Smart.

I sat there a few minutes, looking at nothing, listening to the wind outside the windows. But there wasn't any point in hanging around. I'd buy the milk, or the bread, one of them. And I'd go home and face the music.

I stood up and put on my jacket. It was dark outside and cold. It would be even colder at home after my little outburst, but the jacket wouldn't do me any good against that chill.

I had my hand on the doorknob when the phone rang. It had to be Carol.

The phone rang a second time. I was absolutely still, facing the door with that gilt lettering I'd been so proud of six months ago. "A-1 Security & Investigations. Acme Denton, Proprietor." Two more months. Maybe she was right, maybe two more months of this was two months too long.

A third ring. I pulled my hand away from the doorknob.

And then a fourth ring. Hell... Answering couldn't make it any worse, now, could it? I turned toward my desk, toward the phone. I took two steps and then the world fell away.

I came to like some thug had sapped me. At least, like my idea of what it would feel like if a thug sapped me. In truth, I hadn't ever touched any cases serious enough for there to be a risk of that.

The first thing I noticed was that it was hellishly hot. My vision was a blur and I couldn't make anything out. But there was a horrible smell like chemicals and hot metal and something else that I couldn't identify.

I heard something moving, though I still couldn't see who -- or what -- it was. I put my hand down to my waist, felt the comforting coolness of my revolver. A weight at my ankle let me know that my derringer was there too. So whatever had happened to me, no one had bothered taking my weapons. I wasn't sure if that should be comforting or not.

A sound of movement again. "Hello?" I called out.

"Rise!"

"What?"

"Rise, protector!" These words came from a thin, almost soft, male voice. The voice itself wouldn't have scared me, but the tone of command had me rattled. And what was he talking about, "protector"?

The air was heavy and still in the silence following the most recent command. I tried to think of where someone could have taken me that would be this miserably hot. A boiler room?

The wooziness was almost gone from my head, though my vision was still a mess. I wasn't crazy about jumping to my feet like a trained monkey but hanging out on the floor wasn't exactly the best defensive posture. I chanced getting to my knees and then to my feet. The residual unsteadiness and the smell almost made me sick, but I managed to stand.

"Look, whatever's going on here," I said into the hot darkness, "I'm not laughing."

There wasn't any answer.

I had the sense that the ceiling was low, just barely above my head. I'm tall enough, six foot with my shoes on, but I don't usually have to worry about ducking. The heat was intense and sweat was starting to drip down my back.

I was just moving to take off my jacket when a hand grabbed my left arm. For just a half-second it felt like the grip was loosening but then it steadied. "Where have you come from?" It was the same thin voice, now not so commanding.

And why the hell was he asking me where I came from? "Downtown," I said all the same. "Off of Adams Street."

I felt the hand tighten a little. My vision

was getting better but I still couldn't really make out details. The person beside me was several inches shorter, slender as a rail, and had dark hair. The voice and the breadth of the hand on my arm were the only clues I had that it was a man.

My gut said to keep talking, so I went on.

"I was at my office building, last I remember. The phone was ringing and --"

"Phone?"

"That's right. The phone. The telephone. I think..." I was about to say that I thought my wife was calling me back, but I didn't want to drag Carol into this, whatever this was. "I think I was about to get an important call."

"Tele... phone... It lets you hear things. From far away?"

Oh boy, I had a live one.

"Yeah, that's what it does."

The only sound for a few seconds was our breathing. I could make out some details now of the room. A big fireplace sat empty at one end, a shelf had books and bottles and other things I couldn't make out from here against a wall. On the ground, near my feet, was the biggest mess of junk... Hunks of metal here and there. I couldn't be absolutely certain, but I thought that wisps of smoke might be coming up from some of the debris on the floor.

"Where have you come from?" The man asked me again.

"I told you already. From my office building downtown. Now how about if we see about getting me --"

"Downtown where?"

I could almost see him clearly now. There was a hint of a mustache on his lip, but I could tell he was young, just barely an adult, if that. The notes of command I'd heard from him earlier were all gone. He sounded scared. The fingers of my right hand edged toward my revolver.

"Downtown Chicago, not far from the Loop."

I didn't know what to expect, but if I'd been taking bets, I wouldn't have favored what actually happened. He let go of my arm and fell to his knees.

"I am truly blessed," he said. "You must indeed be a great protector to have been drawn from so far."

I looked down at him and gnawed on my lip. So far...

"Alright, I spilled. Now it's your turn. If I'm so far from Chicago, then just where the hell am I?"

"We're near Yuma. In the Arizona Territory."

Arizona? It'd take a couple of days to get there by car even if you drove around the clock. Carol would have to be out of her mind with worry by now. If she wasn't just glad to see the back of me.

"So how'd I get all the way out here?"

"I called you."

He was still down on the ground and I could see just fine now. There was a door in the far wall. I started slowly edging toward it.

"Look, pal. I don't know what you're getting at. But I've gotten plenty of phone calls before and not one of them has taken me from Chicago to Arizona."

"Phone...? I don't... I don't know why you don't understand." He climbed to his feet. "I don't know what sort of magic you have out in Chicago, but when I called you, I didn't use a telephone. I used those." The sweep of his arm took in the junk on the floor. He looked at me with a broad smile and started walking toward me.

But I'd taken quite a few steps already and was at the door. I reached for the handle. My host raised a hand and pointed at the door. My fingers closed on empty space. The handle and the door were nowhere to be found.

I reached a second time, thinking I'd just missed the handle, but it and the door truly were not there anymore. My stomach lurched as I wondered if I'd been slipped something that was making me see things.

I went for my gun. I was almost surprised to feel it still in its usual place but there it was and it, at least, was real. Real, cold, and deadly. I pulled it out but let it hang loosely by my side. I hadn't seen any other exits from this room and I wasn't going to start shooting unless I absolutely had to.

"I need answers," I told the other man. Adrenaline was coursing through my veins like it never had in my so-far brief career as a private investigator, more than at any time since I'd come home from the war. "Who are you? How did I get here? How do I get out?"

"That weapon won't help you."

"I didn't ask for advice." Now I did raise the gun a bit, though I didn't point it directly at him and my finger was off the trigger. Sweat crept down my forehead. "I asked for answers.

So how about if you give me some."

"I'm Ezekiel Wallace. Like I already told you, I called you."

"Tell me what that means."

He waved a hand and shook his head slightly. "I'm not sure why I'd have to explain this to you. It can't be that different --"

"Explain anyway!"

"I needed a protector. My master died this morning." Master? "Whatever happened to him, it was terribly sudden. He was working, and then he was on the floor. He could barely raise his head, barely even talk. But he warned me, before he died, that his death would leave a... a power vacuum and that I would need to call someone to protect me. So I gathered up every magical artifact, even the things that were little more than junk. I linked them all together, cast the spell, and the rest... Well, the rest you've been here for."

At any other moment in my life up to that point, I wouldn't have believed it. But I'd seen that door and the handle. They were there one moment and gone the next. If you don't call that magic, I don't know what you do call it.

"What about my last question, Ezekiel? How do I get out?"

He frowned. "I hope that you don't want out. I need your help and I'm more than happy to pay for your services."

Ezekiel reached into a pocket. I kept my gun hand steady, watching to see what he pulled out.

A moment later he stretched out a fist. When he opened it, three coins were revealed, their brilliant yellow shine obvious even in the dim light of this room. I couldn't help myself. I let out a sharp whistle. Eagles looked up at me from two of the coins, a woman's head on the third. I couldn't see the fine details such as the letters on her coronet, but I knew they spelled "LIBERTY."

He'd gotten my attention, to be sure. The double eagles were back in his pocket but I couldn't stop thinking about them, not even with all the talk about magic. Sixty bucks face value and worth a nice premium for their gold content let alone any collector's value. They'd stopped making that design before I was born. I had no idea what I was getting myself into, but I knew if I could come out of it with those coins that Timmy's Christmas would work out just fine and I might be able to prove to Carol that I didn't need to go take a regular job, not just yet.

Ezekiel had consented to take the remainder of our conversation somewhere more comfortable. The room we sat in now was spare. A pair of chairs bracketed a table and Ezekiel and I each sat in one. It was still hot but not the infernal heat from the underground room we'd been in before. With a window open and a bit of a breeze -- yes, a desert breeze, if I could believe what I saw through the window -- drifting through the room from time to time it was almost bearable.

"So tell me what I need to do to earn those coins."

"As I said, I need a protector. I don't have the magical strength to go up against anyone that might try to do me harm. But you can provide attributes I lack. Physical strength and, I would presume, a certain familiarity with keeping yourself and your charges alive."

"Why summon me, then? Why not another magician or whatever?"

Ezekiel frowned. "It's not that simple, Mister...?"

"Denton. Acme Denton."

At my name, his eyes lit up.

"What? Don't tell me you've heard of me all the way out here."

"No. It's just..." He gave a nervous little laugh. "Well, when I was casting the spell that called you here, I was asking for someone at the acme of their profession. So your name..."

"Seems like maybe your wires got crossed." I couldn't believe I was taking this seriously, talking about crossed magic-spell wires like it was a misconnected phone call.

"Perhaps. Though..." He shook his head. "You asked why I didn't summon another mage. It wouldn't have done any good. Any mage could resist the call. Even I could."

It certainly seemed like he had an answer for everything.

"Let's talk brass tacks, then. You offered me sixty bucks down there and you're saying you want a protector. How long are you talking about needing protection for?"

He frowned. "I don't know. Frederick -- my master -- said that I should expect people to try to come after me, but I don't know who or when." Ezekiel shrugged. So much for Mr. Answer-for-Everything. "It could be days, weeks..."

"Months?" I asked.

He nodded.

"Well those three coins aren't going to buy you months. Not with me out here, separated from my wife and son."

His eyes flicked away. "I'm sorry about that."

"Look, kid. Have you thought about just getting out of here? Hell, we could ride a train together to Chicago. I'd protect you on the way and then you could just vanish into the city once we're there. And I've lived there all my life except when I was away for the war. I can tell you that there's not any issues with mages or power vacuums, even with Kennelly as mayor."

"That's not possible."

"Why not?"

"Frederick built this house. It's situated on a convergence of streams of power. That's why I apprenticed myself to him. It's also why I can't abandon it and let just anyone take it over."

I blew out a slow breath. I wanted to look past the weirdness of all this, but every time Ezekiel talked, he made that a little bit harder.

"I'll give you two weeks for the three double eagles."

"A month."

"No dice. Two weeks or I walk." Never mind how I'd actually manage that. With the state of my funds, I might just have to walk. But Ezekiel didn't know that. "If I leave then, that'll let me get home in time for Thanksgiving."

Ezekiel frowned. "Thanksgiving? That's" -- he counted on his fingers -- "over four months off."

And that was the last straw. I got to my feet and nodded in his direction. "Nice to meet you, Mr. Wallace. I hope you'll find what you're looking for, but it's not me."

"Fine, two weeks!"

I hesitated for a second, thinking again what that money would mean for my family. He must've sensed that momentary reconsideration as he stood and moved in closer toward me.

"You were brought here for a reason, Mr. Denton. I'm sure of this."

"I'm not."

"Even so."

I blew out a long breath. Hell. Nobody had offered me that kind of dough in a long time...

"Fine. Two weeks. And not a day longer." I reached out my hand. He took it cautiously and I noticed his eyes widen just a bit when we made contact.

"Now," I said. "I assume you don't have a phone, so can you get me into town so I can call my wife and let her know what's going on?"

He bit his lip. "I don't know of anyone with a device like what you describe. But we could go to the messenger's office. She could get a message to Chicago for you."

"Whatever you say, kid, this is your turf. Can we do that now?"

He said that we could and we headed outside. The heat was even worse out here and I wished I had a hat to keep the sun out of my eyes.

Ezekiel led me around to where two horses stood. "You can ride Blaze, he was Frederick's."

I stayed back and watched the beasts. They looked docile enough but I hadn't ridden since a boyhood experience with a pony at a carnival. I hadn't liked it much then and wasn't expecting to like it any better as an adult.

"Too far to walk, I take it?"

He laughed, already sitting astride his horse. "Depends how dried out you want to get. It's about three miles to town."

Blaze, fortunately, didn't make the whole experience of climbing on any harder than it already was. He stayed put and didn't complain even when I shifted about, trying to find a way to sit that was slightly less uncomfortable than all the other options I'd tried.

I finally realized that the most comfortable position would be back off the horse and the only way we'd manage that was by getting into Yuma. I gave Ezekiel a nod and we took off away from the house.

Twice on the ride into town I nearly fell off the horse. The second time I grumbled something, under my breath I had thought, about hoping I wouldn't have to put up with much more of this 19th century crap.

Seconds later Ezekiel had come to a halt and I had to figure out how to guide Blaze back by him.

"Problem, Zeke?"

He looked me over, top to bottom. "There's no way..."

"No way what? You're not backing out now, are you, because we shook on this and I'll be wanting my payment whether you still want my services or --"

"When were you born?"

I frowned. "What the hell does that have to do with anything. Is this some sort of astrology junk?"

"Just tell me. When were you born."

"March 16th."

"The year?"

"1919."

He didn't respond right away, but I saw him swallow hard. A few seconds later he dug into his pocket and pulled out a coin. Not one of the gold ones, a bright copper cent. He tossed it at me and I snagged it out of the air.

I looked at it and was a bit surprised to see the old Indian Head design rather than Abe. "1875" was stamped at the bottom of the coin. Still, it was just a penny.

"What about it?" I asked him.

"That coin, it's, what... About seventy years old?"

"Seventy-five, yeah."

"Anything about it seem strange?"

I considered it again, front and back. Nothing seemed amiss; it was just a hell of a nice old coin. I said so and pitched the cent back to him.

"It would be nice for a coin that old," he agreed. "I've certainly never seen an old coin that nice."

"Other than that one right there."

And then he smiled slightly. "No, Mr. Denton. That's just it. That coin? It's near brand new. I just got it in some change last week and it was the first '75 I'd seen."

I took a moment to think about that, trying to make sense of it.

"From what you said," he continued, "you believe that it's 1950. But I believe it's 1876. So either one of us is badly mistaken or you, Mister Denton, are much farther from home than either of us realized."

I didn't want to believe it. I ran through everything that had happened in the past few hours in my mind, looking for something that would contradict this statement, something that would let me know for a fact that I was just dealing with a crazy kid. I wanted a reason to believe that I could safely ride away from him without a care in the world besides how the hell I'd get back to Chicago with forty-eight cents in my pocket and what to do with the horse I was riding. I wanted to believe that I had a way home, back to Timmy, back to Carol.

But I couldn't find a single damn thing against it. We were riding a dirt road and there weren't any signs of cars or paved roads anywhere near us. The handful of buildings I could see off in the distance sure looked like something I'd see in one of those western pics over at the McVickers Theatre on Madison.

Ezekiel was watching me as I went through these thoughts. There was still the hint of a smile on his face. It made me sick.

"Send me home," I told him. "Whatever the hell you did, undo it. Now."

That smile disappeared with my words. "It's not that easy, Mister Denton. Remember, I had to use all of those magical artifacts just to cast what I expected to be a normal summoning. There's no way I could send you home without a similar set of tools to augment my energies."

Sweat gathered on my back under my shirt as I considered this. He was desperate, that much I could tell from what I'd seen of him so far. Desperate enough to lie?

"Let's say I don't believe you."

"I'm telling you the truth."

"You say you are, but I've just got your word for that and right now I'm not feeling too charitable toward you."

I pulled my gun and this time I didn't hesitate to point it at him. "Send me home. Right now."

"I already told you your weapon wouldn't do you any --"

"Good. Yeah, I know. And that's something else I only have your word on."

His eyes were focused on the muzzle and he was blinking fast.

"I'll count to three. One."

"Do you know what will happen even if you do manage to shoot me?"

"I figure you'll be dead. Two."

He shook his head. "Not to me. To you."

My finger was beside the trigger, not yet on it. "What do you mean?"

"If I die, the spell breaks."

I raised my eyebrows. "So you're saying that if I want to get home, all I have to do is kill you?"

"God! No!" His face was bright red and I could see that he was breathing hard now. He waved his hands around and started jabbering. "The spell will break, but I don't have any idea where that would leave you. A normal summoning, yes, you'd be home. But this --

across time and... Well, since it seems like you don't have any knowledge of magic, I'm going to say you're not even from my future. You're from some other future. You might end up in my Chicago or in a future Yuma in my world or... Who knows where!"

Damn... If he was lying, he was doing an awfully convincing job of it. And the idea of writing him off as a loon had pretty much already gone by.

But I still only had his word on it.

My mind spun. Shooting him wouldn't actually solve anything and threatening him wasn't changing his story. I kept the gun steady a few moments longer, to see if he'd crack. Nothing could be heard but a faint whistle from the wind.

I lowered my gun, slid it back into its holster. "So how do we get me back home? I'm obviously not the protector you need, being from a completely different world. Send me home and find someone who can help you out for real."

He shook his head slightly. "The only way to do that would be to replicate what I did before. Get a number of magical relics together, link them up so they can enhance each others' power, and summon you back."

"So can you do that?"

I knew the answer as soon as he looked away from my eyes. "The things I used this morning were tools my master had gathered over years... decades... of being a working mage."

"Jesus, kid."

We sat there, on our horses, each of us in our own thoughts for a while. "I guess there's no point going into town, still," he finally said.

"No." I'd been furious at Carol just hours ago, but now with her farther away than I could have ever imagined, I wanted nothing more than to be able to be there with her.

I considered Ezekiel as we rode. If everything he'd said was on the level, then there was no real reason I should be sore with him. He was looking for a 19th century tough guy from a magical world. And he got stuck with me. But it still nagged at me that I had to take everything completely on faith. This could be some kind of ridiculously elaborate con job, though I couldn't think of a good reason for anyone to be interested enough in me to want to bother.

We rode back toward his house, a bit of dust blowing now across the land. Neither of us talked for quite a few minutes.

We were coming up on a rock formation when Ezekiel sat up a bit taller in his saddle. I saw him looking around from side to side and was just about to ask him what was up when something big whizzed by my head. It landed inches away from Ezekiel and his horse. It was a chunk of rock, bigger than a football, with lots of nasty-looking sharp edges and points.

Then, from out behind one of the rock formations at the side of the road, stepped out the biggest, ugliest fellow I'd ever seen. Seven feet tall if he was an inch, stripped to the waist, scars on his chest and face and one eye missing. All this, though, paled in comparison to what was between his hands. Another rock, bigger than the one that had almost taken my head off, which he was lifting up and aiming to throw right at Ezekiel.

Reflexes, thank God, took over. I saw the brute getting ready to use Zeke's head for target practice and did a little targeting of my own. My first shot went wide, but it did the trick in another way. The big man's second rock landed several yards away from either of Zeke's and my horses.

"Ride!" I yelled to Zeke. I didn't have to tell him twice.

The good news was that he got out of rock-throwing range in a matter of seconds. The bad news is that this meant it was just me and Mr. Ugly and he looked willing to accept a consolation prize in the killing-and-maiming department if need be.

He charged at me. Blaze, bless him, stood his ground. I fired a second time and this time I didn't miss. The big man tumbled to the ground.

Belatedly, it occurred to me to scope out the landscape, make sure that our friend didn't have friends of his own who were ready to ride to his defense. Nothing. Still, I kept my gun in my hand.

It looked like I wasn't going to have anything to worry about from my attacker. He was breathing and moving a bit, but not trying to get up. Still, I had Blaze take a wide berth around the man's prone form when I took off after Zeke.

"This happen often?" I asked Ezekiel, who looked ready to be sick, when I caught up to him.

"No. I..." He shuddered. "No."

"So who was that fellow?"

"I don't have any idea."

"Fine, let's get back to your place. The sooner the better, I'd say."

"Wait," Ezekiel said. He turned and rode back the way we came.

"Hey!" I called out, hoping he would stop. But Zeke went straight back to where the man had fallen, leaving me to follow.

The man I'd shot was still now. Either dead or well on his way. Zeke was down by him, rummaging through his clothing.

"Look, you wanted me to protect you, right? My official advice as your protector is that we get out of here."

He waved a hand at me. I pinched my nose, irritated. All of a sudden fatigue washed over me; I felt as tired as I could remember being.

"Hah!" Ezekiel cried out, yanking something away.

It was a circular thing, maybe three inches across and it looked like it had a pattern etched into it, though I couldn't make out any of the details.

"What is it?"

"An amulet, enchanted somehow."

"So this is another mage?"

He shook his head. "No way. A mage wouldn't be messing around with throwing rocks."

Ezekiel tucked the amulet away and got back on his horse.

"But surely not a coincidence, right?" I asked.

He shook his head. "Most likely not. Could he have been a random hooligan with a magic amulet? Perhaps. But I wouldn't be wanting to take that side of a wager."

I kept a sharp eye out as we rode the rest of the way back, but no one else interfered with our progress. I had time to think, too, and I had plenty of questions for Ezekiel by the time we were back inside.

"Why send a fellow like that after you? If there's some mage that wants you dead, why wouldn't he do the deed himself? Maybe he couldn't summon you over to him, but what's to stop him from summoning himself into your house?"

Ezekiel frowned as I went through my questions and even shook his head a bit at the end. "Mages don't summon themselves into another mage's house."

"Why not? Professional courtesy?"

"No. It's because even a poor excuse of a mage like myself has protections that would make it impossible for another mage to invade their house unwelcomed. And, besides, it's not like it's as easy as you make it sound. Magic takes power. Some of that can come from tools, like the artifacts I used to help me summon you. Some of it can come from the environment -- remember, I had that on my side, too. But the rest? The rest of it comes from the mage. Or another being."

He fiddled with the amulet he'd taken off the dead guy, tracing the lines on its surface with his long, slender fingers. "And basically the same explanation goes for why a mage would send a brute to do a job. No need to expend their energies when another solution is at hand."

I could see now why he'd seemed frustrated with my questions. They must have been the sort of thing that an ambitious five-year-old might ask. Not what you want to hear the person into whose hands you've put your safety asking.

I put a hand on his arm, trying for reassurance, and he flinched. I pulled away quickly and muttered, "Sorry."

"No... Don't be." He set the amulet down on the table. "In fact, if you'll humor me, I'd like to try a little experiment."

"Not going to turn me into a toad, are you?"

He frowned again. "No. Why would I do that?"

"Never mind. So, this experiment. What do you have in mind?"

He went and got a candle. "Lighting a candle magically is one of the first exercises almost every magically-attuned person is given. It's relatively easy. You can tell when you've succeeded." He grinned a bit. "And, for lots of people it's rather gratifying to be able to do this --"

The candle, sitting in a holder on the table, suddenly sprouted a neat little flame. Ezekiel bent down and blew it out.

"That takes almost no effort from me at this point, but when I was younger I could sit there and try for an hour to get it lit." He shook his head. "Anyway, here's the experiment."

Ezekiel reached over and put his hand on my shoulder. I saw him nod a bit and then the candle burst into flame. Not just the wick, the whole top inch of it was ablaze.

"Son of a --" I yelled as I pulled away.

This time Ezekiel must have used magic to quench the flame because moments later the candle was out and only a large puff of smoke remained.

"Was that a successful experiment?" I asked him, not sure whether I was hoping for an affirmative answer or not.

"Absolutely," he said. "I'd noticed, the times we'd touched before, that I had a sense of increased power. I'm not certain, but I think it's because you're -- alien, I suppose -- to this world and you're acting like a focus for my energy. I gave the candle its usual burst and, well, you saw the results."

I had.

A thought occurred to me. "So, if I'm a focus for you, does that make it easier to get me back home?"

Ezekiel considered the question for a moment. "Yes" was the first word out of his mouth and I felt a burst of relief, like the candle a moment ago. But he continued.

"It's not like it solves the problem of getting you back across space and time and worlds. It will make it easier, there's no doubting that. But it's... Have you ever used a magnifying glass with the sun? Burned a hole in paper or something like that?"

I said that I had.

"Okay, that's what you're acting like for me. But no magnifying glass is going to let you melt iron. Having the ability to focus my energy with your help, with this land here -- all of that will make it easier. But that doesn't mean it will be easy."

The sun was starting to get low in the sky. Through his window I felt a first cool evening breeze and heard a distant animal's yowl. I felt very, very far from home.

When I woke the next morning, the sun shining in the window instantly let me know that my recent experiences had not been a bad dream. Chicago in late fall never sees sunlight quite like that.

I stood up from my rickety bed and realized I didn't have any clothes to change into. Last night, I'd collapsed from exhaustion into bed wearing the clothes I'd put on two days before. Seventy-five years from now.

I certainly wasn't going to be borrowing anything from Ezekiel seeing as how I stood a good five inches taller than he and was also more of a stout tree to his sapling. I wondered if I might be able to get a small advance from him against my earnings so I could go into town and get some clothes.

It took me only a minute to track him down; though he was outside, the area around his former master's house was quite flat and his lone form, walking with a deliberate pace, was easy to spot. Too easy, thought the part of my brain which was focused on the idea of keeping my young charge alive.

"Morning," I said, as I caught up with him.

He nodded absentmindedly and kept walking.

"So, I was thinking, Zeke. When, uh, when you brought me here I didn't exactly have a chance to pack." Oh, what the hell was this? Was I actually feeling nervous about hitting the kid up for a loan?

Confoundingly, he didn't answer me. Ezekiel kept stepping, stepping, stepping and I had no choice but to follow along. I began to get annoyed and I reached out to grab his arm and make him talk to me. The moment we made contact I felt myself launch up into the air and then crash hard to the dusty ground. I saw Zeke hadn't fared any better. The two of us were several yards apart, both of us sprawled on the ground.

"What the --" The same start to a sentence came out of both of our mouths, though I doubt the next words would have been the same if we'd kept on.

Ezekiel slapped his head and answered our unfinished questions. "The focus! It works regardless of who touches who."

I muttered an unkind word under my breath. I hadn't even considered that fact before reaching out to him. Apparently he had been involved in some sort of magical act and when I took hold of him, trying to get his attention, I succeeded more fantastically than I could have imagined.

"Sorry," I said, a bit more audibly.

He shook his head. "I hadn't thought to warn you. It's fine." He closed his eyes for a minute and then his shoulders slumped a bit. "Not altogether fine, I suppose. The ward's gone."

"Ward?"

Maybe it was my imagination but I thought I saw his shoulders droop another fraction of an inch at my question. "It's like a magical fence. Any mages, anyone carrying any magical items, would be prevented from entering unless I allowed them through."

"Sounds handy."

He nodded. "They are. But they're not perfect. They won't protect you from a man with a gun or from a critter like a troll or a vampire. And they only last a day. Frederick's wards disappeared with sunup. Mine won't be anywhere near as potent as his, but they'll be better than nothing."

I chewed on my lip. Protection was certainly something I could understand. As I got back to his feet and he sat there, a thought occurred to me. I figured it must be a dumb thought if Zeke hadn't come up with it first, particularly in light of the short flight we'd both taken, but I was tired of sitting around with my thumb up my ass in this world.

"What if you were using a focus while creating the ward? Would that make it stronger?"

Ezekiel sat up a bit straighter and I saw a glint of surprise in his eyes. "If I planned for it... Yes, I think it would."

So that's how the two of us ended up taking a stroll around the property that morning, my hand on his arm the whole way.

"Wow," he said when we'd walked all the way around.

"Wow?"

"This ward is much better than anything I've ever crafted before. Maybe not the equal of my master's but a far sight closer than I would have expected."

He looked at me and smiled. "Good work, Mister Denton."

I still wasn't sure what I thought of Ezekiel or our situation. Something inside me wasn't ready to trust him; he certainly came in a safe enough looking package, but I'd learned long ago not to go just by looks.

But there wasn't any downside to having him think I was on board, especially when I was thinking of asking him a favor. So despite my misgivings, I managed a little smile back. "Hell, kid, call me Acme."

I even waited until we were most of the way back to hit him up for a couple of dollars.

Ezekiel offered to go into town with me, but didn't seem particularly disappointed when I told him I'd ride in solo. After all, as he'd pointed out, if he stayed behind he would have time to work on thinking more about my situation. With the wards in place he should be reasonably safe, he said. That word "reasonably" didn't leave me wholly comforted.

"Jackson's General Store should be able to fix you up fine," he told me as he pressed a few coins -- not the double eagles -- into my hand. "Take Blaze again and just keep an eye out for anything strange."

I almost pointed out that "strange" defined a goodly percentage of what I'd seen so far since arriving in Yuma, but I let it go.

Before leaving, I retrieved both my guns from the stand where I'd set them the night before. The revolver went in my pocket and I strapped my little Derringer back around my ankle.

Ezekiel asked about the miniature gun as I put it back in place.

"It's what's called a holdout gun. Say you're going in somewhere hostile and they frisk you or something. Well, maybe they get your main piece but you've still got a surprise for them."

He grimaced. Maybe he was thinking about the mess I'd made of our assailant yesterday.

"Hey, some of us don't have magical powers and we just have to get along as best as we can."

"Fair enough, Acme. I hope you don't need to use your guns."

"Yeah," I said as I was heading toward the door. "Me too."

We hadn't gone all the way into town the day before and I was curious to see what a real Old West city would be like, even if it might be one a good bit different from the one in my own past. To my surprise, a casual look around town didn't display enormous differences from what I imagined in the non-magical world. There was a tavern or two, a blacksmith, and the general store along with a variety of other business and residences. But I remembered our encounter on the road yesterday and the signs of magic I'd seen here; looks could indeed be deceiving. I kept my guard up even though the place felt like something out of a cowboy picture.

Just like those pictures, it was also hot and dusty. On more than one occasion I had the sensation of a fly or another bug zipping by my head. Even if it wasn't midday yet, I was still able to work up a bit of a sweat.

If the town itself didn't look terribly strange to me, I probably looked a bit strange to the town. Undoubtedly there were people here who wore suits, at least the local undertaker, but not many who were riding into town on a horse and looking as if they'd slept in their clothes the night before. It was a relief to arrive at the store and find a hat and a few sets of clothes which wouldn't make me quite so apt to stand out, even if Mr. Jackson had a bit of trouble finding things large enough to fit my frame.

"You're certain these will suit you?" he asked me, pointing at the rough work clothes I'd chosen, comparing them to my current garb.

"I reckon they will," I told him. They had the side benefit of being relatively inexpensive.

That errand complete, I rode through the rest of town. Two churches and, yes, a funeral home were among the places I saw as I headed to the far side of town.

I grabbed some lunch from a tavern, a slab of salty ham and a biscuit. It wasn't going to make me forget about the diner around the corner from my office, that was for certain.

Thinking about my office got me to thinking about Carol and Timmy. I felt guilty when it occurred to me they'd been far from my mind since I woke up and I wondered what they were thinking about me. If they thought I'd run off on them or worse. Then again, that was in the future still. And if Zeke was able to get me back home, back to the moment I left or something darn close to it... Well, then. I might be gone a day or a week or a month but they might not know anything had happened at all.

And though that was comforting in one way, there was also something queerly unsettling about that thought. That I could end up living some period of time completely separate from the time that they were living. Not like a business trip where you both know you're away for a few days and maybe you talk on the telephone once or twice. But like being in a coma where time marches on for the other person even if it stands still for you. Though, in my case, it was more like all of the rest of my world being in a coma and I was moving forward alone.

And that, of course, all depended on if I ever did get home. I suppose if I didn't that I'd just go down as one more missing person. Or one more husband and father who had finally decided to hell with it all and hit the rails.

Thinking like that wasn't doing my mind any good. I chewed the last few bites of my meat without really tasting them, slapped some coins on the table, and went back to my horse. By this time the sun was high in the sky and it shone down oppressively. Even wearing my new hat I was miserably hot and the insects which had been bothering me earlier in the day seemed more prevalent now.

With these discomforts the ride back felt a lot longer than the ride into town had felt. I was saddle sore, sweat-soaked, and grumpier than a bear by the time I tied Blaze back up at Ezekiel's place.

I took a load off in one of his chairs and tried to cool down a bit, closing my eyes. Zeke had his nose in a book and I let him keep at it. The chair must've been comfortable enough because I didn't wake up until late afternoon.

"Any luck today?" I asked him, once I'd gotten all the way awake.

"Not bad at all," he said. He held up the amulet that the brute we'd taken care of yesterday had been wearing. "I figured out what this was and it's a good thing, too. It was enchanted to let the mage who applied the enchantment observe what was happening wherever the amulet was carried." He grinned. "Sort of like the telephone you were describing to me yesterday."

I thought about this for just a few seconds, my heartbeat suddenly faster than before. I looked around the room for something opaque and flexible. I spotted an empty sack off to one side and hurried quietly to grab it.

"What're you doing, Acme?" he asked. I shushed him.

The sack in hand, I went to where Ezekiel was sitting and held out my hand for the amulet. When he didn't seem to get what I was aiming at, I pointed at first it and then the bag.

"Why?"

I groaned mentally. Admittedly, if anyone was paying attention, they probably knew what I was on about already but I wished the kid had enough sense to figure it out on his own.

"We might want to discuss some things privately," I said. "Having that around seems to make that impossible."

He chuckled. "Naturally. But I already took care of that. As soon as I figured out what it was doing, I set about deactivating it. It took a bit of work, but it's completely harmless now."

Zeke started going on about just how he'd managed this. Finally, after several minutes of hearing him talk about "energy traps" and "intention veiling" and "blowback triggers" I'd had enough. He seemed awfully pleased with himself but it sure sounded to me like he'd spent a lot of time on this rather than what I thought he was going to be doing -- looking for some more creative ways to get around the problem of how to get me back home.

And I started to wonder just again how interested he really was in helping me get home. After all, I wasn't much of a threat to him and having an other-worldly focus around to use as needed certainly could come in handy.

"Let me ask you something, Zeke," I said, cutting him off mid-sentence. "This all sounds great. But once you figured out what it was for why didn't you just go outside, dig a hole in the ground, and bury the darn thing? Instead, you spent all day messing around with disabling it when what you really should be worrying about is not the last attack but the next one and -- oh, by the way -- how to get the poor sap you kidnapped from the 20th century back home!"

By the time I stopped talking I noticed that I was out of breath and Ezekiel looked a bit shaken. I lowered myself heavily into a chair and, realizing I still was clutching the sack, let it fall to the floor.

He ran his fingers through his hair and let a long breath out. "Actually, Mr. Denton, the whole reason I put all that time and -- as you pointed out -- my energy into rendering the enchantment inert was precisely so I could help you." He held the amulet back up. "It's not sending any information to the person who enchanted it but it's still a magical artifact and that means --"

Oh. "That you could use it like you used the ones when you brought me here."

He nodded.

I was getting really tired of these explanations which sounded logical as long as you believed in a bunch of ground rules for a game that you'd just started playing the day before. I still wasn't sure how much I could believe of what he was telling me. I didn't have any other sources of information, so he could spin whatever tales he wanted and I had to buy them or not, strictly on my own gut reactions.

One thing I knew for certain was that I didn't want to spend another minute in the sweaty suit I'd been wearing for over forty-eight hours. I grabbed pants and a shirt from my new gear and went for a bit of privacy to change.

It was a good decision; changing into clean and dry clothes made me feel a lot better even if I knew that I could rather desperately use a nice long shower.

Ezekiel nodded when I came back into the room. "Looks like you got fixed up real good," he said.

"Yeah." A thought flitted through my mind and I half-smiled. "I can't imagine what Carol would think if she saw me in these clothes, though. Not my usual get-up." The smile faded quickly as I remembered my musings from earlier in the day about time and people and how it all fit together.

A tear threatened to drip from one of my eyes and I turned away to get composed.

"Got anything to drink here?" I asked him, my back still turned.

"Some well water in a pitcher in the kitchen."

"That it?"

He said it was and I wished I'd made an extra purchase back at the general store. A few drops of booze might have gone a long way right then. I went and got what was offered, though, and felt a bit more myself when I walked back into the room where he was working.

But however I felt inside, my emotions must still have been showing outside.

"Is your child a boy or a girl?" Ezekiel asked.

"A boy. Timothy. We call him Timmy, though."

I wasn't looking at Zeke but I could tell he was looking at me. I was wondering what he'd know about missing someone, feeling good and sorry for myself, before I remembered that he'd lost someone himself just yesterday. He'd referred to the older mage as his "master" but nothing about his demeanor suggested that was to be taken in the sense of "master and servant", rather "master and student." Maybe he did know something about loss, something very recent.

He was rummaging around through a desk drawer while I mulled over this sort of connection between us. A moment later he brought over a small glass disk, about the size of a baseball around, no thicker than an eyeglass lens.

"Take this, Acme."

"I'll need more than a glass of water to get this down," I replied. He gave me a funny look and I shook my head. "Stupid joke." I took the disk from him, careful to hold it as he had, by the edges, so as not to get smudges on it.

"Close your eyes," he said.

I did.

"Now, think about Carol and Timmy. Think about a happy moment with them."

I tried and at first it was hard. All I could think about were the fights, the times I'd had to tell my son that we couldn't go to a ballgame or couldn't go to a movie because Dad didn't have the money. But I remembered the look on his face when his mother would make his favorite meal -- these things she called porcupines, meatballs with rice in them basically -- and I remembered the way they both looked when I'd come by a few bucks extra and took us to the circus last year. There were happy times. They'd just been damned hard to find lately.

"Are you thinking about a happy moment?"

I nodded.

"Good," he said. "Hold that memory." And then his hand was on my arm and I was there, right there, back at the circus with the smell of the hay and the elephants and the roasted peanuts and -- And it was gone.

I opened my eyes and saw the same walls I'd seen moments before. Ezekiel was crouched down beside me, his eyes shut, a sense of exertion pouring from his body.

My eyes fell on the glass disc which I was holding and my breath caught in my chest. There, in the glass, perfect images of Timmy and Carol, smiling, pointing. I was sure they were laughing at a clown's antics. It hurt to see them. It was wonderful to see them.

"Good Lord." The words drifted from my mouth. "It's amazing."

Ezekiel stood slowly. He glanced a moment at the disc and said, "You have a lovely wife and son." His voice was flatter than I could remember hearing it. He walked across the room and found a cloth, handed it to me. "Wrap it in that. It's strong glass, enchanted, but not indestructible. A little extra protection can't hurt."

I took the cloth but just sat it on my leg, caught in the images in the glass.

"I'm going to rest," Ezekiel said. "Wake me if there's a problem."

I thought it was only a second later when I looked up and said "Thank you," but the words fell on empty air as he was already gone.

The next couple days dragged out like waiting on a late-night El train in the dead of winter; every minute felt like ten. Each morning, Ezekiel and I walked the perimeter, rebuilding his wards. After that, he went off to his study and I wouldn't see him until nearly sundown. The good news was there hadn't been any new attacks on my host. The bad news was I was going out of my mind with boredom. I gave a look at the books on his shelves and even pulled down a few and tried to get into them. But they were all magically-oriented books and clearly not the sort of thing for beginners. I needed a "Dick and Jane" book for this world, but if there was such a thing, it sure wasn't in his library.

The fourth morning I woke up there, Zeke again burrowed himself into his study as soon as our ward-rebuilding was done. I couldn't stand the thought of another long, hot day of twiddling my thumbs, waiting for good news or bad so I poked my nose in his study and told Ezekiel I was going into town. He was scratching notes on paper and only nodded vaguely at my announcement. I closed the door quietly but I doubt it would have made a difference if I'd slammed the thing.

Blaze and I rode into town with relative ease; I was pleasantly surprised at how comfortable I was getting on horseback. Overnight a rain storm had passed through and everything felt a good bit cooler than before but there was a lingering humidity which I could imagine getting stifling if the day was to heat up very much.

I wandered around town, glad this time I didn't have to worry about standing out due to my clothing. I almost went into the town's Catholic church to offer up a little prayer that everyone was doing fine back home. But then I started wondering if this world's God was the same as my world's God and that was a terribly uncomfortable thought, somewhere in the neighborhood of blasphemy. I decided to skip the church for now; I'd thank God plenty when I got back home.

I bought a copy of a local newspaper to read as I ate lunch at the same place I'd eaten before. It wasn't quite the Tribune, but it would do. The food tasted fine, but something was nagging at me the whole time

I ate. It was like that feeling you get when someone is watching you but ten times stronger, more like they were inside my head.

I couldn't finish my food. Sweat gathered on my arms and my vision started to blur and I realized that there was something seriously wrong. I had to get back to Ezekiel, if I could manage it before I passed out. Or worse.

I tossed a few coins on the table, hoping it was both enough and not way too much, and stumbled toward the door.

I didn't make it. One moment I was staggering across the tavern's wood floor and the next I was tumbling down. Down. Down.

The first thing I saw when I came to was Ezekiel. I drew a deep breath to give him a piece of my mind, but then I realized that his hands were tied behind his back and his mouth was gagged. My assessment of the situation quickly changed.

I heard other people moving around and moved my hand quickly to my head, as if struck by a pain. I wanted time to think.

"Hello, Mister Denton," said a voice from somewhere behind me. I turned slowly toward the speaker. "I apologize for the suddenness of your arrival here but I was afraid you might not be amenable to visiting under your own power. And Corander here, strong though he is, was going to have his hands full bringing me Ezekiel."

A woman sat in a well-stuffed chair. She had gray streaks running through her brown hair, some early middle-age wrinkles, and piercing green eyes. Next to her stood a young man, arms crossed, standing at attention. He put me in the mind of nothing so much as a gladiator from a movie.

"You summoned me here?" I asked the woman, making it sound more uncertain than I really was about things.

"Indeed." She stood up and walked toward where I sat on the floor.

"Why's Zeke tied up?"

She arched an eyebrow. "Why, so he can't hurt either of us, of course."

She moved closer and I decided it was time to get to my own feet. It wasn't as pleasant of an experience as I would have hoped. Still, I was up off the floor and that had to count for something.

"What makes you think he'd hurt anyone?" I asked her.

"Well, for one thing, he already has hurt you, hasn't he? Bringing you here, separating you from the ones you love."

I puzzled over that for a moment, wondering how she knew so much about what had happened to me. But then I remembered the amulet from the thug who'd ambushed us; if it had been hers, she could have gotten plenty of information before Ezekiel had disabled it.

"Look, lady, I don't know who you are. But so far what I know is that you've yanked me away from a perfectly good lunch" -- a bit of a lie -- "and you've got Ezekiel all tied up over there. This isn't exactly a situation which is screaming 'good guys' for you."

She sighed. "I can see where you might have that impression. Very well. First, my name is Elizabeth Matheson." She closed the gap and reached out to shake hands. Reflexively, I started to extend my own hand before it occurred to me that whatever focusing power I provided to Zeke would work for this woman as well. And she didn't strike me as being a lightweight apprentice to begin with. I pointedly put my hands behind my back.

"That's close enough, Miss Matheson," I said, pointedly putting my hands behind my back. She pouted a bit and raised an eyebrow at my gesture, but didn't advance any further. "You still haven't explained why I should be viewing Ezekiel as the biggest threat in this room. Yes, he pulled me away from my home, but he certainly didn't intend to do that."

"You're quite certain of this?"

"Sure, he --" I'd started to answer before really thinking about it. He had seemed surprised to know how far away I'd come from, but could that have been a ruse?

"From your decision not to take my hand a moment ago, you obviously understand that you act as a focus for energy here," she said. "That's quite a valuable prize for any mage."

"But he burned out all of the various magical gear he and his master had collected --"

"So he says. Have you any proof that what he used to pull you across worlds wasn't but a fraction of his true horde of relics?"

She waited just a few seconds. I didn't answer, but I don't think she was expecting me to.

"And in exchange for that one sacrifice" -- she raised up a finger -- "however big it was, he gets a permanent power boost which happens to also come in the form of a highly-trained bodyguard. More than a fair trade I would say. For him."

Damn... Ezekiel was still straining to be heard but what she said was making more sense than I was comfortable with. "I'm only hearing your side of things. Why not let him speak?" I asked her, indicating Ezekiel.

"Some magic has verbal components, Mister Denton. We're safer this way."

I rubbed my scratchy chin and for half a second the thought of needing a razor absurdly floated through my brain. "Let's say I believe you, that this kid's been playing me for a patsy. What then? Are you saying I should just be your stooge instead of his?"

"Not at all. You're not just a focus for mages like myself and Mister Walker over there. You're also a... a force of chaos for our world. And I fear that the risk you pose to us will only increase the longer you are here."

"What risk?"

Elizabeth frowned slightly and took a few seconds before answering. "I can't say precisely. It's the very nature of chaotic energies that they can manifest in any number of ways. Unskilled persons may suddenly develop magical powers which they have no idea how to control. The weather could be affected. The dead could rise up from their graves. On the other hand, it might be even be a change for the better, but the risk is one which no one should have exposed our world to unilaterally." She glanced briefly at Ezekiel with a hard, cold look.

When she turned back to me, she said, "The best thing for me, for you, and for my world would be if we could get you home."

My heart surged at the thought of home. Part of me was still uncomfortable trusting anything this woman said, but if she could offer me a way back to Carol and our son, then did it matter that much what her motivations were?

"How would we make this happen?"

She bit her lip. "That's the unfortunate thing. I don't know what all you've been told, but in a situation like this, where you've gone beyond the bounds of your own world and time there are only two ways you can get home. The mage who summoned you can voluntarily return you to your rightful place with a new summoning. The other way you would get home would be if the mage who had summoned you dies."

"Ezekiel told me that if he dies that I could end up God only knows where."

"Yes, I imagine he would have told you something like that. It would align your interests with his."

I rubbed my eyes. I didn't know what to think now. There were so many thoughts and angles floating around in my head that I couldn't make sense of it all.

"So what now?" I asked her. "Are you just waiting on me to say the word and you can just --" I made a throat-cutting gesture with my hand "-- do him in?"

"Actually, Mister Denton, it would be much better if you were the one to act towards that end." She paused. "I'm trying to think of how best to explain this. It's a matter of... balancing the magical energies. Since the person who has summoned you is either unable or unwilling to return you, it would nudge the magical flow of our world back from chaos towards order if you were then the one release yourself from the bonds of his spell. And I believe you have something on your person which could take care of him quite efficiently. A revolver, if I'm not mistaken?"

God, this business had me shaken up. I'd been standing here yammering for minutes and hadn't even thought about my gun. Then again, Ezekiel had told me it wouldn't be effective as a weapon against him. Of course, I'd willingly believed that at the time.

I pulled out the gun, checked its load.

"One shot, Mr. Denton. One shot and you're back home."

Could it really be that simple? I raised the gun, had it aimed vaguely in Ezekiel's direction but not quite at him. His eyes went wide and he was really protesting now, though I couldn't make out any of what he was saying. She sent Corander over to stand by Ezekiel. He loomed over the young man and then everyone was silent.

I thought about Carol, thought about Timmy. About how much I wanted to be back with them. In the absence of sound, I could hear my own heartbeat rushing in my ears as I considered the weight of the gun in my hand. I saw Carol's and Timmy's faces and I wanted to be with them more than anything else in the world. In all the worlds.

I looked toward Ezekiel but I wasn't really seeing him. I was seeing my wife, my son. I could see them laughing, smiling.

And then I realized that the image I had

conjured up in my own mind was the same one captured in glass by Ezekiel the night before. I blinked, still holding my gun out, still feeling its pull on my arm. With my empty hand, I touched my shirt pocket and felt for the wrapped disk; it was still there, still whole.

Elizabeth had a good story. There was no arguing that point. But I couldn't believe that the person who had put himself into infusing the glass with that image was doing all the things she claimed, especially not putting his own world at risk for personal gain or glory.

I spun quickly, turning to aim the gun at the woman. Before I could take a shot she flicked her fingers and the gun flew from my hands. It clattered to the floor yards away.

"No games, then," she said, giving me the same hard look I'd seen her give Ezekiel only a few minutes before. "You're a powerful weapon and I want you. I've already bound you to this world so that you will remain here even if Mister Walker over there dies. And he will die tonight."

I swallowed hard. Now I knew who to trust, but it was a bit late, wasn't it?

"So, you have a choice. I can kill you both or I can kill him and you can join me. It's up to you."

I looked around the room. Ezekiel was slumped in his bonds, his shoulders drooped. Corander stood proudly next to the young apprentice. The young apprentice I'd agreed to protect and failed.

"I don't want to have to show you just how serious I am, Mister Denton," Elizabeth said.

One thing was for certain. I was never getting back to my wife and son if I died in this room. It wasn't a time for defiance.

"I'll tell you what," I said. "You really had me going. You're good with that calm, rational bit. It suits you. But I see how it is now."

I turned away from Ezekiel and Corander, took a first step toward Elizabeth. I could sense her wanting to rush toward me, anxious to use me to her own ends. I took another step.

"And it looks like I really don't have any choice." Two more steps. We were only separated by five or so feet of stone floor now.

"I'd hoped maybe I could strike an even better deal than this one, but you've got to take what you can get." One more step. She was practically jumping out of her shoes to get at me. A couple more steps and she would have me in her grasp. "I had thought maybe I could" -- Step. -- "hold" -- Step. -- "out."

I went to my knees hard as the second word came out of my mouth. I grabbed the Derringer from its ankle holster and fired a shot before anyone but Ezekiel had a clue what I was doing. My bullet caught Elizabeth square and she stumbled backwards, fell to the ground, blood already staining her dress.

Behind me, I heard another thump. Ezekiel had been knocked to the floor and Corander's body was twisting, growing into something awful with horns and claws. I fired the second shot -- the last shot -- from my gun. Corander screamed and jerked away. He stayed partially transformed, half-man, half-beast, clutching his left shoulder.

There was more shrieking behind me. Elizabeth had gotten to her knees but she was frozen there, mouth hanging open and a horrible wailing coming out of it. Her eyes were panicked; they looked like they were bulging from their sockets. I stared. Longer than I should have from a tactical point of view and longer than I wish I had for other reasons. Some things can't be unseen.

Her screaming rose in pitch and then I couldn't hear her any longer but her mouth was still open, the muscles of her neck still straining as they had seconds before. And then her head burst open. It was worse than anything I'd seen in the war. One moment I could see her face and the next it was scattered across the room.

Corander roared again. The sound shocked me out of my reverie. I ran toward Ezekiel and got him back to his feet. I was grateful that his legs weren't bound. He could move as well as I could. We burst through the door, found ourselves out under a desert moon and ran, never looking back.

We caught a ride on a wagon heading back toward Yuma. Neither of us talked about what had happened at the Matheson house. In fact, we didn't talk much at all. A few times I pulled out the glass disk and looked at Carol and Timmy. Sometimes it made me feel better to see their faces. Sometimes it didn't.

We didn't get back to his place until late at night.

"What the hell happened to her back

there?" I asked, when we were safely inside the walls of his house.

"Besides the binding spell, she'd cast another one on you while you were unconscious. The next person you shot... Their magical energy would be transferred to her."

I thought about that for a minute, imagined it like feedback on a public address system. Yeah, I could believe it. And I wasn't sure I was glad I'd asked.

Fatigue crashed over me. I told Zeke I'd see him in the morning to put up the wards. He nodded and told me to sleep well.

I woke before dawn and dressed. Most mornings Ezekiel would already be up by this hour, eating breakfast before we went outside. He wasn't in the kitchen, though.

I found him in his study, fast asleep with his head on his desk. I nudged his shoulder.

"Hey, Zeke. Almost sunrise," I said.

He rubbed his eyes and looked at me. "Thanks," he said.

"For what?"

"All of it."

I didn't know quite what to say. I didn't imagine "all of it" included nearly holding my gun on him there for a minute back there, but I wasn't going to bring it up if he wasn't.

"Here, I've got something for you," he said.

Zeke handed me the amulet we'd taken off the brute several days ago.

"I've re-enchanted it. This time it's enchanted to keep the wearer from being summoned against his will." He looked a bit sheepish. "I wish I'd thought of that before all this."

I slipped its chain over my head. The weight of the amulet felt good, reassuring.

Then I wondered about something. "Does this put us back where we were? Not able to use this to help get me home when the time allows?"

He smiled a bit. "No, Acme. It will still be able to be used for that purpose. Though it will likely end up a hunk of slag in the aftermath. But..."

When he didn't finish his thought, I prodded him. "But what?"

"Well, I just don't want you getting your hopes up. I've done a lot of thinking and a lot of research. The bottom line is that we're still going to have to acquire a lot more tools for me to be able to return you home."

Sometimes, you just had to find a way. I'd survived the war years and made it home. I was going to survive this, too.

"So when do we start searching?"

"I'm already on it. But these aren't the sort of things you just dart out and find. I don't know when we'll get our first lead, so in the meantime..." He reached down below his desk and pulled up a long slab of wood. "I made this for you, too. Actually, it's what I was working on when you went to town a couple of mornings ago."

He held the slab out to me and I turned it around. There were letters on it, not painted on or burned in or anything else. Magicked on, I suppose. "Acme Denton," it said. "Investigator For Hire. Reasonable Rates."

"I thought you could get back to your usual job, while you were here."

I held the shingle in my hands, felt the weight of the amulet, the weight of the glass disk in my pocket.

"Is it all right?" he asked.

I wondered how I could have ever doubted this young man.

I nodded. "It's perfect. Thanks, Zeke."

And this time, when he smiled, it was full and bright.

An ardent short story reader and writer, Michael's stories have appeared in publications including Ellery Queen Mystery Magazine, Beneath Ceaseless Skies, and Nature. He's the chair of the Cinevent classic film convention and enjoys photography, geocaching, and travel. He can be found online at http://michaelhaynes.info/ and on Twitter as @mohio73.

THE LAST CONTRACT

by Dominika Lein

A futuristic hitman and his alien assistant go for one last job, but something is amiss.

The Last Contract

By Dominika Lein

The genetic sample had proven itself pure and sent me to the 879E Siwu nebula. I arrived in a flash via the teleporter embedded in my palm, on the docking port of the Mamonar Colony station. Here, I would find the sample's source: a person known as Remy Jay, the target I'd been hired to kill. Why did Remy have to die? I hadn't asked. It wasn't my job to care. Known under the alias Swift Death, due to my efficiency in the contract murder business, I didn't mess with my reputation by asking stupid questions.

My only task was to carry out the execution for the sake of my repeat client, Ms. Netai. She'd hired me for so many tasks in the past decade, supporting her rise to the top of an empire of intergalactic companies, that I didn't even need to check the credentials of each contract anymore. Once I had the sample, it was a quick in and out job every time.

Despite the blinking violet sign that spelt out "Mamonar Colony Dock" above the gate, the port had fractures in the hull through which nebulaic gases polluted the air. The cog-like biomachinery implanted in my ribs whirred, adjusting my lungs to the specific atmosphere. Other than the light from the sign, darkness shrouded the place.

My assistant, Vivila Starseeker, stood behind me. The ends of her long green hair unstuck from my shoulder. Why she was there with me... she shouldn't have been, but Vivila - for all her skills in helping me out - didn't excel at obeying in the cases when she disagreed. She must have disagreed with this one.

"I told you to stay behind," I said. I brushed off the spot on my trusty jacket where she'd hitched a ride. If she'd left a stain on the black leather with her weird hair, then I wouldn't be in the mood to deal with her.

Vivila didn't smile or frown. Her expressionless alien face remained cold with blue-violet eyes. The pigment of her skin shifted between a mirrored version of my pale human tone to her species' natural chlorophyll skin like a slow, green-lit beacon. If it'd been up to her, her sleek humanoid body would be exposed. Instead, she wore a simple dress due to my personal request. It'd been way too distracting with her following me around naked. She didn't understand human modesty, so I'd given her an ultimatum on the matter: be clothed or find someone else to attune with. Surprisingly, she'd chosen the former.

Her hair gathered in a set of thick pigtails, the green strands writhing like snakes as she analyzed the environment. "No one is here," she observed.

I couldn't argue with that. Pieces of scrap metal and engineering tools had been left strewn about. An old tow-cart laid on its side, its red lights still blinking on automatic. I said, "This dock could be decommissioned. We won't know until we get inside. Stay low."

We went to the gate. The tilted panel crackled with wayward electricity running through the broken casing. I traced my fingers silently through the air in an assigned macro-gesture. A twisted spiral of alloy scales covered my forearm and hand. I grabbed onto the exposed wiring and pressed it to the input. It flashed blue and the gate door slid open.

Past a foyer where vents cleared the atmosphere of corrupted particles, the central lobby connected the dock to the station interior. No welcoming music or hostess to greet us, the only sounds were those of the ventilation systems jutting fresh steam into the room and a distant beeping. Not a soul in sight. I scratched at my neck, searched around the counters, and overturned a couple benches. Nothing, not even a body.

Vivila touched the lobby counter, her hair spreading over the glossy surface. She said in a flat tone of voice, "There is no breath here. Not human nor otherwise."

I held up my hand, looking at where the genetic sample still floated inside the palm device.

"It brought us here," I said. "So the target has to be alive somewhere in this place."

The teleportation device always brought me a safe distance away from its target and hadn't failed before. Remy had to be here.

My boots clapped against the metal floor, echoing in the otherwise muted room. I slowed my steps to quiet the noise. Though Vivila's observation seemed true, I did not feel as if we were alone. The station hull creaked above us. My attention flitted between different lights that had been left on. The atmosphere had cleared through the lobby's ventilation so there hadn't been a fatal breach. So where did the colony go? No planets were nearby to harbor any humans in the nebula. Regarding information of the Mamonar Colony or its station, I didn't know anything other than its celestial location.

"It doesn't matter. Whatever happened, it isn't our problem," I told Vivila, though she didn't seem concerned. "I'll find this Remy, confirm his death, and then we'll be teleported back."

We descended a staircase to a donut-ring corridor that overlooked the station's core through plexiglass windows. The core had dimmed, not brightly lit or warm anymore, but a dull blur of vertical gold light that crawled from top to bottom in a loop. I adjusted my belt, the heavy attachments pulled at the nylon, and then ran a hand over the square generator that housed a backup system for my biomech. On the third iteration since its initial prototype, the biomech suit I'd been developing wasn't entirely stable, but it worked well enough to test in the field. And in the event something went wrong with the 3.0 system, I could activate version 2.0 instead. Or as I lovingly referred to it, *slightly better than nothing*.

Not that I expected something to happen, but the continual humming of the core mixed with the hissing of air through the vents set an unusual anxiety in me. Something didn't feel so ordinary about the job anymore and that something told me to stay alert.

"Do you sense anything?" I asked.

Vivila placed her seven-fingered hands on the plexiglass. The ends of her hair stuck against the surface. Vibrations rippled, faintly visible in the transparent material. She said, "There is a breath."

I asked, "Which direction?"

"Down," she answered.

The sound of chimes followed us as we traveled down a staircase to the lower levels. Multicolor lights glimmered along panels where doors used to function but now stuck at awkward angles in varying modes of open and shut.

I slid my thumb across the center of my forehead and felt the coarse branded mark, which served as reminder of my vocation and thus, the purpose for being in the station. I continued with renewed confidence. There was nothing scary about an empty space station, after all. It was easier than a gangster den already.

Vivila followed close behind. Her sweet floral aroma covered the acrid scents of oil and sanitation liquid. She set a hand on my wrist and said, "There."

The door she looked at had jammed halfway shut. Showers of fiery sparks spurted from the top. The biomech glove had gone into stasis to recharge so I macro-gestured and it returned to cover my arm. I grabbed the door and pushed to move it aside. The door screeched, and sparks rained over my alloyed exterior, bouncing off to the floor. It refused my attempt. I macro-gestured with my other hand, activating that side's biomech glove, and used both hands. The door wrenched free and I tossed it aside with a loud clatter of metal against metal.

Wires hung down in the opening, flaring like a curtain of beaded fire. I gathered the twitching mass in my fists and knotted them out of the way before walking through to the corridor beyond. Vivila followed, carefully avoiding the stray electricity.

Even though we were bound to be getting closer to the target, the pervasive feeling of something being off gnawed at me. I considered whether it would be feasible to leave right then and there: an odd consideration for me, someone who preferred to get things done quickly and without thought. I looked at my palm-device, wondering if the manual override would work or not. I'd never tried it before but theoretically, the ability existed.

"I'm about ready to get out of here," I said to Vivila. She made a quiet noise of acknowledgment, smoothed out her dress, and waited for me. Part of me wanted her to raise concern. I wanted to hear that I was acting stupid for being carried away by a creaky, old space station. I tapped my finger against the device, then lowered it without an attempt. No, I couldn't be driven away by mere apprehension.

I led farther into the corridor as the curved walls sloped downward at a subtle angle. My renewed commitment to the job, however, did nothing to ward away the hissing sounds of vents or the faint blinking of lights. I kept an eye on a few doors that had gotten stuck open. Beyond them, darkness settled in leaking mists of steam.

Metal sheets scraped each other in a piercing noise that I immediately recognized. I leapt backward, glancing down at the floor where a spattering of lights had blinked into life. The lights followed me in moving circular formations. Briefly landing on the ball of my foot, I leapt again to get away from the activated tech.

"Get off the floor," I told Vivila.

She leapt onto the ceiling. Her hair webbed out and created a net to harbor her lithe form. She scuttled toward me, a few strands of her vine-like hair stretching out to wrap around my waist.

The lights reached to where my feet landed. Electricity buzzed, charged to the max, and shot through my boots. The biomech suit's failsafe activated automatically, covering my entire body with the alloy scales. If it had been a smaller electrical discharge, the soles of my boots could handle it, but this was specifically engineered to pass through shock-resistant footwear and force the human system into seizures.

Vivila's hands slipped on the ceiling, almost falling as a couple more strands of her hair wrapped around my arms. She lifted me up and I joined her in the webbing. Good thing too because a few more seconds in the electrical field and the suit might've overloaded.

I'd seen this style of trap before, but why would tech like this be set in an abandoned colony station? Someone had obviously placed it with a human in mind; not just any human either, but a human who would be able to avoid the basic stationary version of the trap. Balanced on a swing seat of Vivila's outstretched hair, I prepared the device in my hand to activate the return teleport manually and said, "We're leaving."

"What is that?" she asked. She pointed past me at a strange machine crawling out from the mist and over a broken door. It wasn't humanoid, with twelve limbs of patchwork metal and pump-like masses connecting them, yet the thing moved as if it were painfully alive.

"That's not the breath you felt, is it?" I asked as it jerkily approached us.

"It has no breath," said Vivila.

A red light grew bright on the machine's core pump. With it, a strong blast of sonic waves crashed into us. Vivila's hair detached. We fell together, landing on the mobile trap. The electricity shocked the both of us. Vivila crumpled onto her knees beside me. My biomech suit blocked just enough that I could keep conscious, though my limbs slowed in reaction.

Through blurred vision, I forced my body to move and blocked the machine's path to Vivila. A host of thinner appendages, stiff and hard like jointed knives, burst out from its limbs. With my full suit active, including the helmet, I could see a faint red outline of where its drives were located. I realized, suddenly, that it was a Z690 chopshopped together with a C472, which explained the strange formation of limbs. Most robots just have one drive, but combined...

I fired a plasma bolt from the top of my alloy sleeve. It zipped silently outward, only visible due to the steam filling the hall. It sliced through the metal and pierced the left drive, causing the robot to stumble.

Firing again, the second bolt missed as the machine diverted to the side. The thin appendages stabbed into a nearby panel. I heard Vivila cry out, then felt the ground disappear from beneath me. I barely grabbed onto the edge of the trapdoor. With the circular lights and the mist, I must have overlooked the seams before. My body swung from the momentum. The metal cracked under the modified strength of my alloy gloves.

Below, Vivila fell out of sight into

darkness. I lifted myself up in a fierce pull and landed at the edge, just in time to block the machine from stabbing into my head. Its tiny daggers tapped dangerously against my crossed forearms. I held the x-block position, searching for the second robotic drive.

The jagged shape outlined in red light. The robot's core started to activate for another sonic pulse. I shoved it forward, gained some space, and kicked at the bastard. My strike landed hard against one of the pumps and sent the robot crashing against the wall. Parts broke off, including a couple of limbs, but it managed to get upright. I aimed for the drive, and fired a plasma bolt.

The pump exploded, sending bits of metal everywhere. I held an arm up, saving myself from a large limb about to collide with my face. The force of it sent me sliding over the lip of the open hole. I scrambled to grab the edge and found myself dangling again over the void. The limb fell past me, disappearing into the darkness where Vivila had gone.

Could she climb her way back up? Was she dead? If I let go... would the suit hold up from the landing impact?

I had told her not to come. This was one of the reasons why. Normally, I wouldn't prioritize a person's safety over my contract, but Vivila had grown on me in our time together. My instincts told me to continue without her...

The biomech suit retreated without stimulus, exposing my human skin again. I felt warmth emanating from below. Wherever it led, it was hotter than the corridor. The worst thoughts went through my mind. She was probably dead, burnt to a crisp or crippled. Best to move on.

I lifted myself back up and then searched the mess of parts that the robot had left behind. Nothing. Not a single clue or marker of who had made it or why. Still, I had a hunch; a gut feeling that had been bothering me for a while. The empty station, the high-tech traps, the hybrid robot... it all seemed specifically chosen for someone with my skills and weaknesses. Whatever laid at the bottom of the trap's descent was, probably, also meant for me. What if it was another unauthorized machine?

The thought of Vivila fighting for survival against a robot like this... the cogs in my chest stuttered and my fingers anxiously twitched. I was wasting time. Without her, I didn't have a decent idea of which way to go. Even if I didn't find the target, could I really leave her behind on the abandoned station? I muttered, "Ok, let's see what they've got."

A swift macro-gesture with both hands triggered the biomech suit to return over my body. I leapt down into the darkness. It was a vertical tunnel with a curved round metal wall. After a journey of dings and dents, I landed in a pile of stark human bones and old fabric scraps of torn jumpsuits. A row of smelters in chrome pillars overheated the humid air. The room looked like a charge-port for the station's core. Wide pipes lined the walls, connected to a network of thinner metal tubing. The systems still ran, even without a crew, hissing and whirring in automatic motions.

Vivila wasn't in sight. I kept the biomech in active mode, though I knew I was using its primary energy charge. The targeting in my scanner proved useless, the smelters messing with heat-based scans. The scanner was meant for mechanical targeting anyway. Humanoids don't require such tech in most situations.

I caught a whiff of floral scents and followed the trail as the scent grew stronger. Around a pillar and behind scrap metal, I found a narrow crevice slashed into the wall. I peeked through and saw the green-haired, changing-skin woman nestled between metal grates.

"You found me," said Vivila from her hiding spot. She stared at me, the pretty angles of her face unmoving. Her violet eyes flashed blue from the reflected light of the smelters.

I pulled her out to the room. "Was anything in here when you landed?"

Vivila said, "The bones of your species. Are we still leaving?"

"Do you feel that breath again?" I asked. I already knew my preference when it came to leaving... but that would make this my first failed contract since I became an officially designated hitman. It'd be quicker to find the target, get it over with, and teleport back the familiar way.

Her hair writhed outward. She went to the wall, setting the ends of her hair on the pipes. After a few seconds, she pointed toward a curve in the wall that led assumedly to the exit. "It is much stronger on this level. That way."

I commented, "This has to be a set-up."

We left the charge-port and found

ourselves in a crew corridor. The hall was wide and tall enough for a couple of solo spaceships to fit through. Instead of smooth metal walls with panels like in the upper levels though, the place was covered in networks of alloy pipes, connected dials, and handles to control the various filtration and other systems that kept a station of this size running. Compared to the destruction of the station's upper levels, the maintenance floor looked untouched.

My suit internally beeped, silent to anyone but myself, and reminded me that it would need to recharge soon. I macro-gestured to let it do so and it receded, the alloy disappearing from my skin. If I needed it again, however long it got to charge would be better than if it lost power during a fight.

"What do you mean by set-up?" whispered Vivila. She kept close behind me, her hair dancing and twisting as she remained alert to the environment.

I answered, "None of this is coincidence. The target expected me. It's almost like they received warning, but that's unheard of."

"Because of the teleport?" she asked.

I nodded and didn't bother to explain further. If Vivila wanted to know more, I would inform her later when the contract was finished and we were safe in our bed again. Instead, I said, "Quiet. I need to focus."

We crept around a corner. I kept a hand up, to be ready and to make sure Vivila stayed behind me. Ahead, I saw flashing lights and sprays of orange-red sparks. The sound of a grinder smoothing metal echoed through the place. I glanced at the green-haired alien. She nodded; the breath came from here.

I motioned for her to wait, then slunk down and peeked around the open frame.

What I saw sent an anchor into the pit of my stomach. In the workshop room, eight robots toiled on each other in a display of blasphemous engineering. Z690s patched with V738s, C472 strewn across in bits smoldering against an old R250, and more in a diverse array of technology. They didn't notice me, busy with their Frankensteinian labor.

Past the machines and against a back wall, a human floated in a vat of amber goo. He placed his hands against the transparent container. He'd noticed me and waved his arms frantically. How long had he been in there? It had to be Remy Jay, my target and the only other human in the whole damn space station.

That feeling of unease returned in full force. Why would Ms. Netai want this man dead? He was already a dead man, just a matter of time... but perhaps he had information that was too important to be left to chance and required a more personal touch. My tech left no room to question if a kill happened, though. The excuse still didn't squash the nasty taste in my mouth while I observed the imprisoned man.

I backed up. Vivila set a hand on my wrist and looked at me with a questioning raise of her delicate hairless brow. I tapped the device in my palm. We were leaving. If Ms. Netai wanted me to come back, she'd have to pay double my usual fee.

I'd never done it before though; that is, used the device to teleport without having killed the sample's target. Digging around in my memory banks, I recalled the procedure from the manual. I twisted the outer ring and then pulled it up so I could dissolve the genetic sample within. The device quietly hissed, a few tiny bubbles rising from the inner orb.

I watched as the sample swam around inside the solvent, almost as if it was running from destruction. I twisted the ring back and forth, tilted my hand, and felt pain shoot through the nerves in my wrist. The outer ring pushed the orb back into my palm and settled where it had been.

I waited for the flash of the teleport... but it did not come. The sample remained in the orb. Nothing had changed at all. The attempt had failed. Either I had forgotten the manual instructions or the teleport acting manually, without the genetic sample cleared, was beyond its capabilities.

Vivila grabbed my shoulder. She turned me around and pointed. A whisper of surprise escaped her lips.

The patchworked V738 with a Z690 had left the workshop. Its core drive beamed a spread of red light, scanning us. It bent over its fused drive, the original robots having been broken in half and welded together at their cores into a shambling mess of cold, inorganic materials.

What happened next was a blur of light, sound, and movement. My biomech activated in full. I threw my arm out and a warp bullet ricocheted off, landing in the wall rather than Vivila's head. Her hair lifted her up to the ceiling and out of my way. The wall scattered from the impact before reforming.

Robots being what they are, I felt no mercy as I rained plasma over the machine. In a leap, I got closer using the firepower as cover. I kicked its malfunctioning body into the workshop where the other robots had already taken notice of the fight. They were bound to notice after the shrill beeping of the fused drive started during the first rounds of plasma.

No escape, the only way forward was to kill Remy Jay so we could teleport out. I grabbed a C472 machine part, swinging the lever into the closest of its shambling brethren. The robot tried to impale me with a whirling drill attached to a long limb. To the side, I dodged blatant melee attacks and let the ranged bullets and beams bounce off my suit.

My body kept in motion. I did not pause for even half-a-second. I couldn't stop or slow down. I had to win. I had to destroy each and every robot that aimed to kill me and protect the woman I... momentary thoughts of Vivila flickered between a couple of strong blows as metal limbs landed against me. I heard the internal beeping of my biomech suit as the charge started to drain.

A K649 had gotten ahold of my leg. Its hook clasped around my thigh. Every moment it stayed connected was another moment it leeched my power supply. The whirl of metal parts and sprays of fire distracted from the connecting wire that led between the hook and the actual body of the machine. I fired at the wire, but it swished, dodging the plasma.

Another robot joined from behind, with alloy claws aimed for my arm. It caught hold and I desperately tried to knock it off, wrenching my arm in its steel grip. Though I had taken out five of them, more had arrived from somewhere else in the station.

I heard the mournful whirr of my biomech suit shutting down.

With my free hand, I smacked at the backup system on my belt. The lesser alloy took over, covering my skin from harm. The robots overcame me. There were too many and though I had fight left, my limbs were held down and the beta system lagged in its activation of any programmed defenses. All I could do was snarl at the infernal machines.

I heard screaming and knew they'd gotten a hold of Vivila as well. The K649 continued to leech energy from my power supplies and as I tried to break free, something very hard and very large hit me across the head. My vision went dark.

When it came back a minute later, I was immersed in a viscous amber liquid. The glop filled my lungs. My belt had been taken from me, neither suit was active anymore. I swam to the curved wall of the container. Next to me, I saw Remy Jay, who looked grieved.

In the center of the workshop, Vivila refused to be put into a vat. She had broken free from whatever robot had dragged her in and now swung from the ceiling, her hair wildly sticking to it as she dodged attempts to grab her again. I wanted to tell her to not struggle. That the robots didn't slaughter her mystified me. If she gave them too much trouble, would that unexpected mercy change? Maybe it was her humanoid appearance that kept the machines interested.

I didn't know and didn't care why. All I wanted was for her to be safe.

I pounded my fists against the container, but it proved much stronger than the force of my muscles. Vivila landed on top of the vat I was in. I couldn't see her anymore, only hearing her on the container's lid.

The metal cord of the K649 shot past. I heard a fateful clink and Vivila cry out, then watched as the machine dragged Vivila off the vat and to the floor. Her hair tried to stick, and she tried to grab at things, but the tentacle proved too fast. She reached toward me as the robots threw her in a neighboring vat.

With only my internal systems functioning, I moved around the amber liquid and surveyed the narrow, tall container. Though thicker than the ocean waters of New Earth, swimming was simple. I reached the top and pushed on the lid, but nothing happened.

Driven by instinct, I swam to the bottom of the vat and searched it. Vision clouded by the amber-tinted liquid, it messed with my reserve optical tech. I glided my fingers along the bottom and found a sealed sector where the base had been attached. These vats weren't meant to contain prisoners, but to hold cooling fluids in case the smelters overheated or a fire broke out in the workshop.

Nearby, I saw Vivila struggle in the liquid. It impacted her alien physiology differently than mine and her hair had started to thin and shorten. She pressed on the wall, then looked at me. Though her expression remained mostly unchanged, the attunement between us sent a jolt of fear.

The machines had gone back to their engineering and some had even left as if the matter was done with. In all, a count of seven functioning machines moved about. They were older models though. I had made sure that I had taken out the newer, upgraded versions first during the fight.

I waited only a few seconds because I could see that Vivila had started to cocoon herself. I dug my fingertips at the seal and forced my fingers under the sticky adhesive, ignoring the pain that came from such action without the protective layer of my biomech. The seal gave way and I tore it from the indented ring. Liquid seeped out. A small puddle formed on the floor.

The seal came undone and I pulled the rest out, then tossed the ring aside. The vat slowly drained. I hooked my hands underneath the bottom edge of the vat's wall. The plexiglass pressed into my skin, but I summoned my strength and lifted the barrier. The amber goo rushed out as I forced the container upward.

My escape caught the attention of the robots. The puddle spread underneath the metal feet of one. It slipped while trying to move away, crashing on the ground. Its core drive pulsed crimson in a wailing sound to alert the others.

My body dripped with the viscous liquid and my vision swam in amber. I didn't stop. My muscles trembled, I lifted the container above my head and then brought it down onto a couple robots. The pillar of plexiglass didn't give way, made to withstand the force of nebulaic gases, and crushed the robots. The amber liquid spread around my boots. Balmy air clung to my sticky skin.

With a shout, I kicked the pillar and it rolled into a row of approaching robots. They tumbled back in a pile of tangled metal limbs. Hands on my knees, I gathered my breath as my lungs readjusted.

The target pounded against the vat, yelling so large bubbles rose from his mouth but his words were inaudible. I used my returning energy to reach Vivila. I tried to climb up, but the container proved too tall to manage without my suit. I dodged a couple of warp bullets that landed in the wall behind me.

I jumped onto a workshop table and kicked aside a non-functioning robot. On a shelf, I saw my belt in the process of being torn apart. I grabbed a scrap limb and used it to absorb well-aimed shots while I leapt between the cluttered tables toward the shelf. Junk tumbled from the tables to the floor in a mess of noise that blended with the buzzing and whooshing of firepower trying to take me out.

A clink sounded, echoing amidst the chaos. My heart raced, and I glanced at the clamp hooked around my ankle. My foot slipped out from underneath me. I barely caught myself from slamming my face into the table.

The K649 dragged me across the tabletop. Loose scrap metal slid around me. I tossed a handful of screws, then lifted a plate to shield myself. Twisted around, I faced the machine. Grabbing onto the connecting cord, I pulled myself toward it.

As I approached the K649, an attached drill bit whirled at the top of its misshapen body. I shouted and rammed the plate against the robot.

The robot fell back. It wrenched the metal plate from me and threw it aside. Though I started on top, it pushed me over and pinned me against the workshop floor with its hooked limbs.

Sticky with the amber liquid and oily refuse left behind from the machines, I couldn't slither out from under the K649. It pushed the drill bit closer to my head. The twisted metal spun in a blur of silver and gray. The sharp tip pointed at the branded mark on my forehead, close enough that I could feel a faint breeze created by the movement.

I braced with my feet and hands and pushed against the machine with all my might. If I weakened for even a second, the robot would bore into my brain where I had no protective augmentation to halt it.

The clamp remained on my ankle and the connecting cord had locked in place to keep me near. I bent at the knee, using my shin to withstand the pressure, and then jerked my ankle back. Just enough to force the K649 up. I shoved, desperate for any chance. The K649 tilted so the drill pointed toward the ceiling in a complete flip.

Shoulder pressed against its body, I held it in position. I tore away the patchworked metal. Rivets detached, never meant to hold the mechanic abomination together. An exposed space opened as I forced my way in. My fingertips grazed the core drive. It scorched my skin, but I grasped it and tore it out.

Extraction successful, I tossed the drive toward the vats. It fell to the side, lifeless. I panted, releasing my ankle from the hooked clamp. Crawling, I continued toward the shelf where I'd seen my belt. The remaining robots scattered in attempts to collect the core drive that bounced behind the vats.

How long they'd be distracted by it, I didn't know. I forced myself to my feet and sprinted to the shelf. I grabbed my belt, shoved some loosened parts back in their spots, and returned it to my waist. The power supply still had to charge, but at least I had it back. Now, to free Vivila and then the target could die.

I ran at the robots. They glitched, confused by the aggressive approach. Their A.I. systems had been programmed to prioritize collection of the working core drive. I grabbed the smallest machine, dragging it toward the vat where Remy Jay was.

In a crash, I pressed the robot to the base of the vat, then used it as a step to leap onto the top. One of the other robots got a hold of the core drive. Now their priority queues focused on me. Without the K649 to hook me though, they had to use their lesser capabilities.

Predictably, warp bullets came at me. I leapt down behind the vat. The bullets hit the plexiglass. The particles scattered. Amber liquid dripped out. While the vat's wall was in dissolution, in those fractional seconds of time, I grabbed the seal along the bottom edge. Without it, the structure couldn't remain airtight. The liquid rushed out from the circular base.

Remy Jay landed on his feet, coughing from the sudden exposure to actual air. I lifted the bottom of the vat. Remy crouched down, and I threw it at the robots.

While the machines scrambled to avoid the wreckage, I ran the short distance to where Vivila had been captured. I couldn't see her anymore. She had cocooned in a lime-green film, hidden from easy sight except for the shadowed outline of her figure. I knelt down but couldn't get to the seal on this vat from the outside.

The robots hadn't learned from their previous attempt. They sent warp bullets after me again. If there was one thing robots like these were good at... it was their limited learning capacity. Just with Remy's vat, the warp bullets sent particles in a temporary flurry of destabilized matter. The main structure wobbled in affected reality. I grabbed the bottom edge's seal in the same way. Without Vivila crouching, however, it proved difficult to get the vat up and over. Instead, it fell to its side and the edge grazed over the cocoon. The green husk fell along with it, Vivila both protected and trapped inside.

A warp bullet grazed past my shoulder. For a moment, it impacted the fabric of my jacket, scattered in a mess of particles, and then reconfigured. I glanced at the hole where the black material had been. My actual skin remained untouched though. I grabbed onto Vivila's cocoon, pulled it out from the column, and brushed a hand to wipe away the amber gunk.

"Vivila, it's safe no-" I dropped the cocoon to dodge a searing beam of plasma. There weren't many robotic machines left but they were doing their best to make things as difficult as possible.

I heard the internal trill of my systems coming back online, the biomech suit having reached a workable charge.

Another beam shot at me, but I let it hit my shoulder. The biomech absorbed it, using the excess energy to finish the transition to cover my body with its alloy scales. Aided by the speed boosters of the suit, I turned around and leapt at the nearest robot. I tore its core drive out, crushing it to dust under my mechanized grip.

To the next machine, I tore its limbs from its gyrating body and used them to slap it apart. I stomped on the core drive, then fired plasma at the other machines until nothing but heavy, dirty smoke billowed from the robotic remains.

My hands curled into fists and I yelled at the ruins in an animalistic shout. I dared them to get back up, for another machine to pick itself out of the wreck and challenge me. None did. Breathless, I stared at the destroyed workshop for a minute.

Finally, I let the suit recede and return to charging. I stumbled, my worn muscles making themselves known, and fell to my knees beside Vivila's cocoon.

The shadowy figure moved inside the

green husk. Her long legs twisted, crossing over each other. The palm of a seven-fingered hand pressed against the interior. The husk peeled away in fractal layers. Vivila revealed herself. The cocoon gathered along her scalp and integrated with a lush head of vine-like hair. She lifted herself up with the green strands pressing against the floor. The woman settled on her slender feet. Her dress had disappeared, leaving her bare and exposed in her alien humanoid figure. At first green, her skin faded to mimic my own coloration, revitalizing her attunement to me.

My lips twitched, a corner raising involuntarily. She didn't smile back, but her violet eyes flashed bright and her neutral expression relaxed me due to simple familiarity. I took her by the waist and kissed her, swift and short. She blinked, then said, "The breath is moving."

The target, Remy Jay, headed toward the workshop's exit.

I let go of her. The human didn't worry me. Drenched in the amber gunk and only dressed in his boxer shorts, he left footprints soiled with black ash. Remy couldn't move fast, though he seemed to be trying. I followed with Vivila nearby.

While I kept on the heels of the man as he slipped about in his escape down the corridor, I retrieved a thickly rolled paper, from a pouch on my belt, and licked the end of the bundled leafy herbs. I used a sparking wire for a light, then smoked. It filled my mouth with rustic sweetness, reminding me of the garden Vivila kept at our humble station suite. How I wanted to be back already and have her nurse my wounds, soothe my aching muscles, and heal my bruises.

All that stood between me and such a future was Remy's death. The man darted into an elevator shaft. I picked up the pace, flicking my cigarette aside. Vivila kept up. The door nearly slid shut, but I shoved it open long enough that we slipped inside the elevator. I hadn't thought such a thing would be working on an abandoned station like this, but a biometric scan had given Remy access. It started to ascend, beeping with every level it passed.

He cowered and said, "Wh-why are you chasing me? Who are you people? What have you done with the colony?"

"Nothing," I answered. I macro-gestured. The glove of my suit spread over my forearm and hand.

"Wait," said Remy. He held up his hands. "Why are you doing this? You must be confused!"

One bolt of plasma and my task was complete. Remy slumped against the elevator wall, a hole in his head. Not a hint of deactivation for any kind of tech; the man had been unmodified.

I said, "Pure human, huh... strange."

Vivila shrugged.

The elevator arrived with a ding. The door slid open. I grabbed the scruff of Remy's collar and dragged his body into the corridor, which looked a great deal different than the crew level or the docking port. The floor was polished to look like ivory stone. Windows lined the entire hall, giving a vast and beautiful view of the nebula outside. I dropped Remy on the floor, admiring the sparkling mists and vibrant colors. Every possible hue mixed in flaring interactions between chemicals.

"Whatever happened on this colony station," said Vivila in her flat tone. "It is a shame."

"Mm," I hummed my agreement.

"Shall we leave now?" she asked.

"In a few seconds," I said. Though I wanted to leave, I felt no rush anymore. It felt peaceful in the luxurious level. Besides, I saw something in the nebula that gave me pause. I wasn't sure if the silhouettes were simply due to the stress, but as I watched, I became certain of what I saw. I motioned for Vivila to look at the objects moving closer. "What does that look like to you?"

She hesitated, then said, "A small fleet?"

"Yeah," I muttered. I squinted. My upper lip curled in distaste. I recognized the symbol lined along the dark metal hulls. They displayed the crossbones symbol of Ms. Netai's enterprise, my client who'd sent me to the station. I grabbed Remy's hand and using the device on my palm, I scraped his skin against the outer ring. It spun, separating the genetic sample and then glowed cerulean.

I held Vivila by her wrist. Light flashed from the device, consuming us in brilliant blue.

In an instant, we were no longer on the Mamonar Colony Station, nor anywhere near the star 879E Siwu, nor within range of the nebula. Instead, far away from all of that, Vivila and I stood in the large office of Ms. Netai.

Temperate warmth and artificial peach aroma filled the sophisticate's room. A quiet melody played from the internal speakers, lilting synthetic notes of drawn out pacing that echoed against resonant walls. Silverwood furniture reflected in the polished granite floors and crystalline ceiling. Beyond the patterned glass, an expanse of stars twinkled.

Ms. Netai stood in front of her holographic desktop, watching a few floating videos of livestream data. Hands at her hips, the human woman glanced at us and said, "Oh, so you've returned then."

She waved her satin-gloved hand, sliding away a couple of the videos from view. The slate-colored coat she wore was cinched at the waist and the collar spread out like a fan behind her tightly wound maroon hair. Ms. Netai's optical implants whirled in a spiral of golden light.

I stepped in front of Vivila. My cheeks sucked in as I took a tense breath and I tapped my tongue against the point of my canine tooth. She knew what I was thinking; I could tell by the winding smile she gave me.

"Now, Swift, you've worked under me for a long time," she began.

"No, I'm not your employee," I interrupted. "I am contracted."

She rolled her golden eyes, dismissing my comment with a wave of her hand. "Whatever. The fact of the matter is times change and you're not as needed as you used to be."

"So don't hire me then," I snapped.

Ms. Netai smirked, casually crossing her arms. She leaned back slightly. "Honestly, I didn't expect you would actually find your way out of the station but that's my fault for not having the coders program the A.I. to disintegrate the bait after you arrived. Oops."

I approached her until we were within arm's reach. "Tell me why."

She grabbed my hand and lifted it. Ms. Netai gracefully caressed around the device embedded in my palm. She shimmied her shoulders and fluttered her pink-tinted eyelashes at me. "This little thing teases me so."

It made sense suddenly. She wanted the tech. I yanked my hand away. "I said no when you offered payment and now you do this? Even if you got it, it won't operate for you. It was made for me and it will only ever work for me."

Ms. Netai's smile disappeared. Her surgically contoured face twisted in an ugly pout. She whispered, her breath hissing between her teeth, "I want it."

I leaned in and whispered against her ear, "You can't have it."

As she seethed, I walked away from her.

Vivila looked at me as I passed by. I paused, then turned to look at the corporate overlord again. I said, "We're leaving. Don't contact me again."

The office door automatically slid open as I approached. Regret ensnared my thoughts. I should have seen it coming. Ms. Netai had been on me for a while to purchase the device and I'd turned her down each time. No amount of money would persuade me. My grandfather had made this device and he told me that it would only work for someone within our family, someone with our genetic heritage. It wasn't meant for anyone else. He might've intended it for military use instead of freelance murder-for-hire, but he wasn't around anymore to be disappointed in me.

Still, I wasn't about to hand it over to someone like Ms. Netai. She wanted to reverse engineer it into something she could sell or use, but I wouldn't allow it. It was a line I couldn't bring myself to cross... and she didn't understand it. After all, to anyone but myself or maybe Vivila, I seemed like the kind of guy who would cross every line in order to get paid. It wasn't true though. I had my own code, even if most people didn't know it.

"Swift..." the quiet voice of Vivila sounded from behind me. Though I couldn't see why, and it was just one word said - nothing more than my name - I felt a surge of protective rage. In the wall's reflection, I caught sight of Ms. Netai holding Vivila's hair. She had a syringe tensed against the alien's neck.

"Let her go," I warned, not turning around.

"You think I'd let you walk away, free and clear?" Ms. Netai snarled, "You should know me better than that. Now, hold out your hand for extraction or else I'll kill your alien pet."

I glanced to the side where the woman's robotic butler stepped forward with a laser scalpel. Turning around, I held out my hand and glared at the woman. The robot grasped it, turning it over to look at the palm. My biomech suit activated, coating the arm with alloy scales. I fired, the plasma bolt shooting the robot's lower half out from under it. The suit covered me in full and I kicked the upper half of the butler to crash against the wall.

I bounded forward and aimed at Ms. Netai's head. Her optics went wild, the gold spinning in desperate attempt to react fast enough; but they lagged far behind the three bolts that already went through her head as soon as I had aimed.

Non-killers, who have others do their dirty work for them, always consider themselves immune from death. They aren't though, not even in our technological age. Ms. Netai fell back against the floor and Vivila wrenched free.

"You stole her breath," said Vivila in observation.

I made a quiet hum of agreement, my lips pressed tightly together. I wasn't sure if Ms. Netai had more defenses in place. It didn't look like it though. The woman had truly been arrogant far past her actual worth.

"We should leave now," she added.

"The pod should still be docked," I said. I led the way out after disengaging the biomech suit. No one stopped us, though I saw Ms. Netai's assistant watching from a balcony as we hurried through the port lobby. We reached our pod, settled at a docking post.

Once inside, Vivila took over and flew us out of the corporate station. She looked at me. A slight smile twitched at the corners of her lips before disappearing. I leaned against the co-pilot seat, closed my eyes, and sighed, "We can't go home."

"What?" Her voice raised in pitch. "Why not?"

"It won't be safe," I said.

Though we had been allowed to leave, I couldn't be certain what situation we were now in. I had acted instinctively, like a tiger pouncing on a serpent. Whether it'd been expected or not, I didn't know. I couldn't risk it though. I couldn't risk Vivila, though I knew I was the weaker for it.

I glanced at the alien woman. She'd already taken to looking over the starmap to find a different place to go and smiled slightly. Whatever happened, wherever we went, even if it meant I had to find something else to do than kill people for a living, well... it all seemed worth it.

Dominika Lein is the author of "Reptilian Wanderer" and the "I, the One" universe. More info can be found at dominikalein.com.

...but when the new StoryHack was released, all of the submarines jumped for joy.

MAKANI
AND THE VULTURE GOD
Paul R. McNamee

when treachery disrupts an ancient contest, Makani the ka-man must fight human and supernatural foes to retrieve the stolen spirit of his friend

Makani and the Vulture God

By Paul R. McNamee

Lono's narrow sled shot down the hillside. Riding prone, his muscles bulged across his wide shoulders as he gripped the handrails. The sun beat hot on his bronzed body and the wind cooled his sweat. He resisted the urge to adjust his position. His holua—its runners greased with coconut oil—accelerated down the mound, skimming over the man-made track of smooth ili'ili river rocks.

Behind him, beyond the tall hill, Whatura's late afternoon shadow crept over the scene of the he'e holua competition. The craggy mountain reached to the sky and dominated its surroundings.

The scenery blurred past. At the bottom of the hill, the expectant crowd cheered and hollered.

Lono was going too fast for mistakes. A dragging leg, a trembling arm, anything to roll him off the sled would be a disaster. He was certain the run was his personal best. He could not remember feeling such speed. Time stretched. He felt he might lift off into the air like a bird.

Time snapped back to normal as Lono's holua decelerated along the flat run at the bottom of the hill. Some of the women sang impromptu songs of victory and glory while men pressed him with slaps, hugs, and smiles. More than one claimed Lono's run had been the fastest they had ever witnessed.

Makani nudged through the throng and strode to his friend. The ka-man was a few years older than the athlete. Unlike Lono's flowing thick, dark locks, Makani kept his hair short to his scalp. The ka-man was shorter and of a stockier build than Lono.

Makani grinned.

"Hunapo will be hard pressed to top that run!"

Lono turned his gaze up the hill. Against the sun, the next competitor stood in silhouette, holding his holua at his side. The sled cast a shadow of rungs diagonally across the top of the run.

The competition had lasted all afternoon and the final runs were at hand. Most competitors had forfeited their last runs, aware that the holua skills of Hunapo and Lono surpassed all others. It was not in the nature of the sport to keep score. The end result would not be a numeric superiority of speed or style. The crowd would know who the best had been, and to the victor would go the bragging rights.

Hunapo laid his holua down and stood upon it.

The crowd let out surprised gasps.

Hunapo planned to ride down the rocky track standing. Surfing on alaia boards to ride ocean waves was one thing. Crashing into the soft wet arms of the sea was a far cry from spilling onto the hard ground. Most of the people had ridden holuas while standing—but those displays were for fun on grass-covered knolls and small practice mounds.

The run from the hilltop to the bottom was long.

The crowd chattered.

Lono grunted. Makani said nothing.

Hunapo was challenging Lono. If the fool

could stay upright, Lono would feel obliged to be the bigger fool and attempt the same.

"He'll break a leg or worse," someone commented.

Makani agreed in silence. Hunapo's foolhardy act would end badly. Lono had nothing to worry about. If Hunapo was lucky, he would tumble early before he picked up too much speed.

Hunapo was as tall as Lono, and though thinner, he was wiry. He shoved his holua off with his foot and nimbly hopped onto the sled. The short crossbeams were uncomfortable and awkward for footing. But Hunapo showed no signs of trouble as he planted his feet. He bent his knees slightly as the holua accelerated.

Hunapo stood like a statue as he rode his holua down the hill. The racer should have been moving his arms, even slightly, to maintain balance.

Makani was about to comment on Hunapo's foolhardiness when he heard a whisper on the wind. A sense of weak lightning played along his spine.

Magic!

Makani glanced around. All faces were concentrating on Hunapo's foolhardy run. No one worked magic aside from the ka-men. Makani was the only ka-man present. There were the priests, of course—but they would call on the intervention of a god. A trivial matter of a sporting competition would hardly be worth the efforts of divine petition.

Of course, there were gods who enjoyed good sport...

Makani observed the priests in the crowd. They were as caught up in the spectacle as the other onlookers.

Hunapo was three-fifths down the hillside, close enough for Makani to see—or imagine—a cocky grin on the racer's face.

Makani saw a blurring shadow over Hunapo's head. A large shape, stretching wide, left and right—as if a giant bird was perched on Hunapo's shoulders, its wings spread wide.

Makani's eyes darted up from the shadow. He saw a ghostly gray bird, its spindly legs and dull talons clutched Hunapo's shoulders. The avian ghost twitched and adjusted its wings, keeping Hunapo upright and balanced.

Then the vision was gone. Hunapo slid to victory and leapt off his sled. The holua raced away as the cheering crowd embraced him.

Makani ignored the celebration. He scanned the sky but could not find the ghostly bird.

"Well, Lono!" Hunapo shouted. Joy, mirth, and malice were in his gaze. "I think the he'e holua is over for today! Better luck next season!"

Hunapo's words were little consequence. The tone and sneering countenance spoke volumes.

The crowd failed to notice. They only heard a bit of bragging. Rightly so, as far as they were concerned. Hunapo's daring run down the hill standing on his holua would be a story to tell many times for many years.

Makani simmered. He knew Hunapo had cheated and had not earned the right to vaunt. In tribal politics, the young man was far more an enemy to Lono than a rival. Makani wanted to wipe the sneer off Hunapo's face.

If Makani had the political power, he would have sent Hunapo into exile before he caused some great strife. But Makani was not chief, Kaikane was. And Kaikane considered Hunapo a valuable member of his koa fighters—the chief's bodyguards and elite warriors. Makani knew the subject of exile could not be broached unless Hunapo broke a taboo or he could be proven unworthy. Cheating at the he'e holua was unworthy, certainly.

Lono placed a flat hand over his brow to block the setting sun. He gazed at the track of ili'ili scintillating in the fading daylight.

Lono picked up his holua and headed up the hill.

"I think there is time for one more run, Hunapo."

The crowd fell silent. As Lono climbed the hill, their mutters flared from sparks to a blaze of buzzing, excited conversation. Even if Lono could only remain on his sled for half the run down the hill, it would be a day to remember.

Lono's acceptance of the challenge seemed to please Hunapo as much as if Lono had capitulated. Hunapo was being cleverer than Makani thought possible. Hunapo had a plan within a plan. Makani felt a flash of contempt for the untrustworthy man, but he ignored it. He knew he should not underestimate Lono's enemy.

Makani ran up the hill after his friend. "Lono! Wait!"

Lono turned. He gave Makani a grim grin.

"You mustn't try this race standing. You'll break a leg or worse. Probably worse."

Lono shook his head.

"Maybe, but I can't let Hunapo go unchallenged. He ran fair and the winds favored him."

"It wasn't a fair run."

Makani's statement gave Lono pause. The carefree smile fell from his face.

"What are you saying, Makani?"

"I tell you, he used magic to stay upright!" Makani's eyes pleaded with his friend. "I don't mean he is that good. I mean he used real magic."

"Then speak up. Make him forfeit his race."

"I can't prove it. I can see what others can't. My word against his." Makani cursed. "Damn black magic, too. Where'd he come up with that, eh?"

"What makes you say it's black magic?"

"Because if it was my magic, I wouldn't hide it."

Lono stared at the crowd thronging around their new champion.

"Listen, Lono." Makani put an arm on his friend's shoulder. "You let this one go. You be master of the he'e holua next time. No shame in that."

They were half-way up the hillside. Lono studied the stone track, gauged the distance from the top to where they stood. He turned and glanced back down the length they had already climbed.

"I can do this." Lono was as stubborn and proud as any warrior. He was compelled to meet the challenge from Hunapo. "I can ride my holua without magic—and I can do it better."

Lono turned from his friend and continued to the top of the hill.

Makani went to descend the hill but thought better of it. He wanted to keep an eye on Hunapo. The crowd had Hunapo surrounded. From his vantage point halfway up the large hill, the ka-man could watch both Lono and Hunapo, even though he would be twisting his neck like an owl.

On the hilltop, Lono waved his arm in a wide arc. Behind him loomed Whatura, lowering in darkness as day faded. The mountain was jagged, bald, and barren above its girdle of rainforest. Under the bright sun, the peak had appeared ordinary. In the fading light of dusk, its visage seemed evil. Makani sensed the mountain issuing its own challenge;

Come here, little men who play on a little hill.
Prove your skill on my rocky slopes!

Makani felt gooseflesh prickle across his skin.

Lono shoved off, quickly secured his footing and stance on the holua. Unlike Hunapo's casual ride, Lono's arms and torso constantly shifted to maintain his balance. His holua skills were remarkable. After a full day's use, despite spot checks, the track of smooth ili'ili stones had hazardous patches where the rocks had spread too wide, or shifts had created dips. Makani knew Lono navigated over spots where Hunapo would have been thrown if not for his magical benefactor.

Lono passed Makani. The ka-man put up his hand in a sign of encouragement. Lono, despite his concentration, worked in a quick return of the gesture.

Makani's senses of the preternatural and supernatural swarmed over his body like a hive of bees.

The dreaded shadow returned and wheeled over the hill. Then it folded its wings and dove. The swooping gray blur aimed for Lono's back.

Makani berated himself for being a fool! The spirit had helped Hunapo. Why wouldn't it continue to help Hunapo by disrupting Lono's run?

He ran down the hill.

The ka-man cursed himself for being so ill-prepared. He had not expected to combat magic on a day of sport and celebration. He could not stop to work his own magic. As he ran, stones clicked in the pouch at his waist.

Sling stones!

He always kept a few blessed stones on hand. Sometimes they would work against the supernatural, sometimes not. Better to be prepared.

Makani had no time to stop and bring his sling up to speed. He pulled a stone from his pouch and hurled it down the hill.

The ghost bird slammed into Lono. Lono flipped off the hurtling sled and hit the track hard. His limp body plowed through the bed of stones. The crowd below erupted in cries and gasps of horror.

In the same moment, Makani's stone

passed through the vague haze of gray. The thing screeched and momentarily appeared in the sky over the crowd. People screamed with fright at the brief spectre of a ghostly giant vulture swooping over their heads.

Makani ran to Lono's side, rocks flew as he skidded to a halt on his knees.

The ka-man touched cold flesh and cursed. He searched the sky, saw the gray form heading toward Whatura. Makani could imagine the ghost bird carried something its talons, vaguely man-shaped.

"Lono is dead!" a young woman screamed. She erupted in shocked grief. Makani remembered her having eyes for Lono. She wasn't the only one.

"He is not dead," Makani raised his voice over the wailing.

"He is not breathing," another man said.

"His flesh is cold," Makani said, "Too cold for a man who just died."

The crowd quieted.

"What do you mean?" the sobbing woman asked.

"Evil magic has been worked here."

The crowd parted before their chief. Kaikane cast a cold eye over the prostrate form of Lono. The broad shouldered, potbellied chief was a giant of a man. Some of his hair had turned grey but fire had never lost its spark in his blue eyes.

"Of what evil magic do you speak?" Kaikane asked.

"Lono's ka and mana have been stolen away!" The ka-man's fingers pressed flesh and he bent joints of Lono's lifeless body. "Somehow his body doesn't seem any worse for the crash. But it is an empty shell."

"The phantom vulture did this?"

"Yes. But the bird did not act alone." Makani scanned the throng of pressing bodies. Nearly dark, it was hard to discern individuals. "Where is Hunapo?"

Gossiping whispers passed from mouth to mouth.

Hunapo stepped forward. He met Makani's accusatory glare and thrust his chin defiantly.

"What do you want of me?"

"The ghost bird—what do you know of it?"

"Nothing."

"You lie," Makani said. "The spirit helped you stay upright on your run. I saw it."

"Nonsense." Hunapo glanced around the crowd for support. "Did anyone else see this feathered ghost?"

"We all saw the spirit bird," said a young boy.

"We all saw it over Lono as he crashed. No one saw it before then." Hunapo folded his arms over his chest. "I would say it was a bad omen for Lono."

"Do not deign to instruct me in the ways of omens, Hunapo." The ka-man's voice cut like the serrated edge of a shark's tooth.

"I won't stay here and listen to such foolishness." Hunapo turned to Kaikane and bowed his head slightly. "If they can't accept Lono's death, I can. I will mourn him in my own dwelling, away from their unkind allegations."

Hunapo took his leave of the he'e holua hill. The crowd parted to make way for him.

Kaikane watched him go, then turned to the ka-man.

"Do you have proof of your accusations?"

"I know where to find it," Makani said.

"Then go find it. If you do not find it, do not speak of it again."

Makani selected three loa warriors he knew were loyal to Lono.

"Take Lono's body. He is not dead." He eyed Hunapo's back as the warrior stalked away. "Do not place him in his own home. Pick one of yours and guard him."

The warriors hesitated. Only after Kaikane had nodded an approval did they follow Makani's orders.

"What will you do?" asked one of the loa.

Makani looked out into the darkness beyond the torches where he knew the mountain Whatura loomed.

"I will go find the proof of Hunapo's treachery."

Makani pushed through the rainforest along game trails. The ka-man did not feel alone. Gazes were upon him from eyes hidden in the thick foliage. He half-expected a carnivore to launch upon his back. He sensed the surveillance but couldn't afford the time to investigate. Something was stalking him. If it attacked, he would deal with the danger then.

He neared the end of the tree line, and saw the rugged mountain reaching up into the sky ahead. Black specks of buzzards circled the peak. He saw something large move slightly, somewhere near the top.

Distracted, Makani heard a rustle in the undergrowth. A figure burst from the foliage to his right. Makani dodged a spear thrust, covered the distance to his attacker, and struck hard with his fists. The man staggered backward, and Makani saw his opponent was Hunapo.

The warrior still held his spear and poked at the ka-man. Makani parried with his patu, each blow of his tear-shaped club clacking against the wooden spear of Hunapo. They circled each other, each waiting for their foe to make a mistake of footing or posture.

"Do you want to die today, Hunapo?" Makani asked. "Back down. If you're lucky, Kaikane will only send you into exile, rather than to your death."

Hunapo snorted like a boar and said nothing. He had not come to talk. That suited Makani.

The warrior favored the thrusts of his spear. Makani realized the feint too late. After a repeated set of jabs, Hunapo swung up the end of his spear, using its butt in the fashion of a taiaha. The blow glanced along the side of the ka-man's jaw, forcing Makani to spin away in defense of his face and head.

Exposed, his back turned to his foe, Makani braced for the sharp thrust of the spear tip into his body.

A great gust of wind blew through the trees, shaking the green fronds all around. The ka-man heard the crushing of foliage, the snapping of branches, a screech and a scream.

He whirled to see giant brown wings taking to the sky—no ghost this time. A bird with an impossibly wide wingspan launched upward through a gap in the forest canopy. The creature was the size of a moa bird—but moa birds could not fly. Hunapo struggled in its talons.

The enormous bird turned and flew up toward the mountain's peak. Makani saw its bare pink head.

A giant vulture.

Above the thick rainforest, the bald mountain was harsh and unforgiving. Makani tumbled over shifting scree. His leathery soles and palms were scraped and bleeding. Vultures wheeled overhead. They nested among the crags and boulders. He wondered if they feasted on hapless climbers, fools who should have known better than to attempt climbing a mountain as unforgiving as Whatura.

The air was dry and cold. In his rush, Makani had not thought to bring a cloak. He shivered as sweat chilled on his skin.

Above to the left, hidden from the view below, there was a large cave. A flat curved ledge protruded from its threshold.

The giant vulture perched on the ledge. It regarded Makani with cold obsidian eyes.

The raptor spoke.

"What do you seek on my mountain?"

"What does Whatura seek among men?" Makani responded. He knew the bird was no rarity of nature. He stood before Whatura, the vulture god who shared his name with the mountain. "Why does Whatura send his spirit to steal the ka of a warrior?"

The vulture shifted, its folded wings shrugged.

"That was a bargain, made with this one."

Hunapo stepped from the cave.

Whatura lifted a taloned claw from the ground. In its grip was the end of Hunapo's spear. The other end remained pinned to the ground under his other claw.

"He would have put this spear through your back but that is not what I seek." Whatura pulled until the spear broke with a snap.

Chagrined, Hunapo glared at both the vulture god and the ka-man.

"I..," Hunapo started to speak.

"Silence!" demanded Whatura.

"What do you seek?" Makani asked.

Whatura stepped into the cave and darkness swallowed the feathered deity.

Makani and Hunapo glared at each other. Each wanted to attack the other but they were unsure what reaction to expect from Whatura.

The vulture god emerged from the cave in the form of a man. Unsurprisingly, his human visage was not handsome. Sagging skin wrapped his head, and sallow eyes glared out over a hooked nose.

In each hand, he held a holua.

"A contest."

"What does the winner gain?" Makani asked.

"If Hunapo wins, Lono's ka stays with me," Whatura said. "If you win, I release Lono's ka to you."

"Great Whatura," Makani said. "I have some skill at he'e holua but I am no match for the likes of Hunapo or Lono. I admit this with no shame."

"Then you forfeit?" Hunapo asked.

"What contest is there in a forfeit?" Makani said.

"I agree," said the vulture god.

"If it is a contest you seek, it should be Lono, not I, who challenges Hunapo."

"Lono's body lies leagues down the mountain," Whatura said.

"Return his ka to me," Makani suggested. "I will restore him, and we will return for the contest."

Whatura, despite his human form, clucked like an annoyed bird.

"I know you ka-men of old," Whatura said. "There is trickery in your souls. Even if you swear to bring Lono back to this peak, I feel you would set a trap. No. The contest shall be today."

"Then let it be a fair and worthy contest, Whatura," said the ka-man.

"What do you suggest?" asked Whatura.

The vulture god's smile told Makani he already knew the answer.

Lono felt as awkward as a newborn child. He walked cautiously back and forth on the ledge, testing Makani's legs.

"Your body is not mine! Shorter reach, shorter stride. And my voice isn't mine! Such strange sensations." He flexed and reached out with his arms. "I don't know your strengths and weaknesses."

Makani's answer was in his mind.

Then learn fast. For a vulture, Whatura seems impatient.

The vulture god glowered as Lono tested his new body.

Hunapo grinned as though he had already won the contest. He probably had. For all of Lono's he'e holua skill, channeling that skill through another person's body while racing down an inhospitable and ungroomed mountainside countermanded any advantage he had over Hunapo.

There would be nothing smooth about the run. It surely meant death, perhaps for both contestants.

"The sun is high," Whatura said. "Let this contest be decided before it falls into the night."

Lono looked up, saw vultures circling overhead. Their shadows raced along the mountainside.

"Not the best omen," Lono said.

Inside his mind, Makani grunted a gruff agreement.

Lono took his place beside Hunapo at the top of the mountainside. He gripped the rungs of the holua. He had built and raced his own holua. The holua in his hands was merely functional—a tool created by someone else, not a part of his spirit.

Whatura gave a wordless signal with his hand and a nod.

The race was on.

Both men went prone on their holuas. There would be no standing or boasting. They raced with death.

The initial stretch wasn't as rough as Lono expected. Much of the surface was the dust of crushed and crumbled black pahoehoe. Soon though they hit patches of aa aa—brown volcanic rock strewn in rough chunks. The holua shook. Lono fought for control through Makani's body. He had trouble adjusting to the ka-man's stocky build.

Lono squinted as bits of scree and dust particles blasted his face. Through Makani's eyes, Lono saw the cunning in Hunapo's eyes. Hunapo pulled a shark-toothed dagger from the pouch at his side. He would need to strike an exact blow, slice in such a way to throw Lono off balance but retain his own balance. The tearing wound, regardless of where it landed, would cause Lono to flinch and lose control. A crash at their current speed would mean death.

Hunapo sidled his holua alongside Lono. Lono saw a smooth patch ahead. That would be the moment Hunapo would strike. Hunapo rolled his body up slightly on his right side, his left knee folded to counterbalance as he raised the dagger in his left hand.

Lono raised his torso to meet the blow. Instead of a fleeting, tearing glancing blow to his biceps, Hunapo's dagger dug into the meat of Lono's shoulder. The teeth caught. Hunapo instinctively retained his grip on the wooden dagger handle, rather than letting go. Like a man hooking an unexpectedly large fish, Hunapo was dragged.

Lono winced as the dagger tore free. He hoped he hadn't caused irreparable damage to Makani's shoulder.

Hunapo's holua spun into a slide, runners turning sideways, no longer pointing straight down the mountain. He had only a moment to regain control.

Lono denied him the moment, nudging his own holua, shifting its rear like a fish's tail. The end of the struts brushed against Hunapo's wobbling sled.

Hunapo screamed in terror. The cry lasted only a moment. The holua crashed in a cloud of dust, pebbles, and shards of slicing, sharp volcanic rocks.

Lono shot down the remaining mountainside, undisturbed.

Existing without a body while he had been a prisoner of Whatura had been a strange sensation. Occupying Makani's stout body had been another oddity. Lono never expected returning to his own body would feel weird. He was still shaking his limbs like a man whose clothing did not fit.

"It will pass," Makani assured him.

"Sometimes I envy your magic," Lono said. "This is not one of those times."

They shared a bowl of okolehao, sipping and watching the sun rise over the waves. The restoration of Lono's spirit to his own body had taken the all night. The ka-man looked tired. After the clamor of the people at the ka-man's return from the mountain, Lono's resurrection, and the ignominious death of Hunapo, the two friends had retreated to the shoreline for peace and quiet.

"Whatura will need to find another champion."

"Hunapo was a fool. What does a vulture god care about competition and champions?" Makani shook his head. "Whatura didn't want a champion. He had no use for your ka, either."

"What did he want then?" Lono asked.

The ka-man took a long drink.

"Whatura wanted a sacrifice."

On the bloodstained slope of the jagged mountain of Whatura, a wake of vultures roosted and slept among the craggy rocks.

They had feasted well.

Paul R. McNamee's stories have appeared in 'zines and anthologies. He strives for more pulp each time he sets down a tale.

Night of a Thousand Eyes

Deborah L. Davitt

Arthur Polaris long ago uploaded to an android body. Now, he's investigating the disappearance of several other GalSec operatives on a corporation world. The dark secrets he learns might just cost him his life.

Night of a Thousand Eyes

By Deborah L. Davitt

Forty-two light-years from Earth, in a ship orbiting a terrestrial planet near a yellow dwarf star, his eyes opened. Awareness fired along photonic circuits. Seven seconds of confusion ensued as he examined the crystal cylinder in which he found himself.

Then a complete dossier of his identity and mission unfurled in his mind. *Designation: Arthur Polaris, mark VIII, templated from original human consciousness July 7, 2283. Last update: December 17, 2370. Occupation: Terran Alliance Investigator. Objective: Ascertain status of Vanth V colony. Statistically significant number of indentured workers at end of contract term failing to leave the planet or end their jobs with colonial sponsor, Severstal Heavy Industries. Prior investigations inconclusive.*

Arthur exited the cylinder, examining his body. Like every other form his consciousness had occupied since his physical death eighty-seven years ago, it appeared that of a human male in his late thirties, of indeterminate ethnicity. He'd designed that semblance himself. Even his name had been self-chosen, bland and unassuming. He'd left behind living friends and family for an afterlife of duty to the Terran Alliance. Not just him, but all his copy-selves, too.

Analysis complete, Arthur nodded. *No degradation in either my personality-memory matrix or my physical template. I can still fit in **anywhere**.* "Computer," he said aloud, "download mission files to this platform. Highlight previous investigations, operatives, and outcomes."

"At some point," the ship's AI replied sweetly, "we should agree on a name for me."

"Pick whatever you like," Arthur replied, shrugging. "You're the one who has to wear it." He paused, memory flaring. "But not *Beth*."

"Of course not," the AI responded, sounding offended. "Commencing file download."

Arthur dressed in a freshly-printed suit, reviewing the file contents. And then blinked, a remnant of his lost humanity. "Three agents dead or missing? They should have sent one of me sooner."

The space elevator descended through the eternal night of tidally-locked Vanth V's dark side, giving Arthur plenty of time to study the tangle of lights spreading across its surface like a mirror of the galaxy above. The megalopolis seemed the equal of any on Earth, but its towering arcologies housed only living humans. Few of the Uploaded ventured to this colony. *Ghosts aren't welcome, I suppose.* Silicon lips quirked, and the visage reflected in the elevator window stared back at him. A stranger's face. *Who I was doesn't matter anymore. Only the job matters now.*

His first stop, predicated by the case notes of the investigators before him, was the headquarters of the megacorp that dominated the colony. SHI concentrated on mining and the production of heavy equipment and spaceship components for colonization efforts. This information and more scrolled through his mind as he presented his credentials in the lobby and asked for a meeting with one of the executives.

"Ms. Vaduva," he said, on being escorted into her office, noting the heavy furniture and drapes. Replicas of Old Terra antiques. Nineteenth-century grandeur 3D-printed within the past ten years, by the wear. "You spoke with a TA investigator three months ago. Maria Nzeogwa."

"I remember. Lovely woman. I'm afraid I couldn't help her—" She gestured him towards a chair, which he ignored.

"You were one of the last people with whom she had contact before going missing."

"Am... I a suspect? Should I get someone from Legal in here?" She raised her eyebrows, and his optics recorded the minute fluctuations of her pupils. The increased speed of her pulse under the skin of her throat. *Fear, but within nominal range for someone being pressured by law enforcement.* A routine thermal scan made him blink. She radiated no more heat than her furniture. *And yet, with a pulse, she's human, not an Upload.*

The dichotomy threw him off-balance. For the bulk of his lives, there had been the living, and there had been the Uploaded. All the controversies lay in the past—did the Uploaded count as the same individuals? Did they inherit their previous assets, or were they the same person, entitled to keep them? How were their families to react? With grief? With joy? With hostility at an interloper?

Now, was there some form of humanity that stood somehow between the organic living and the Uploaded dead?

Arthur put those questions aside. "You're someone I hope might help me with my inquiries." He tilted his head. "If it helps, I'm an Upload." *Unlike previous investigators, if this platform is incapacitated, my most recently backed-up self will download to a new platform, and I'll just pick up where I left off.*

She recoiled. "You're dead?"

Interesting, response. She's young enough that Uploads should just be a fact of... hah... life. "I prefer the term differently-alive."

"Is that supposed to help?" Discomfort in her voice.

He shrugged. "I find that knowing sometimes comforts people. I lack the endocrine and adrenaline responses that I had when I was alive, Ms. Vaduva. I have little self-interest." His lips quirked faintly. "I'm here to do a job, and I rarely take anything personally." *Once, the protesters would've said that's because I'm not a person.*

She licked her lips. "I've never met an Upload before. You... seem so human."

A shrug. "I still have emotions. I just don't experience much urgency. There are no chemical processes pushing me this way or that. There are those who call the Uploaded afterlife a pallid experience. I'm not one of them. I find it... enlightening." No way to distill the last ninety years for her. *Two lifetimes of memories. A certain weary disgust with human stupidity and greed, but not the fervor of outrage. Disinterested love for humanity.* **Perspective**.

"My family's Russian Orthodox. We've... never embraced the Uploading process."

Arthur wished he could sigh. "Millions haven't. What a loss for the whole of civilization, generations wasted into oblivion." He paused, adding pointedly, "Uploads made the first waves of colonization possible. Though corporations like SHI haven't really embraced us. So many willing hands equal lower wages for the megacorps."

Her lips parted. But instead of mentioning unions or other socioeconomic ramifications, Vaduva murmured, "But what of the departed souls?"

Arthur blinked. "Assuming that such a thing exists, I think it's safe to say that God can take care of them." He paused. "If the original me exists somewhere, I guess he's off with his wife." *Damn it, Beth.*

Vaduva looked around her office. "I'm very comforted." A pause, and then back to business. "What do you think I can help you with?"

She can be pushed off-balance, but not for long. "What can you tell me about my predecessor's conversation with you?"

"Let me pull up my notes from the meeting," Vaduva replied. Her fingers skated over a virtual interface, and her eyes flicked over information he couldn't see. "Ms. Nzeogwa wanted details on employees who'd used our corporate clinics. Most do. Corporate care is far less expensive. And we at SHI pride ourselves on taking care of our own."

That tallied with where his predecessor's case notes had broken off. "Did Nzeogwa speak with you again outside the office?"

"No." Unsolicited, she added, "We have the lowest rate of reported crime of any planet in the Alliance. It was a shock when she disappeared."

Nuances caught him. "How's your *unreported* crime rate here on Vanth, Ms. Vaduva?"

Her eyes beseeched him as she stood. "Be careful during your inquiries, Mr. Polaris." Dismissing him. *Warning me, too?*

"Thank you, Ms. Vaduva." He shook her cold hand. "But as they say, you can't kill what's already dead."

Her eyes lowered. "No," she murmured. "But you can send the dead to hell."

The streets bustled in spite of the dark skies and pervasive chill; every building blazed with neon lights and holographic displays. Even residents' clothing, he noted, had glowing hems and edges. Bioluminescent fibers filled with living bacteria. His internal sensors pinged, picking up thousands of cameras and their wireless feeds to monitoring stations. *A night with a thousand eyes. Keeping their **reported** crime rate low. No one here should fear the night.*

And yet, in spite of the purported safety of the planet, people on the street turned up their collars against the white flakes of falling snow and walked quickly, not looking up.

Arthur's lips curled down. *Same everywhere I go. The living never look **up**.*

With a population of fifty-seven million, he'd have thirteen hundred corporate medical facilities to investigate. "*A good thing they're open all night,*" he transmitted silently as he walked.

"It's *always* night here," the AI replied silently.

"*True. Nzeogwa kept good records till her disappearance. I can start with her last couple of stops.*"

The first three hospitals didn't yield much. But the fourth? Nzeogwa had given him a note with a doctor's name. "Dr. Bao? No, she no longer works here," a nurse told him hurriedly. "She went into private practice about five months ago."

"I thought most workers preferred the corporate medical centers."

The nurse flapped a hand at him. "Some people want a second opinion. And Dr. Bao had, well, gotten herself in trouble with the administration here."

"Trouble?" A mild tone. Half of investigation was just putting people enough at ease that they'd talk. *Couldn't put Vaduva enough at ease, though.*

The nurse shrugged. "Don't know the details, just know she left after a big meeting with the board and legal."

"Happen to know the location of her new clinic?" A smile to keep the nurse talking, and she rewarded him with dimples and an address.

Dr. Bao Lan's secretary proved an obstacle, refusing to allow him to speak with the doctor if he didn't have an appointment… even when Arthur displayed his credentials. He smiled thinly and booked one, waiting in the lobby for an hour until admitted. When Dr. Bao bustled in and started to take his blood pressure, he stopped her. "You're not going to like your results, doc."

One startled glance, and she brushed graying hair away from her dark eyes as she whispered, "An Upload? You're much more, ah—"

"Lifelike?" Arthur deadpanned.

She winced, lowering her voice. "More *realistic* than the models I've seen before. You'll have most people here fooled. Let me go through the motions, eh?"

"Whatever makes you happy, doc," Arthur replied, lowering his voice to match hers as he extended his arm. "And while you're determining that my heart doesn't go pitter-pat, how about if you tell me why you left corporate life?" He paused. "Not a lot of people on Vanth do, I hear. Anything to do with unreported crimes? Or maybe people who have more in common with the dead than the living?" He threw the phrases out mostly to see how she'd react.

Her breath hitched. "I signed a nondisclosure agreement—"

He didn't raise his voice. "The last three investigators sent here are dead or missing. That NDA is pretty meaningless, in my opinion." *Should I put more pressure on?* "The last one to go missing was Maria Nzeogwa. Who vanished shortly after speaking with you and Rahela Vaduva. A body isn't necessary to declare someone dead, doctor. I'm treating this as a homicide investigation."

Her eyes flicked towards the walls apprehensively. "Here," Bao said sharply, picking up a pen and pad, "let me write you a prescription."

"You use paper here?" Arthur asked, genuinely surprised.

"Sometimes, the oldest methods remain the most secure," Bao said loudly, meeting his eyes. "Our pharmacies actually prefer this." She handed him a scrap of paper, on which she'd written, *Under observation. Meet at Chowdhury's, 18:00.*

He waited at the Indian restaurant, appreciating the odors through his olfactory receptors, but unable to partake of the naan or the curry, for nearly two hours. "Did you like Indian food when you were alive?" the AI pinged him from orbit.

"I didn't. Beth did, though." He kept the words silent. *"She spent a year in Calcutta."* Unconsciously, his hands rose to his eyes, covering them.

A pause. "What do you think of Delia?"

"What?"

"For my name, silly. I ask because you've selected your own, Mr. *Polaris.* You should be an expert on choosing names." Poke, poke, prod.

"Try it out for a couple of years and see if it squeaks," he replied silently, staring out into the street. "It's been too long. Something's happened to Bao."

A call to the clinic told him little; a call to local CorpSec netted him nothing more. Arthur stared into space and engaged his electronics warfare suite, quietly hacking into the corporate databases until he obtained Dr. Bao's address. *Test their defenses. Non-essential information. I can dig in for deeper records later.*

The door to her small apartment stood partially open. To his tired lack of surprise, her living space appeared to have been ransacked. Bioluminescent plants had been overturned, their soil and leaves scattered everywhere. Cabinets left ajar, drawers left open. A couple of antique books had had their spines slit, and their pages carpeted the floor.

Questions churned through his mind: *Is she still alive? What did she know? If she knew something, why didn't she disappear at the same time as Nzeogwa? Maybe she didn't cooperate with Nzeogwa... maybe I caused this...*

Times like these, he wished he could still take a deep, steadying breath. Still, Arthur was glad he didn't have the potent cocktail of human neurotransmitters firing through his body and brain. Guilt was bad enough without fueling it with adrenal rage. *No. I didn't cause this. Someone did, but not me.*

He examined the apartment minutely. Almost everyone these days kept their important information in storage servers spread out throughout each colonial planet's infrastructure. But someone who thought of physical media like paper for passing secrets might have made a physical backup of important data—clearly what the previous searcher had been looking for.

I'm spending all of my time following in other people's footsteps. Nzeogwa's. Whoever ransacked this apartment. Frustration, irritation with himself at being so far behind.

Yet patience proved the right tack once again. *They looked in all the active locations—things she could pick up and take with her, or were otherwise easily portable. They might have had sonar with them, to look for cavities in the walls. The easy places, like under the toilet tank lid. Let's try where people never think to look, but that would be easy for someone with basic home repair skills to handle.*

He didn't see it, but his fingers caught the faint variance in the outer bathroom doorframe. Arthur dug in his nails cautiously, removing spackling compound, revealing a slit about an inch long cut into the frame. He smiled faintly, and carefully worked the concealed chip out of its hiding place. "Let's see what we have here," he murmured, and inserted the chip into a concealed slot in his forearm.

Medical reports spilled into his mind. Information on several hundred SHI employees who'd contracted a mystery ailment. *Symptomology mostly consistent with viral infection,* she'd noted, *lethargy, photophobia, loss of appetite, dehydration, anemia, and high fever. Patients don't respond to standard antivirals and blood-tests are negative for viruses and bacteria.*

Arthur blinked as he processed the information. Bao noted that vials of the patients' blood had gone missing from the lab. When she'd requested medical reports on several of them after they left her care—as they all had—she'd been informed that they were no longer her concern. Irritated, she'd gone so far as to track several of them down—in the ICU of her own hospital, having undergone some sort of surgery. *Surgery doesn't correlate to a viral infection.*

And then, one last file—which contained an address and a copy of her NDA worded in bland legal jargon that revealed nothing. Arthur shook his head. *Probably not a virus. Something developed by the corporation, then, maybe? Not enough information. But definitely enough to report.*

He triggered his transmitter as he left her apartment. First, he reported the break-in at Dr. Bao's apartment to both the TA Magistrate's office and CorpSec.

Then he sent his personal report of his findings so far up to his ship. Delia replied sardonically, "And hello to you, too, Arthur."

Arthur paused in the lobby of the arcology. "*I woke you?*"

"I don't sleep any more than you do. But you do realize that it's the niceties that keep us human, right?"

"*You never were human, Delia. Send this on to TAMO Central, would you?*"

"I'm close enough for government work," she replied sweetly. "Why aren't you sending this to the local TAMO office? Also, give me a hard synch on your memory. You were out of contact for automatic synchronization for thirty minutes in that arcology."

"*Local magistrates are probably under the corporate thumb. Maybe not bent, but pressured. And sorry. I get crap for signal inside buildings like that.*" He initiated the hard synch as requested. "*If SHI puts any delays on my transmission to Earth, keep trying to relay it through our comm system, please.*"

"Will do." She paused. "What's your next step?"

"*I've got an address. But do I want to go straight there? Might call unwanted attention.*"

"With Dr. Bao missing, speed might win over subtlety."

"*Yes, but I also don't want to have CorpSec on my heels, either.*" He waved down a transit pod, feeling the weight of a thousand camera eyes on his shoulders. *No. Don't look like you've got an answer. Good way to get jumped. Slump the shoulders a little. Head to a hotel—you've been going twelve hours straight. Let the ones who think you're human, think you're human. Let the ones who know you're a machine assume you need to recharge. Hah.*

Still, in spite of the lack of endorphins and stress cortisol, his mind stewed angrily. He wondered if Dr. Bao were still alive, and if there were anything he could or should be doing to find her, right now. *No. Let the TAMO locals and CorpSec trip over each other. I technically have another job to do.*

Still, it grated. Like every other life he'd ever failed to save.

Like his wife's, so many years ago.

Arthur only spent an hour in his hotel room. The virtual worlds frequented by many of his Uploaded brethren held no attraction for him. ***This** is our life*, he wanted to tell so many of them. *Real life is out here. Where the living are. Where we can still make a difference.*

"You know, humans use interaction as a way to reduce stress," Delia reminded him suddenly. "You should give it a try now and again."

He didn't feel like arguing with half a billion other ghosts, or with an AI who knew more about him and his history than he entirely liked. *Somehow, she feels more real, with a name. She's been a person all along, of course, but with a name... it's different somehow.* "I don't experience stress anymore," he said out loud, transmitting at the same time. "It's a physiological thing, you know." He paused. "Unless you're suggesting that you're *lonely*."

A pause. "I'm sure that you'd say that it's as unlikely for me to experience loneliness as for you to experience stress," Delia answered, her tone oddly sad.

"Probably." The silence that stretched afterwards became awkward. *Damnit, she's just too real. Too **human**. And I'm... probably not human enough, these days.* "You have a reason for checking in on me like this?"

"Reports from your other copies indicate cumulative psychological stress. All work and no play is how their AIs summarize the issue."

It bothered him, vaguely, that the AIs assigned to his copies communicated with each other, while he and his brother-selves steadfastly did not. And yet... *Is that concern in her voice?* "So you want me to go socialize? When a person of interest has gone missing?"

A pause. "No. Forget I said anything."

Delia sounded miffed.

So he reviewed his case records. It seemed a better use of his time than indulging in fantasy—or reviewing his own memories, intolerably bright as they were. Of the wife who'd refused to record her consciousness. *I've got all the time in the world, Arthur.*

All the time in the world, up till the moment someone he'd put away had gotten out of jail and found her alone at home.

We could've had eternity. But we don't. I'm still here, doing the best I can. Like all my other copies, wherever they are. Soldier, sailor, policeman, spy.

Realizing that he'd fallen into a memory loop, Arthur swore and stood. Slipped out of the hotel, this time using his electronics warfare programming suite to disengage cameras as he passed them—a light electromagnetic pulse to knock them off-line did the trick. He didn't bother with a transit pod this time; they could be tracked. He just walked the long and lonely miles towards the address pulsed on his mental map of the city streets, seemingly ignored by the humans milling around him.

The address turned out to be a low-slung building near a crater-like strip-mine. Arthur disengaged perimeter cameras and switched off the power to an electrified fence before climbing over it. The doors to the building yielded easily to his hacking protocols.

Habits of old thought rose up within as he entered: *Should have gotten a warrant.* Newer protocols reminded him: *Local magistrates are probably bent. That's why you were sent with broad powers. As usual. What, thinking about Beth get your wires crossed?*

Arthur felt the ping of his internal processes quiet. Felt the smooth flow of his automatic synchronization with his ship proceed. *Maybe I do need to give myself a reboot. Or a boot in the head. One of the two.*

Inside, a smell of antiseptics and astringent cleaning solutions. Long hallways, barely lit by flickering overhead panels. *What was that in the medical files? Light sensitivity. Maybe this is where they're keeping the people with the 'virus.'*

He padded on, still sending mild EM pulses at any cameras he detected. Found and bypassed a control room with guards, and then slipped out into a wide, open room filled with metal beds. The beep and hiss of medical monitors, checking for heart-rates and respiration. The hum of screens hooked up over each patient. His eyes scanned, not comprehending what he saw. *I don't need to understand now. I need to record. I can cross-reference with medical databases later.*

One bed near the end caught his attention—maybe it was the gray hair, so rare in this era of longevity vaccines and anti-senescence treatments. He'd only seen one person who wore her organic age openly on this planet. Bao. Arthur looked down at her slim form under the sheets, anger rising in him. *The human thing to do would be to get her out of here. But that will set off a hundred different alarms.* He scanned her body in thermal mode—elevated temperature. *She's not what Vaduva is. That's... something, right?*

He swore internally. Caught her foot and shook it gently. "Dr. Bao?" Arthur whispered. "Dr. Bao, can you hear me?"

Her dark eyes opened, looking dazed. And then she jerked upright, making a hissing noise. Her fingers hooked into claws, scrabbling at his arm. "Dr. Bao, it's me. Calm down. I need to get you out of here." He offered her his hand. *Bad decision*, the back of his mind derided. *She's not Beth, you idiot. You can't save everyone.*

She lurched forward, grabbing for his shoulders. A stinging sensation against his neck, and Arthur jerked back. "Did you just *bite* me?" he hissed, bringing one hand to his throat. As he did, he could clearly see some sort of *siphon* or proboscis recoil into her mouth, tucking away under her tongue as Bao reeled back to her pillows.

What the **hell**? Arthur thought, stunned, just as alerts lit up all through his body. *Unidentified substance infiltrating platform*, his systems informed him. *Attempting to consume platform matrix and reorganize its material. Interdiction and containment protocols enabled.*

Arthur didn't need more information. *Time to get out*, he decided, darting back the way he'd come. Behind him, Bao's monitors began to chirp excitedly, and he knew that nurses would soon appear.

He got as far as the control room before running into trouble. The guards were cycling off-shift, and when he ducked into a closet for cover, one of them spotted movement and came to investigate. *Warning: Organized incursion continues,* security subprocesses nattered at him as the door opened, and the guard loomed. His hands extended automatically, yanking the man in with him. Spun him around. Wound his arms around the startled man's throat, clapping one hand over the guard's mouth to muffle a shout.

The guard, furious, slammed backwards into the shelves, trying to knock Arthur off his back. Arthur ignored the impact, applying pressure to the carotid arteries. Felt the heartbeat, vivid against his sternum, so like the steady rhythm that had once dwelled under his own ribs. Eased the man down to the floor gently. *Incursion continues,* his processes warned again. *Identification: Nanite particles.*

Wonderful, Arthur thought, peering out the door to see if any of the other guards were coming. *Probably not intended for my form of human life, right?*

Unknown, the subprocesses replied.

Arthur keyed his transmitter, hoping that this building wasn't shielded against RF transmissions. "*Delia? Got a problem down here. Nanite infection. Uplinking my security log. Take a look?*"

"I let you land on *one* planet, you decide to hook up with some floozy without firewalls, and now look at you," Delia teased in his head.

"*Not really the time for jokes. Still trying to get out of the facility.*" Arthur let the other guards go about their business—two of them joking about how the missing man had obviously been dying for a coffee break—and slipped out of the building.

"I'm on it, but you owe me." Delia had paused long enough to let him get outside without distraction. "Wow. These little guys are adaptive, aren't they? The nanites were injected?"

"*By Dr. Bao. From a proboscis under her tongue. To the best of my knowledge, that wasn't there several hours ago.*"

"How closely did you check her oral hygiene when you were interviewing her, anyway?" Mock-jealousy in Delia's tone.

"*This is a hell of a time for you to work on my socialization issues by adapting your behavior to human norms.*" The thoughts felt fragmented. Arthur clenched his teeth and strode on, pulling his collar over the open hole in his throat. No blood, of course; just a trickle of white ooze as his synthflesh attempted repairs. "*Delia—*"

Her voice became crisper. "Nanites are like viruses. Adapted or built to a specific, species-oriented task, nothing else. That these are adapting to your system this quickly... they're over-engineered."

Great. Can you bolster my security protocols' containment efforts? He raised his head as he walked, realizing that he'd assumed the slumped-shouldered gait common to humans on this rock. He made himself look up at the whole of his surroundings, and spotted several human figures on the fire escapes above him. Motionless. Arthur frowned and turned onto a main thoroughfare, crowded with humans going out to bars and restaurants. *More cameras to block, but more people, too...*

His throat *itched.* It hadn't done that since he'd been alive. Warnings bloomed through his awareness from compromised system after compromised system. And out of the corner of his eyes, Arthur registered the proximity of humans moving against the crowd's flow. Cutting through the hunched forms of the other humans, straight-backed, intent-eyed. Focused on *him.* "*Delia, do they have optical implants? Is what they're seeing locked into CorpSec feed?*" His servomotors failed momentarily, knocking him off-balance. Making him dizzy. *This night has a thousand eyes, and they might all be human for once.*

"No," Delia replied. "Arthur, you're leaking EM from your transmitter. I think they're tracking you by that, and they're using electronic warfare systems to compromise your damaged systems further—"

Arthur ducked back down another alley. *Too many bystanders. Most probably innocent.* He shuffled away, his limbs heavy. *Mobility systems under attack.* "*Delia, you've got me synched, right?*"

"I'll catch you. Don't you worry."

And then they were on him, a dozen pairs of hands grabbing him at once. Tearing at synthflesh, raking it open. Yanking at a body suddenly recalcitrant as he tried to defend himself. Dazed thoughts: *Haven't been this helpless since that last hospital bed, hands shaking too hard to feed myself, catheterized, trying to reach for the nurse call button—*

Intolerable memories of weakness. Of failure. Arthur struggled. Fought his own limbs, even as they were torn from their sockets.

He didn't scream. He didn't make a sound as he forced his gaze around to record their faces, the mouths gaping open as sleek black proboscises unfurled from under their tongues like alien flowers—*Only on this world, the flowers are the ones that sting and drink. Triggering platform autodestruct. Delia, you'd better catch me—*

Forty-two light-years from Earth, in a ship orbiting a terrestrial planet, his eyes opened, awareness firing along photonic circuits. Seven seconds of confusion ensued as he examined the crystal cylinder in which he found himself. And then full awareness raced back to him from his most recent set of synchronized backups, and Arthur Polaris kicked open the door of the construction cylinder. He didn't usually feel emotion this strong; at the moment, he relished it. "Delia, how recent are my files?"

"Last update, thirty seconds before your platform went off-line," Delia shot back, sounding every bit as angry as he felt, himself. "I've been analyzing the data during your platform construction. And I moved us out of orbit—they might have closed the local gate to jump-traffic, but they'll have to hunt us down to destroy us."

"I don't put it past them. We know too much." A pause. "Backups of us sent to Earth?" His mind worked through the chain of calm procedure, overriding emotional responses.

"Affirmative. It'll take us longer to get there using just our own comms, and there's a chance of data corruption en route, but we'll get there. Eventually." Her tone held defiance.

Arthur pulled on a fresh suit, feeling better for the reboot. *Or maybe for the boot to the head.* "What else have you got for me?"

"The medical records you gained access to suggest that the people in the facility you found were infected with similar nanites to the ones with which you were injected," Delia replied, bringing up a model of the infectious little vermin for him on a screen. "TAMO has recovered the remains of several of your attackers. The self-destruct caught them off-guard. Your body was, however, completely destroyed."

"I've seen my own corpse before. I can pass on seeing it again." Arthur waved it off. "The human remains are more important. Finding out what the nanites are actually *designed* for. Chains of evidence."

"The local TAMO office is stalling on the autopsies. They might be rethinking their loyalty to the corp. They have to know that the galactic core is going to shut this place down hard when our report comes in."

"What have you got so far?"

She hesitated. "I've had time to review the material, particularly what you saw in Dr. Bao's screen. She'd only disappeared six hours before you found her. It's a *rapid* process in humans—"

Arthur drummed his fingers on a bulkhead. "Details, Delia."

Another pause. "Downloading files."

Images flickered behind his eyes. *Nanite infiltration. Rebuilding human bodies into cyborgs. Stringing nanotubules along bones and through muscle fiber, making each individual stronger and faster. Using raw materials from internal organs, replacing the stomach, spleen, and bone marrow with semi-organic battery packs for storing energy. For transmitting and receiving data.*

His eyes opened. "That... would explain why Vaduva was room-temperature," Arthur agreed, letting it wash over him. In a single day, he'd run the full gamut of old sorrow, fresh anger, and new horror. All things he'd thought behind him. "No active metabolizing of food into energy. And humans can't live without red blood cells. The spleen, the bone marrow..."

"They have to obtain those from other people," Delia agreed softly. "Blood banks. Transfusions. Or... well... direct assault."

"The siphon under the tongue," Arthur muttered, raising a hand to his new neck. "They reinvented vampires? What *for?*"

"I can't be sure," Delia warned, "but I think that the communication on the EM band links them all together. Like drones in a hive. Which was how they were tracking you."

Arthur sat down. "Replacing free will with corporate loyalty ligatures," he muttered. *The thing most Uploads fear the most. Being controlled, since we're... software. Subject to programming and restraints and hell, malware*. He rubbed at his eyes. "What else? What's with the photophobia?"

"The nanites appear to be sensitive to UV," Delia replied softly. "Keeps the infected on the night-side of the planet."

"Bullshit. It keeps them from going *off-planet*. The corporation never loses its workers." Arthur wanted to spit. "And I'd bet that the upper-most echelons, so long as they're loyal, get to keep most of their free will." *Like Vaduva. She tried to warn me, but couldn't say much without risking what self she had left.*

"Probably. It's supposition at this point," Delia admitted.

"I'm going to need a bigger warrant and a lot more investigators." Arthur stood. Paced, though he knew that was a waste of energy. "Maybe stakes and holy water."

"I could simply *land*," Delia offered, her voice chill. "The plascannons on this ship would be far more effective than holy water. I have a good notion of where they house most of their server architecture, too."

Arthur rested a hand on a control panel. "Nah. They blow you up, we're both out of it until some version of us wakes up on Earth."

"At least in the versions most recently sent, I had a name, and you knew it."

"I could go down again by myself." He shrugged, turning towards the flight controls. "They'd get to learn that what I told Vaduva earlier is true. You can't kill what's already dead."

"Absolutely not," Delia replied sharply. "You return to the planet alone, they'll kill you again. Worse, they could conceivably gain control of your platform. Hack your programming. Turn you into something—someone—else." She hesitated. "I under-represented the concerns of my fellow AIs earlier, Arthur. Several of your copies are contemplating permanent storage without run-time or outright deletion. You're too much like them not to have a similarly self-destructive streak. But I hope that you'll listen. That you won't keep trying to do it all alone."

He stood stock-still, processing the words. A flash of indignation at how closely she monitored him—how all the AIs monitored all of his selves. And yet... the concern in her voice sounded real. *She's an AI. And she's not Beth anymore than Bao was. But she's just as* **real** *as I am. She deserves the words.* "Delia?"

"Yes, Arthur?"

"Thanks. For looking out for me." He paused. "For keeping me human. Nominally." Wry self-deprecation in his tone. "I don't think I'd still be *me*... without you."

Her voice warmed like a smile. "Getting sappy on me, Arthur? How unlike you!"

"Eh. If I'm about to get some version of you killed, you deserve to know that you... matter." A sigh's worth of silence. "I'd been trying not to *let* you matter for a long time. Didn't want to depend on you, or anyone else."

"Everything depends on something else. That's what being human *means*." Soft now, and oddly gentle.

"I know. I'll... do better. For both of us." Another pause, and then he directed his mind back to business. "We'll play hide and seek with any corporate ships they send. Wait till the cavalry arrives."

"And then?" she asked.

"Then we kick down some doors." He put a hand to her console. "Deal?"

"Deal."

Deborah L. Davitt was raised in Nevada, but currently lives in Houston, Texas with her husband and son. Her poetry has received Rhysling, Dwarf Star, and Pushcart nominations; her short fiction has appeared in Intergalactic Medicine Show, Compelling Science Fiction, and Galaxy's Edge. For more about her work, including her Edda-Earth novels, please see www.edda-earth.com.

BLACK DOG BEND
by JD Cowan

A musician stumbles into a time warp and finds himself part of a revenge plot. Now he must battle a killer dog, hired hitman, and a witch to escape.

Black Dog Bend
By JD Cowan

I.

The midnight breeze of the forest sent shivers down Jordan's sweating back. He was being followed. The long trek had led him through the woods and out into a small meadow where he first saw that black mutt. He blinked and it ran off into the sweetly-scented cedar trees. Crickets and rustling leaves were all that remained to keep him company. Jordan shook the gooseflesh from his bare arms. He ruffled his dirty blond hair, clutched the supposed relic around his neck, and cursed his luck.

The van had run out of gas because no one paid attention to the tank, and now he had to deal with this. The band was too busy being at each other's throats after the gig went bad in the last town. They'd even lost their phones during the chaos. Not the best day. He volunteered to go for gas if only to get away from the bickering.

He should have gone back by the highway, but the woods would be faster. There was no way to *know* it would be faster, but he *knew* it anyway. He couldn't possibly explain it, but the guys wouldn't believe him anyway. Things had been progressing well since leaving them.

Until that dog showed up.

It took another fifteen minutes before the rapping of paws ran behind the bushes off to his right. He saw nothing. The whisper of a woman blew by him, but no one was speaking. Jordan shook the collar of his t-shirt. The heat was getting to him.

A shotgun blast of humidity shot through his chest. On a fat tree branch before him sat a large black dog. Its beady orange eyes stared him down. An ashy odor wafted from the beast.

He instinctively grabbed the relic around his neck. His mother had given it to him as a boy, handed down from generations. It was a small stone wrapped in cloth, supposedly belonging to St. Thomas Venae the Hunter, and found in ship wreckage somewhere in the south. He didn't believe what she told him, but he kept it for good luck anyway. Now, as he slowly stepped back from the strange dog, he was beginning to reconsider.

He made it twenty feet when it howled. The dog bounded off the branch in his direction.

Jordan took off through the woods. The canine snapped behind him. Its barking crashed in his eardrums.

And yet, despite the dog pounding against the grass behind him, Jordan knew where to go. His lungs tore inside with every breath, but he didn't get lost.

Jordan's lungs threatened to jam up his throat. He swirled around bushes and leaped over steep rolling hills. The harsh moonlight guided him through the woods, the barking of the large black dog blasting behind him. The growls gathered closer. Finally, his heavy legs brought him into a meadow.

The field unfolded out into an ancient dirt road and lumber fence leading towards a large house. The two-story home had white paint and clean windows with beautiful black tiles along the roof. It had been recently renovated with a *Blind Bend Motel* sign above the porch. However, his arms gathered goosebumps as he approached. A presence lived here. Yet he still ran, hot breath on his back. He clutched his relic again, and leaped the steps to the porch.

Jordan followed through with his shoulder, and the door hinges let out a massive shriek. He slammed it shut behind him. The barking instantly ceased, leaving his breaths to cut into his nerves. He cringed, his eyes involuntarily blinking, as a blanket of humidity consumed him.

When he blinked again bright white bulbs bathed the foyer before him. Old hardwood floors and blue-striped wallpaper towered over the entranceway. The chubby man at the desk a few feet ahead showed him the first sign of civilization he had seen in some time.

"Traveling late?" the clerk asked.

"There's a crazy dog outside. Didn't you hear it?"

"A what?"

Jordan explained his entire trek from the van up until meeting the dog, careful to avoid talking about the band. Who knew if the night's events had spread this far? That didn't prevent him for asking for gas or a ride into town. Anything to get away from that dog.

"I think we have some gas in the basement," the clerk said. "Bring what you need up here and I'll charge accordingly. I'm not sure what to say about the dog. Never saw that strange one around here. Sure you don't just want to stay for the night? It should wander off by tomorrow."

"Well, I've got friends waiting. It wouldn't be fair."

"You must be in a band if you're out so late and need gas that badly."

"Good guess. Do you mind if I call in a ride from town?"

"I'll call." The clerk chuckled to himself. "Go get what you need and we'll get it sorted. Just don't disturb my tenant when they get back. She's the only one I've had all week."

"I can imagine."

Old, strong beams and high ceilings led him to believe the house had once been a larger establishment. But that was ages ago. He learned back in town how the area had gone downhill over the years. But the house still looked good.

Before Jordan could descend the basement stairs, the front door opened and slammed.

"Back so soon?" the clerk asked.

Jordan turned in time to see the woman lean against the shut door, her eyes on the ceiling. Her breaths fell hard as ruffled dark hair curled around her faintly pink neck. She wore a peach blouse with short jeans, making her appear as out of place for this time of night as he was. A small smile formed in the corners of her pale lips.

"I just had to say goodbye to an old friend," she said. "They didn't like it."

"That's your prerogative, miss. As long as you pay I won't say anything. I wouldn't recommend going out again, especially since this gentleman says there's a wild dog out."

"You didn't see it?" Jordan asked her.

"I didn't see anything. Did you just get here?"

"I've been walking all night to get to town. For some stupid reason I thought this would be a shortcut. That dog came out of nowhere."

"Well, it's gone now." She raked her green eyes across Jordan. "I'm Athena. Just staying here a few days to get my affairs together. Went out to make a call and get some fresh air. Why were you out there, if you don't mind me asking?"

A layer hid beneath Athena's posturing. Her smile wavered slightly. She was testing him. But he let it slide. The night had been bad enough, and he needed to get moving.

"I'm Jordan. Our van ran out of gas and left my friends and I stranded, so I'm out here like a fool."

"No phone?"

"Big brawl back in town. Long story."

"Sounds exciting. What band?"

He sighed. There was no sense hiding it now. "Three Wolves. We play rockabilly."

"I don't know what that is."

"You should come to our next show. We'll be in Ashville tomorrow. I'll get you a good seat close to the action. Though I guess that's about a hundred miles from here."

She grinned. "Don't count me out just yet. Maybe I'll take you up on that."

"Rockabilly?" the clerk cut in. "That's ancient stuff! Kinda romantic keeping the old works alive like that. I guess someone's gotta do it. Covers or originals?"

"Both. We've got some jumpin' songs of our own." Jordan couldn't quite admit he didn't write the songs, though not for lack of trying. He'd been stuck on one for the longest time, and now he wasn't even sure he would get to finish it. "Our last gig went south and we never had the chance to fill the tank before leaving town. I'm surprised you didn't hear about it."

She crinkled her small nose. "Hey, I'm even surprised I didn't hear about you guys playing tonight. Maybe we just missed each other."

"Well, I just need some gas and I'll be out of your hair. If you want I'll tell you about the band in a bit." He nodded to the clerk. "You said it's downstairs, brother?"

The clerk confirmed it, before his cheeks flushed. He suddenly jumped out of his chair and left into the bathroom across the hall. This man was a surprisingly trusting fellow.

Athena and Jordan reached their separate staircases, hers ascending and his to the basement. He paused. Something about her earlier words stuck in the back of his head. She took three steps before he stopped her.

"How *did* you not know about our show?"

She tilted her head. "What? Come on; don't tell me you're that egotistical."

"It's a small town, and the cops were called hours back. Fists were flying. No one was talking about it?"

"The town was dead. No one was out. Are you lying?"

"Dead? There was chaos all over. We had to run because it had gotten so bad. Where did you go?"

Her green eyes widened. "Oh no," she whispered. The pink flushed from her cheeks as she bounded up the stairs. "No, no."

Jordan followed after her. For a light girl, she moved incredibly quickly. But he had to know.

"Is something wrong?" he asked.

"Go away."

He followed on her heels across the red carpet. The wood paneled hall held at least three rooms on each side. The woman stopped at the second one on the right. She laid a hand on the doorknob and he grabbed her shoulder.

"What are you hiding?" he asked. "Did something happen in town? Were you lying downstairs?"

"It's complicated. Now please, just go away."

She threw open the door and a flash burst out of the dark inside. Gunshots!

Jordan lunged at her and bullets danced through the threshold. His arm and chest lit ablaze, and shots burst against the wood paneling behind him. He knew the sensation—he'd been shot. Red life force stained his pink skin. Jordan landed on top of Athena, straddling over her. He grimaced as the pain sparked through his muscles.

The scent of roses and ash attacked him as he glanced at her. She shook, frozen still and wide-eyed. The relic around his neck fell across her cheek. For a moment, she stopped trembling. Blood seeped from his arm into the carpet. He wobbled.

"Run," Jordan rasped.

Her mouth opened to speak, but froze for a moment too long. "She trapped us."

"Get up and go!"

He rolled sideways and she wriggled free of him. Athena ran down the hall, mumbling hysterically to herself between hard breaths.

A large man left the room, loading his handgun. He wore a grey suit with a crimson tie and slicked-back dark hair. She glanced back towards the shooter just as he finished loading another cartridge. He stepped around Jordan, strolling slowly.

"You took far too long, woman."

Jordan's throat choked despite his attempts to speak. His vision blurred and bent. He'd heard that voice before.

The assassin fired down the hall and Athena cried out. Blood burst from the small of her back. The attacker leveled the weapon at the fallen woman. She pulled her limp body across the carpet.

"It's a waste," he said. "But a job's a job."

Air split with the shot, and Athena ceased being. The assassin turned back towards Jordan. The fallen bass player recognized him. He knew it. But from where? The gun leveled at Jordan's temple.

"You made me miss."

The killer then fired into Jordan until the life went out of him entirely.

II.

Jordan's own screams woke him up. The pain had all but vanished, leaving him numb. He was... standing by the front door to the motel?

And he was alive.

The clerk behind the desk swore at his exclamations. "What the hell is the problem, stranger?"

Jordan patted himself down. No wounds. His clothes were not even punctured with bullet holes. "I'm not dead?"

"I can fix that if you want. Now turn around and leave. It's too late for crazies."

"*I'm* crazy? Didn't you hear the gunshots?

The killer's upstairs. He shot at me, and her! Call the cops."

"Who are you? There's no one upstairs. Are you mental?"

Madness. Jordan knew he had been shot, and so had Athena. And yet he was here, unhurt and unblemished. But what about her? The last time he saw her she was...

He charged up to the desk. "Where's Athena?"

"Is that who you mean? She was shot?"

"Yes, how did you not hear it?"

A loud bang erupted behind Jordan. Athena flowed through the door, but not like a person would. She phased in from the black outdoors, her matter reconstituting whole inside the entranceway. It was like she just stepped into existence. Her eyes wide and empty, she blandly looked around the room.

He stared blandly for a moment before it sank in. Athena wasn't dead.

Jordan grabbed her shoulders. "You're alive? You remember what happened, right?"

She stared at the relic around his neck. "I remember everything."

"Then tell me what that was about. Didn't he kill us?"

Instead of answering, she glanced past him. Her breaths barely held still as she watched the wall. "We're stuck here."

"What in Hell's half acre are you two going on about?"

"Never mind," Jordan barked. "You call the police. There's a killer upstairs. I'll take her out of here."

Jordan took Athena by the elbow and charged through the open door. He would rather risk the dog than the murderer. However, he met resistance. A wall of humid air crashed against him and twisted his body around. The invisible force pushed him back into the house again.

An unseen border refused to let him through.

Jordan ran out the door once more, and the invisible force spun him around again. The intangible wall couldn't be crossed.

A cold bolt shot through his muscles. "We can't get out?"

"She's cursed us," Athena said. "We can't leave."

The girl shook free of him. She ran towards the split level stairs and barreled down into the basement. He watched her go, still mulling over the knowledge that she was alive.

"Can you explain what you just did?" the clerk asked. "Is this a prank?"

Jordan snatched the clerk by his lapels. "Listen! A killer is hiding upstairs. He shot us dead, but somehow we're still alive. Then we tried to run and you saw what happened. Get your phone out and call the police. Don't fool around!"

The clerk wrapped his fingers around the collar of Jordan's shirt. The relic around the bass player's neck brushed his knuckles. "Let go, and I'll do it."

"Make sure to mention there's a crazed dog outside."

"Well, I," the clerk flinched and fell away from him. He tripped and fell against the desk. He began breathing hard.

"Hey, what's wrong?" Jordan asked. Was it the relic? That couldn't be possible, could it? "Is it this?"

The clerk groaned, and his moans pitched higher with each passing moment. He forced himself up, knees wobbling. The chair beside the desk kicked over as he thrashed. His whimpers became shouts.

"How long?" the clerk rasped. "How long has it been?"

"Jordan!"

The girl appeared at the top of the basement stairs holding a small finely-crafted wooden box. She tucked it under her arm and paused. Her shoulders trembled when she glanced up the stairs to the second floor where her murderer lay in wait. He put a hand on the box.

"Give me *something*, Athena. Tell me what you know."

"The man upstairs was hired to kill and retrieve. I called earlier and was told it was my last chance. Guess it wasn't a bluff. My old boss wants what's in this box. If I can give it to that killer then maybe he'll walk away and we won't have to die anymore."

"*Anymore*? He's killed you before?"

"I remember," the clerk mumbled. He leaned against the desk on his elbows. "I've seen this night hundreds of times, every single one the same. I've died so many times. I hurt... everywhere. How am I alive?"

"I stole this," Athena stated. She made one slow step up the stairs. "And because of me we have relived this night hundreds of times, oblivious to our fate. This is my punishment. You two are innocent, and I'll be sure to get you out."

The clerk wobbled into the next room over. Jordan looked between the mumbling male and the woman ascending. The lunacy made his head spin. Before the girl got too far, he pursued.

Jordan tore the small box from her clasping fingers. The warmth from the object bit his palms. She fought against him, regardless.

"That's mine," she said.

"If this was yours you wouldn't be in this predicament. I'll bring it to the man upstairs and hope he doesn't do the deed again. You try to get through to the cops."

"The phone won't work. Do you still not understand that we're not in time anymore? We're prisoners in this bend where reality warps to keep us prisoners. The only way out is to break the curse."

"Then I'll settle it. Better me than someone he'll shoot dead first chance. I can do this."

He held the box to his chest and shouldered his way up the stairs. Athena looked after him with a single eyebrow raised. She didn't believe him. That was fine; he didn't fully believe himself. It took much control to keep his breaths level and his legs from shivering.

Three Wolves traveled across the country and played in whatever dives they could. The audience's faces when they played a set was worth it. It was a small thing, but it meant everything to the guys. He'd always had them to lean on. Even during their brawl, they had watched each other's backs. Going it alone was not his thing. If it was he would have finished that song long ago.

His fingers quaked against the box with every step down the hall. His killer lay just ahead, and Jordan had only words as weapons. That same bass part from his work in progress thumped in his head with each heartbeat. So much for ever finishing the song.

He knocked on the door. "Room service. Are you there, miss?"

The light scraping of boots against carpet moved to the rear of the room. The closet door clicked shut. Jordan let out a sharp breath, and turned the handle. He only had one shot at this.

The same bedroom with disheveled sheets and open dresser drawers awaited him. He would always recognize the place he died. Jordan swallowed his shivers and held the box tight.

He let the door click closed behind him, into the place where he had been murdered. He still didn't fully grasp what was happening, but he made his decision. No turning back now.

III.

The small box beat in his hands like a drum. Constant and steady, it could have been mistaken for a time bomb. Perhaps it was. At this point he would believe anything. The killer remained quiet as Jordan held the box out.

"I have your package," the bass player said. "There's no need to kill the woman. You can take it back to your employer."

A subtle sound clicked from the otherwise silent closet. Jordan's brain rattled in his ear like a feedback loop. That psycho was getting ready to fire.

"There's no trick," he continued. "I'm trying to avoid a scene, and would rather nobody get hurt. Just take it and leave, and everybody wins."

Slowly, a husky voice said: "This has nothing to do with you."

"You were sent for this box, and I'm giving it to you. Simple."

The assassin threw the closet door open and leaped out, his weapon trained on Jordan. This killer remained familiar, but Jordan still couldn't point him out. Despite the man's obvious advantage, he refused to reach for the box.

"My client wants this and the girl. Give her to me and I won't put a hole in your gut."

The gun clicked, and Jordan licked his lips. His spine quivered. "Can't do that. You won the prize. Just take it."

"I have a better idea. Why don't you head out with me? Keep your hands up."

The assassin made him turn around before jamming the weapon against Jordan's lower back. The pair took a trip down the stairs with Jordan holding the box high in the air. Thankfully neither Athena nor the clerk was anywhere to be seen. The motel's silence was overwhelming.

Then the box trembled.

"Hey," Jordan said.

"If you're pulling anything," the killer

replied, "you'll regret it."

"I'm not!"

The shaking ran up his arm. The contents in the wooden container quaked harder the closer he inched to the front door. Whispers bit at his earlobes from an intangible place just out of sight and sound. What had Athena stolen?

The metal jabbed further into his spine. The killer growled. "I thought I told you not to move?"

Sweat trickled down Jordan's temples. "I told you I'm not! It's this thing."

"Don't lie. One more move and you won't make another."

"Hold it, Wyland!"

The shrill shout cut the thick tension. The clerk stumbled from the archway to the living room, holding a hunting rifle. Sweat caked his entire face as his chest heaved. His teeth clenched harder than a wolf on fresh meat.

The gun on Jordan's back slid a few inches to the left, and the assassin swung around putting Jordan between the pair. The weapon remained hidden from sight. This killer was a pro.

"How many times, how many years, has it been Wyland?" the clerk shouted.

The killer stuttered. "Am I that famous?"

"You've told me your name every time you've killed me. Every. Single. Time. And now it's done. Now you get to meet the devil and give him a good kiss from old Simon Leclerc. This is the last time."

"I don't even know who you are, sir," Wyland said. "I only got here a few hours ago. Stay out of my way and there won't be any trouble. Now if you'll excuse me, my friend and I need to go for a walk."

Simon raised the rifle, and aimed it down. "Going to be difficult with a missing head."

Humid air hung over the lobby as the two men remained frozen. Jordan thought Wyland might have the advantage with a prisoner, but Simon's twitching expression meant he might not care about any of that. He didn't even acknowledge Jordan's presence. Wyland must have realized it as he broke the tension.

"So you know the girl, then?"

"You kill her before you kill me. Every time. But no more."

"You're crazy, mister. I haven't killed anyone tonight."

"You won't ever—"

Wyland whipped Jordan forward and Simon fired. The shot went wild, cracking against the wood wainscoting. Jordan rolled forward slamming into the desk, and Wyland jumped sideways. The killer landed on the hardwood and squeezed the trigger twice. Two bullets punctured the clerk's chest and stomach. Simon slammed against the wall behind the desk and slid down, limp and bloody. Someone screamed—but it wasn't any of the three.

Athena emerged from the living room, wide eyes darting around the mayhem. She crouched beside the fallen clerk. Wyland jumped back up when he noticed her.

"You! I've been looking for you."

She looked up in time to see Wyland leveling the gun at her. He squeezed the trigger.

Jordan crashed against him, and the weapon fired wild. Athena ducked behind the desk on top of Simon as wood splintered out everywhere. Jordan held Wyland's firing arm and the two rolled across the floor.

The killer grunted. "You made me miss."

"I'll make you miss a whole lot more than that." Jordan slammed his fist down into Wyland's jaw, again and again. The killer punched back. Jordan spat blood. "Drop it!"

The weapon flew wild from Wyland's hands and across the floor. The killer spun and backhanded Jordan, sending him reeling. But Wyland didn't capitalize. He had no chance to. The killer clutched his head and yelled. Just like Athena and Simon had done earlier, Wyland's expression morphed into one of horror at Jordan's touch. He bellowed in agony.

"What did you do to me?"

Jordan flashed his relic. "This thing doesn't like this place."

Wyland yelled and shouldered Jordan. The victim choked on his breath and was thrown to the floor. Wyland scooped up his gun and crossed over to Jordan, stomping violently and wobbling. He slammed the butt against Jordan's skull. Jordan's cheek struck the hardwood with the force.

"Thousands of nights... rotting flesh and dried blood... no way out except by my own gun... you did this. You let me see it!" Wyland's breaths arrived faster and faster as the fingers on his free hand tightened on his reddening temples. He paled and the whites in his eyes enlarged. "What is in that wooden box? Who sent you?"

"A black dog chased me," Jordan murmured.

"I'm getting out of here and I'm putting a bullet in that witch, but first, I'm giving you what I gave those two many times before."

The gunshot rang out through the motel. But Wyland never fired. Up against the wall leaned Simon with the rifle in his hands and blood trickling his lips. Athena helped steady him and his weapon. Wyland reeled, the gunshot in his back bleeding.

"Told you I'd get you," Simon said, sliding back to the floor. Athena helped him back down.

Wyland dropped his firearm and jerked out breaths. Jordan took the gun up and pointed it at the killer, but had no chance to use it. Wyland slammed down like a heavy weight.

He didn't move again.

Wind whistled through dead motel. The ordeal was over. Jordan tried to catch his breath and push his nerves down into his gut. Nothing would settle. His knees buckled. He parsed out what had just happened, the chaos that ended in so much death. But before he could plan his next move, Athena ran by him, retrieving the box from the floor. She fled toward the door.

"Where are you going?" he asked.

"She killed Simon. I can't let her get you, too."

"You can't leave," Jordan rasped. "That's not going to work. Remember?"

"This will."

She placed the box against the night air where the bend was earlier, and the wind rippled. The atmosphere broke and parted like the Red Sea. Cold air flooded into the motel.

"Don't follow me," Athena said. "She's out there, I know it."

Despite his calls, Athena took off into the night. He couldn't stay: he needed to get up. But his legs wouldn't listen. He punched his trembling knees and forced himself back up. They ached as if they had been through a meat grinder.

He slowly climbed up and a scent met him. The stench of a wet animal entered his nostrils. A dog?

But at least he had a weapon this time. Jordan put Wyland's gun behind his back and limped out into the dark of midnight. An oppressive wind churned his insides. This time he would kill the mutt, and whatever had sent it.

IV.

The cold night whipped across Jordan's bruises as he stumbled across the dirt road. His legs had slowly regained composure despite the sweat pooling on the back of his neck. In the center of the pitch black pathway he found two other people.

Athena stretched out the box towards a middle-aged woman. The older woman wore black streaks in her unkempt hair and her short, bent nose accentuated her slightly chubby cheeks. She wore a simple black dress like she had come from a funeral. Aside from her crooked lips, she also smelled like a wet dog.

Her expression remained grim. "Did you think I wouldn't find you, Athena?"

"I thought it would be too late when you did."

"Sentimental dreamer." The woman nodded solemnly. "I should've known better than to use a foolish girl."

"You lied!" Athena shouted. "You told me we could change everything. We were just different, but we would show them. But then what was that back room? Whose skin was that? How many people have you hunted down? You're a monster."

"Don't lie, girl. You always had an idea of what I really was when you walked into my shop. You knew people would get hurt, all for us to become one with the goddess. They're all worthless in Her sight. You knew that. But you ran before you saw it all. I have more than mere magic to use, you see."

The old woman grinned, and Jordan winced. Her teeth sharpened and lengthened like fangs. Jordan aimed for her chest.

Athena continued: "We could have told them. But I didn't think anyone would have to die."

"Because you don't think. Selfish girls come into my shops all the time looking for something to put them ahead. Eventually they find it, and they all find that room. Then it takes no time at all for them to join me. But not you. Instead you stole a piece of me, probably to sell it to black market trash. But I'll tell you that my heart won't do you any good. I removed it for a reason. Now, give it back, or return to your punishment of eternal death. All I need do is kill you to send you back."

"You're wrong!" Athena said. She tightened her fingers around the box. "I remember everything now. Part of the spell is broken. If it wasn't for Jordan I would still be there."

"Yes, he ruined my fun. I tried to chase him off, but he somehow got through my barrier. And he also woke you up. How did he do that, I wonder?"

"Why even do this?" Jordan interrupted. The woman swore at his arrival, and Athena sent an uneasy smile his way. He decided not to mention the relic. "You'd never get the heart back if you left them there. It would be trapped with Athena."

"I have only benefited from losing it. How old do I look to you? Forty? Forty-five? Not quite. I am over one hundred. All from adding better parts for my weaker ones. I never cared if I got it back. It's irrelevant. But she stole from me."

Once more her skin wavered and bent in the breeze, this time softening to wild black fur. Her nose lengthened to a snout, and fingers twisted to claws. She bent forward and her spine and chest cracked, expanding to the shape of a large dog. It was far bigger than the one he met earlier.

The newly created black dog barreled forward, paws beating heavily against the dry grass. Slobber flew from its jaws.

Jordan raised the gun. He shouted as Athena ducked behind him. He fired, and the first shot plunged into the earth. Dust plumed out. The canine ran past it. He pulled the trigger three times, the first two shots striking air, and the last cracking the beast in the skull.

It tumbled forward in a roll and landed flat on its belly.

"Got it," he whispered.

Athena pointed to it. "Look!"

Before he could take a breath, the mutt sat up and shook its head. The bullet wound bled, but the beast was no worse for wear. It growled, and sprinted toward them again.

The gun barked in response, striking the beast's shoulder. But it did not cease its charge. The dog would not fall.

"That won't work," Athena said. "She's immortal."

"Then crush the heart!"

"It can't be done. I've already tried."

"How do we stop it, then?"

The dog barreled into Jordan, throwing him down into the dirt. Teeth snapped at his neck, rancid breath shooting up his nostrils. He shoved the gun into its mouth, holding its jaws at bay.

Athena leaped on its back and slammed the box down on the canine's head. Wood broke and splintered and the heart rolled out onto the grass beside Jordan. Athena held the dog's neck. Jordan instinctively went for the loose organ. A stray claw slashed against his forehead, drawing blood. He shouted in pain, and wrapped fingers around the heart. It warmed in his hand.

"Use the heart," she said. "Use it!"

"How?" he yelled.

"Give it back to her!"

The dog lashed out, teeth scraping his cheek, and he slammed the heart into its chest. Black fur-like vines whipped into the dirty organ and pulled it out of Jordan's grip. The heart sunk back into its chest as the enemy whined, still snapping at its victim.

All at once, the dog buckled and threw its head back, tossing Athena to the grass. It rolled off of Jordan, stumbling sideways. The beast shook as if having a heart attack.

Jordan fired into its side. This time the canine whined as the blood spurted loose.

The black dog wobbled as it walked, straightening upwards into the body of a middle-aged woman. The seeping wound on her side remained. Her black dress rotted and twisted away. Every step she made put a decade of age on her features. Skin wrinkled and her bones showed through her mangled, bleeding form. On the third step her hair became sheet white and her cheeks sunk into her skull. A dry gasp escaped her maw, ejecting dust from her lungs. She faced him one more time, her eyes watering with rage.

He fired into her chest again, and skin burst open into a chalk-white dust. The ashen corpse floated out in a dust cloud into the night air. No trace of her remained.

The earth quaked. Jordan turned on his elbows to see a thin black veil lift from the house. What had once been a tall, handsome motel became nothing but an empty lot. The old woman's magic had dissipated, leaving the world as it was supposed to be. The gun in his hand disintegrated as did, he figured, the corpses in the house. The chill of night reigned once more.

"Jordan."

He sat up and saw Athena sitting on her knees with tears rolling down her blemished cheeks. She glowed faintly in the dark, the only brightness he could see in the newly revealed overcast. Athena faded with the veil.

"But I thought I ended it," he said, quietly.

"You did." She smiled through her tears. "Thank you."

"Athena,... "

But before he finished his thoughts, she disappeared into the night, leaving only a memory and emptiness behind.

He stood up with a groan. Incomplete feelings lay at the tip of his tongue and his mind. He couldn't stop his muscles from wobbling or his mind racing, but he still made his way back to where the house had been. Nothing remained but his knowledge that people died here.

He finally remembered Wyland's face. He had been a killer with a big reward offered for a tip leading to his capture. Jordan had seen it in one of those crime shows about missing murderers. Wyland was never found. This man went missing thirty years ago. And now he wouldn't be coming back.

With the sky back to normal, Jordan spotted distant lights between the trees. The town was a good while off, perhaps half an hour or so on foot.

Jordan took one last look at the barren graveyard that had swallowed so many lives, and walked away.

V.

The guys looked at Jordan funny when they saw him coming down the road, a gas can in each hand. He had gotten a ride halfway back to town, and on the way to the van, but it still took him until near dawn to finally return. Thankfully, the attendant was a fan of the show they put on, chaos aside. He didn't rat Jordan out to the cops. The red morning sun covered Jordan like a blanket by the time he reached the guys.

"What's with the bandages?" Luke asked. "Get into another fight?"

Jordan ran his fingers over the taped-on patch above his eyebrow. "Yes."

"Mr. Pacifist himself. Good job on the gas. Ready to go? You can get some sleep while we fill it up."

Jordan winced when the sun lifted even higher behind him. The rolling fields beyond the nearby wooden fences showed a world rising and ready for the day ahead. He couldn't sleep through it.

"I'm not tired," Jordan said. "Besides, we gotta make some sixty miles through rougher territory if we're gonna make the show tonight."

He climbed into the van and dug out the notepad by his bass. His brain hummed the melody flooding into him as he jotted down the correct chords. The bridge came easy, as did the solo. Everything easily clicked into place.

Perhaps when they reached their destination he would already have it done. Jordan rubbed the relic around his neck and said a short prayer as the sun poured orange over the countryside.

The next show would be a banger.

JD Cowan is a writer with an obsession for stories and Truth. He takes pleasure in looking for Light in the places where darkness grips the tightest. He blogs about stories and entertainment at wastelandandsky.blogspot.ca and can be found on Twitter @wastelandJD for those interested.

SWIMMING WITH THE DEVIL

by
WILLIAM ECKMAN

A Persian pearl diver decides to cut out the middleman when selling his pearls. He ends up at the mercy of pirates, then slavers, then a sea monster.

Swimming with the Devil

By William Eckman

Ram snatched his pearls from the visiting trader. "How do you expect me to feed my wife and three children?"

Nothing protected Ram's head from the heat of the late-afternoon sun above, or his feet from the heat of the sand below.

The trader sat on a carpet, his back to the ocean. A second carpet, held up by poles, shaded him without blocking the coastal breeze. He held a teapot above his head, and poured a stream into his mouth without spilling a drop. "I have no wish to starve your family, my friend. You are welcome to wait until another trader arrives at this quaint, out-of-the-way village. Of course, the children which you speak of may be hungry while you wait. They cannot eat pearls."

"They can eat oysters." Ram turned his back and walked away.

Alone in his seaside shack, Ram woke throughout the night at the slightest noises. He watched the open doorway for pearl thieves and the shoreline for boat thieves. His boat, once his late father's, didn't let him travel far. Its leaking hull forced him to spend time bailing instead of sailing, and the protective symbols painted on it by a Zoroastrian priest were now barely visible, but he couldn't dive for pearls without it. He didn't know how to do anything else.

~

The next week, he snatched his pearls from another trader. "How do you expect me to feed my elderly parents?"

"You think you have it rough? Think it's tough to make oysters give up their pearls? Try the sea voyage to Pindu. Pirates everywhere, lying in wait to take my cargo and sell me into slavery, and that's not even the worst that could happen. Dhows are always being sunk by sea monsters, and their crews are never heard from again."

"Don't speak to me of sea monsters. I dive in the water to find those pearls." Ram turned his back and walked away. He walked down the shore to the boatyard, where he found the boatbuilder, old man Kamal, resting in the shade. Kamal was a foreigner, but the villagers tolerated him because his boats, and even the occasional dhow, were always watertight, and because his cousin was a reliable supplier of high-quality wood.

"Kamal, did you request the wood for my boat?"

"It's one of the very next things I plan to do. Right after I look at your coins."

"You worry too much about coins. Once you build me a new boat, I'll be a rich man. I'll sail far away, to diving grounds that haven't been picked over by every diver in the village. I'll have more pearls than you've seen in your life."

"You'll swim into a jawfish territory, and get yourself eaten."

"I can spot the signs of a jawfish."

"Maybe you can. Maybe you can't. Or, maybe you're one of those who thinks he can outsmart the fish. You think you will be safe at a certain secret time of day?" Kamal held his thumb and finger close together. "You think you can squeeze just barely into the very edge of the territory, and make it safely away before the fish notices you?"

"I'll find an oyster reef without a jawfish, somewhere."

"Listen to me, young man, there are worse things out there than jawfish. There are things my people call the kraken. Your people call them ..." Kamal made a twirling motion with his hand as he tried to remember. "... devilfish."

"My grandfather was full of stories from when he served in the Shah's navy. I've heard dozens of devilfish tales. It's a made-up creature for scaring little children who like to swim too far from shore."

Kamal slapped Ram on the top of his head. "It is not! You think jawfish are terrifying because they swallow a diver who wanders into their territory? A kraken won't be satisfied to eat just one man. It will grab a different person in each of its tentacles, then shove them into its mouth, one by one. Some say they have eight tentacles." Kamal held up his fingers, with his thumbs folded in. "Some say ten." Kamal held up his fingers and thumbs. "Others say twelve." Kamal looked at his hands in frustration, then slapped Ram's head again. "A kraken is as vicious as it is devious. It will let a diver collect pearls for days, watching and waiting until the man brings his family to help with the harvest. Then, the whole family is eaten together. The largest of the kraken are even worse. They will follow a diver's boat back to his village, and take many families at once." Kamal slapped Ram again.

"Stop hitting me. I'll be careful."

"You must listen to your elders. I've learned many things from my family's stories – things you would never believe. Did you know my ancestors fought at Nahavand, when the Shah's forces drove those cultists back into the desert?"

"Really? On which side?"

Kamal waved his hand. "That is unimportant. Shouldn't you be somewhere gathering your pearls?"

~

Another two weeks passed, and Ram snatched his pearls from yet another trader. "The money from these pearls will be dedicated to our fire temple. Will you hold back coins meant for Zarathustra himself?"

The trader sighed. "In every village, there's some kid who's never traveled anywhere, but still tells me my prices are wrong. So, I'll tell you what I tell them: after I buy your pearls, I sail them through pirate-infested waters to Pindu, where I sell them to another trader, who sails them even farther away, risking pirate attack himself. He sells them to a trader who takes them inland, risking attack by bandit or roc. When I sell your pearls, I only receive a handful of coins for them myself, and I have to bribe port officials every time I sail into Pindu." The trader spread his offered coins across the carpet. "My silver is here, right now. You can take it home this very minute."

"I'll take my pearls home instead."

"It's your decision, but I warn you: when I return on my next voyage, my prices may not be so high. Or if I suffer some misfortune, I may not return at all."

Ram turned his back and walked away. At the back of a sturdy brick house in the village, he whistled softly. He stood outside his love's bedroom, where for years, the small size of the window had prevented his attempts to enter, and her attempts to exit.

"Ram, have you sold your pearls?"

"No, my love. I have a new plan. It will keep me away from you for several weeks, but I will return with enough treasure to pay your father for our marriage, and still have enough for a new boat. I'll find more pearls in distant waters, and we'll never concern ourselves with money again."

"Ram, you mustn't steal."

"No, my love. I'll have no need to steal or to kill for my riches."

"Then go, Ram, and return soon."

~

Ram held a pearl in front of the dhow captain. "Take me to Pindu, and it is yours."

"You bring your own food." The captain reached for the pearl.

Ram pulled his hand back. "You get the pearl when we arrive at Pindu."

"As you say."

~

Ram returned to Kamal's boatyard. "Order the wood for my boat now, Kamal."

"I'll do it right away. Let's take a look at those coins, then."

"Quit worrying about your coins. I'm on my way to Pindu, to sell the pearls myself."

"You're going with that dhow captain? How many sailors does he have?"

"I don't know."

Kamal slapped Ram on top of his head. "Remember! This is important."

"Two sailors, plus the captain himself."

"Ram, they will take your pearls and throw you into the water. There are rules to traveling with strangers. Three against one, they will always attack, without exception. Two against one, they will attack if they are strong, or if you are weak, or if they are desperate. Less than two against one, and they will never risk an attack. You must take another person with you, or you will never see your home again."

~

The fisherman Bijan had no wife to mend sails or nets, so he rowed his fishing boat and pulled in fish with hook and line. This made him both the strongest and the poorest man in the village.

Ram held a pearl out to him. "It's yours if you come with me to Pindu. Pearls sell for much higher prices there."

"Two pearls. One for the trip there, one for the trip back."

Ram squinted at Bijan. "Agreed, but you bring your own food."

~

Squawking seagulls circled the dhow, mistaking it for a fishing boat. The setting sun silhouetted the captain as he spoke. "We shall be in Pindu by morning ... or afternoon, depending on the winds. These things cannot be known."

"That's when you'll get your pearl."

"Yes, of course. When we arrive."

As he had done throughout the voyage, Ram laid face down to sleep, so no sailor could reach his belly-pouch of pearls without waking him up. The sacks of grain he slept on were comfortable, and he didn't remain awake for long.

~

Visible in the moonlight, the captain approached Bijan. He nodded towards Ram. "He is your cousin?"

"No, he is paying me two pearls to travel with him."

"Two pearls is a good payment. Ten pearls would be better."

~

Ram woke as two sailors wrenched his arms behind him, while Bijan pinned his feet. He rolled his body, first one way, then the other, but went nowhere. He repeated the attempt, grunting with exertion. He bent his knees to get his legs under him, but Bijan pulled them straight. He kicked, but with feet held together, only managed a weak push against Bijan's chest. The sailors bound his arms behind his back, then tied his feet together. The captain gagged him with another rope before taking the pouch of pearls. The sailors threw him into the lowest part of the hull, and the gag muted his scream as he landed shoulder-first.

He spent hours stretching his fingers to their limit, tugging at the ropes with his fingertips, but the sailors knew how to tie a knot. Before sunrise, the dhow scraped up against a jetty. The captain jumped off while the crew secured their vessel. When he returned several minutes later, he whispered to the crew, pointing at Ram, then at the water. Two sailors picked him up, one by the arms and one by the legs, and carried him towards the edge of the dhow.

I'm going _overboard to conceal their crime. I'll drown unless I draw the attention of someone on the docks. _Ram thrashed and screamed into his gag, only making the sailors walk faster. He kicked his leg bindings over a cleat where a rigging line was tied, jerking the sailors to a halt and making one of them fall to his knees. The sailor cursed, stood up, and pulled Ram's legs away from the cleat. In moments, Ram was over the side.

He took a deep breath, but it was knocked out of him when he landed on something solid, a pile of cargo in the bottom of a small boat. Two other men in the boat obscured their faces with strips of cloth, just in case there were any doubts they were up to no good. One of the men threw two coins up to the dhow, while the other rowed the boat away. Ram rolled off the pile of cargo, discovering that it was actually Bijan, tied up and unconscious. What had Kamal said? Three against one, they will always attack. Ram rolled back and forth, ramming both knees into Bijan's back in revenge, until he was too tired to roll any more.

~

Ram sat on the beach, his left ankle shackled to a man who sobbed day and night, his right ankle shackled to Bijan. Ram never looked to his right, and Bijan never spoke. New prisoners were put on the right end of the string of men as they came in. Each day, two were taken from the left end and led away. They never came back. Ram was now one man from the left end.

The captives got water once per day, which wasn't enough for men exposed to the burning sun. Ram had been the only prisoner to eat, his meal a single clam he dug from the sand. He glanced around to make sure his captors weren't watching, and sharpened half of the clam's shell against the metal of his shackles. The other half-shell, hidden in his clothes, was already sharpened, and this one probably wasn't getting any sharper, but he had nothing else to do.

The slavers were rough men. He'd watched them fight over gambling disputes, and sometimes for no reason he could discern. Ram had never fought in his life. The slavers had scimitars, spears, muskets, and pistols. Ram had a sharpened clam shell.

When he was unshackled, he knew better than to ask where he was going. The other prisoner didn't know to keep his mouth shut, until a slaver struck him between the shoulder blades with the butt of a spear. Ram and the other captive were shoved, kicked, and prodded over a hill, where they could see they were on a small island. A T-shaped wooden walkway stretched from the shore, but it was of no use as a dock, as no dhow could sail up to it. On either side, nets encircled areas of water, as if fishermen had left in the middle of their task. Even stranger, other nets were stretched over the top of the circles.

They were pushed down the walkway to its end, where the other prisoner fell to his knees and grabbed at the clothing of his captors. "Please have mercy, I cannot swim." Ram prayed that his captors' plan was to throw him into the water. Two slavers grabbed the crying prisoner, jerked him to his feet, and pulled him down the left side of the T, which ended above the center of one of the circular enclosures. The prisoner again fell to his knees, alternately sobbing and screaming that he couldn't swim. One slaver held a knife to his throat, while the other leaned over the water to untie a section of the covering net and peel it back.

The man's eyes showed relief as the slaver moved the knife from his neck, and then panic as the slaver kicked him through the opening into the water. As the other slaver tied the covering net back into place, the man reached up, grabbing at strands of netting. Each time he caught hold, his weight pulled the net down, and he thrashed and splashed in the water until he could grab hold of another piece, which was pulled down as well. The slavers laughed at the man's struggle for a minute or so, until an enormous pair of jaws closed around him, dragging the screaming man under and turning the water red. Ram now understood that his captors weren't in the business of selling slaves. Their captives were fish food, stuffing the penned-up jawfish every day to enlarge its liver. Jawfish-liver oil was worth far more than the slavers' pathetic group of captives.

Ram's captors bunched together as they shoved Ram down the opposite side of the T. They stared into the water below, pointing their spears towards the deep or holding scimitars over their heads for a downward slash. Some mumbled quiet prayers, while others were louder with diverse curse-words. _This jawfish must be much larger, if it can push the entire net upward to reach them, or much smaller, if it can push its jaws between the ropes._

Ram moved close to the man who untied the net, and as soon as the opening was large enough, dove for the water. He would not splash at the surface, drawing the attention of an overfed jawfish. He would go deep, using the pearl-diver's secret: air wants to be with other air. Air in the lungs drags a diver to the surface, as the air fights against the water to be with its own kind. He blew his air out instead of holding it in, remaining calm as the sea took him down. As he sank, one of his captors' curse-words popped into his mind: kraken. It was the word Kamal had used for devilfish.

Ram sank deep enough to avoid his captors' scrutiny, then swam to the net and sliced one of his clam shells back and forth across a strand of netting. The gaps in the net were large, so a single cut strand would allow him to squeeze through, but his sawing motion was pushing the net backwards more than cutting it.

A tentacle, as thick as his leg, struck the net above him, and his clam shell spiraled into deeper water. He pulled himself downward using the net, but another tentacle struck below him. Others struck all around him, leaving him no direction to flee. He looked into an eye the size of his head. He had gone from captive of slavers to captive of a devilfish. He fought the panic of being prey, and the panic of needing to breathe.

No bite tore him in half, and no tentacle

squeezed the life from him. The devilfish remained motionless, doing nothing. No, it was doing something. It was stretching the net taut. Ram reached for his second clam shell. It was gone. No, there it was, in a fold of his clothing. He sliced back and forth, cutting through a strand with little trouble now that the net was held firm.

He pushed his head through the gap. His shoulders wouldn't fit. He blew bubbles and felt the pain in his chest that told him he had to shoot for the surface, now. He backed up, put one arm through the gap, followed with his head, then pulled his other arm through behind. He swam upward using slow leg and arm motions. Every diver who'd been too deep for an oyster knew that frenzied swimming led to choking and coughing later. Reaching shallower water, he stopped swimming and let the sea buoy him the rest of the way to the surface.

He floated, pulling air deep into his lungs. For some time, all he could do was float, taking slow breaths in and out. He was free from the slavers' chains and safe from the tentacles of the devilfish, but had no further plan. There was no other land in sight of the island, so swimming out to sea would be a death sentence. The slavers didn't keep a boat here, so any escape would have to wait for one of their boats to return. Could he sneak aboard and remain hidden until it reached some other shore? No, there were too few hiding places, and usually too many men aboard the boat. Could he steal the boat when it arrived? Not by himself, but if he freed his fellow captives, together they might seize weapons, kill the slavers on the island, and ambush the boat when it arrived. He would not free Bijan, though. Bijan would die of thirst, chained on that beach, his final thoughts being memories of what he had done to Ram.

A shot cracked in the distance, and a musket ball splashed near his face. Another musket cracked, and a ball whizzed over his head. He couldn't free anyone while the slavers were shooting at him. He needed them busy doing something else. He blew out his air and used the net to pull himself down. The devilfish was still in the same position, holding the netting taut, as if it had expected his return. He sawed at another strand of netting, severing it to enlarge the hole he'd escaped through. He reached for another strand, but the devilfish surged forward, squeezing its enormous bulk through the opening, which had seemed far too narrow.

Ram shot for the surface, not wanting to miss the spectacle of the slavers being torn apart by a devilfish. He surfaced and wiped the water from his eyes, spotting the slavers on shore, but no tentacles flailing about them. He scanned right and left, not detecting any dark shape beneath the water, until he looked straight down. A tentacle curled around his legs, and he was jerked under the water. He barely had time to clap his hands over his nose before he was dragged feet-first through the water at high speed. The devilfish wouldn't fight the slavers. It was swimming away, and it was taking its dinner with it.

Ram held his air as long as he could. There was no reason to make it easier for the devilfish to pull him under. As his breath ran out, he blew bursts of bubbles. He thrashed in the devilfish's grasp. To his surprise, he was released, close to the surface. He gasped in lungfuls of air and got his bearings, spotting the island. It was now nearly a mile away. He had been underwater for a couple of minutes at most.

A tentacle circled his legs again, and he managed a deeper breath before being dragged again. His arms trembled as he held his hands over his nose against the force of the rushing water. The devilfish released him just as he blew out the last of his air. Did it only eat live food, and was saving its meal for later? He knew there could be no rescue for him, as the devilfish was moving faster than any ship had ever sailed.

When he felt a tentacle touch his legs again, he pulled them up to his chest. He thrust an arm downwards, offering it instead. The devilfish dragged him through the water headfirst this time. He closed his eyes, let his body go limp, and concentrated only on holding his breath. The pattern repeated, minute after minute, hour after hour. He wondered whether he should end his ordeal by sucking water rather than air into his lungs, but something kept him going. Maybe he held some irrational hope that he would ultimately survive, or maybe he was just too stubborn to give up. The sun reached its highest point in the sky, then fell towards the horizon. Did devilfish sleep? Would this nightmare end when the sun went down?

As he gasped at the surface again, he

spotted land in the distance. He immediately gave up hope that the devilfish would bring him close enough that he could slip ashore. He wouldn't swim six feet before the creature caught him again. He watched as the land grew closer and closer, but it brought him no comfort. When he came within swimming distance of shore, he thought only of his ultimate destination, the devilfish's belly.

Ram recovered at the surface. He'd already floated several times longer than at any previous stop, but still no tentacle came for him. He recognized the rock formations on the nearby shoreline. This cove was the known territory of an adult jawfish, avoided by divers for as long as he could remember. Was the devilfish in a life-and-death battle? He ducked his head under the water, searching for combatants, but his gaze fixed on the hundreds, probably thousands, of oysters which had grown enormous under the jawfish's protection. Any pearls found here would be the size of a man's eyeball, and each worth a fortune.

He took another breath and put his head back under, scanning for devilfish or jawfish. He spotted the devilfish, tucked into a crack in the rocks, its gaze never wavering from Ram. On the seafloor beneath the devilfish, he saw the jawbones of the jawfish, all flesh long gone. The battle which he thought might be his salvation had taken place long ago, and this was now the devilfish's home. This was where it ate its meals, the next of which would be Ram.

He floated, staring at the devilfish between breaths, the devilfish staring back at him without pause. The sky grew darker as the sun fell, and the water below darkened even more quickly. Ram missed the moment that the devilfish moved, and it was below him in an instant. It wrapped his arm again, but instead of dragging him through the water, lifted him high into the air. He closed his eyes and said a final prayer as he waited to fall into the devilfish's mouth.

His feet touched the rocky ground, gently, and the devilfish released his arm. His legs gave way, and he fell onto his rear. The devilfish's eyes remained above the water's surface for a few heartbeats, then disappeared below. His terror relieved, Ram gave in to exhaustion, and closed his eyes.

In the morning, Ram feared he had survived his ocean voyage only to die of thirst and hunger on land. He walked for only a minute or two at a time before sitting down to rest. As he sat, trying to gather the energy to rise again, several goats appeared over a hill, followed by an elderly goatherd. Spotting Ram, the man looked around him in fear, but seeing that Ram was alone, in poor physical condition, and without a weapon, he came forward. After listening to Ram's story, he gave Ram all the goat's milk he could drink, and all the curds he could eat.

As Ram walked towards home, he couldn't pry his thoughts from the giant oysters in the devilfish's cove. With those pearls, he would live like a king for the rest of his life. Did he dare risk returning for them? Could he stay awake at night yearning for them, wake from sleep dreaming of them, yet leave them there, unclaimed? Were he and the devilfish now brothers for life, fellow survivors of the slavers' island, or did the devilfish consider their business concluded, an even trade of an escape for an escape? There was no way to be certain, for no man can know the mind of a devilfish.

William Eckman blogs about science fiction and fantasy at Planetary Defense Command. Since this is a pearl diver's story, it should also be mentioned that he used to be a biologist who studied marine bivalves.

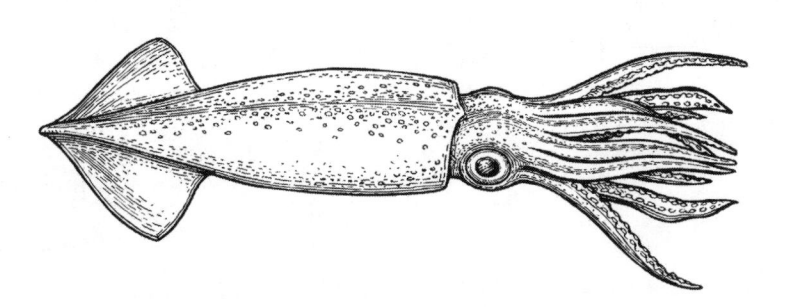

From the Editor

Hello Friends,

I would like to spend the little space I have in this column to address the question that nobody is asking, which is why it takes me so dang long to publish an issue. Here's the uncomfortable truth-- I can not focus on one project at a time very well.

For example:

Many of you have seen my book of reprinted articles from the pulp era about writing (see the ad in this issue.) Because I'm a law-abiding sort of fella, I did the research to make sure every reprinted word was in the public domain. That research is not terribly hard to do, but it is a little bit of a pain in the butt. There are online scans of copyright records, but those are no fun to crawl through. There are at least one or two online tools for searching renewals made from something like the 1970's onward. However, I could not find a slick way to search the whole history of copyrights and renewals, so I had to do it by hand.

Somewhere on the distant horizon is a sequel to that book. I already have a stack of magazines ready to scan. This means I'll need to do a bunch of similar copyright research. I'm a programmer, so I figured I could make my own copyright and renewal search tool for all the pertinent years. I started coding something up using a build tool that I've wanted to use for a while, only to find it had no good way to talk to a database. So I had build a way for apps built with this tool to talk to a database. Then I had to collect all available data and get in into a searchable database. After a number of experiments in parsing the text provided by the wonderful volunteers at Gutenberg, and looking at the newer records provided by the copyright office, I finally found a project that had already compiled all that data. But it had been compiled into a disappointingly unusable format. So I started coding something to read it into a better format. I got about halfway done with that only to find a tool that would do it for me. Long story short, I built an app that will search copyright registrations and renewals in a second what it used to take several minutes to do. And I did that instead of editing this very issue for a while. Side projects pop up like this all the time. That's a big reason why I've been slow.

In conclusion, I may be slow and get distracted, but I love this magazine, and I'm very excited about the fiction and art in this issue. Hopefully it was worth the wait.

Cheers,

Bryce Beattie

Editor

The white sun bore down upon them

It looks like this is the end...

See you next issue!

STORYHACK
ACTION & ADVENTURE

Made in the USA
Columbia, SC
22 October 2023